Becoming Cinder

Books by Christine Marshall

Becoming Cinder

White as Snow

Forever Sleeping

RISE OF THE GIANTS

BATTLE OF THE GIANTS

LAST OF THE GIANTS

The Last Mapmaker

A Series of Intentional Disasters

Volume 1 & Volume 2

Promised Beauty

Final Lock

NOBLESTONE and the Lost Dwarves

Becoming Cinder

A retelling

Christine Marshall

*This book is dedicated to
all the fairy tale lovers out there.
Don't be mad when
this book makes you cry.*

Chapter One

"Jessamine, dear, show a little more dignity with your food, please," my father, the King, admonishes with his deep voice.

My mouth stretches into a wide smile with my lips open, revealing the chewed-up eggs and toast inside, then snicker. A decent sized egg chunk lands on my plate, and saliva drips down the front of my pale-yellow day dress.

He rolls his eyes at me. "Teenagers."

"What?" My eyes widen, all innocent. I blink a few times and grin.

He chuckles and returns my smile. With food in his mouth. His eggs land in his salt and pepper beard that matches his short hair, instead of on his plate.

My mother bursts into laughter, her long brown curls exactly the color of mine bouncing with every guffaw. Before we know what's happening, all three of us practically roll on the floor.

We're breakfasting in the palace dining room. Rich mahogany dominates the space, and anything that can be is lined, curtained, or cushioned in velvety purple and burgundy. Even the floor has a thick, soft eggplant colored rug. Plush pillows line the window seats and cover the bases of all two dozen chairs evenly spaced around the enormous table. Silver candlesticks, dishes, and utensils are arranged in perfect place settings in front of each chair. It's ridiculous. Apparently, that's how the King and Queen are supposed to dine. Even if the meal is just sunny side up eggs with fruit and toast for breakfast.

"We must pull ourselves together…" Mom says between deep breaths and chuckles. Once she gets started, it's hard for her to stop sometimes.

After Father finishes his breakfast, he leans over my mother, wraps his arms around her shoulders, and kisses her on the head. She smiles up at him with love in her chestnut brown eyes. His own sky-blue eyes are all sappy looking.

Gag. Seriously? Talk about showing dignity. No one wants to see their parents look at each other like that.

My father takes his leave, off to accomplish a kingly activity of some kind.

"Are you ready to work on your training today?" Mom stands and pushes her chair close to the table.

A woman from the kitchen staff drops off a picnic basket, and my mom hooks her arm through the handle.

We exit through the mahogany doors of the dining room into the entry hall. Our feet echo off the pale marble floor and bounce off the walls up to the two-story ceiling. Our enormous family painting hangs at the top of the wide, matching marble stairs to my right. I nearly bump into a statue of a dragon that was recently gifted to my father.

"Careful, Jessamine," my mom pulls me away from the statue at the last second.

"Why is this thing even here? I mean, I get it. Our crest has a dragon on it. And our kingdom is called Dragovalon. But still." I pause and study the statue from top to bottom. "It seems a little… much."

"At least it is not life size!" Mom gives me a wicked grin.

I roll my eyes.

Mom pulls me toward the grand, two-story wooden doors at the front of the entry hall. Anthony, the butler, is nearby, as usual. It's like he materializes out of nowhere sometimes!

He bows. "Your Majesty. Your Highness." Then he pushes one of the massive doors thicker than my own body open and we step outside.

A deep breath fills my lungs with the warm humid air and the right-after-rain smell coming from the cobblestone circle in front of the palace. The familiar almost-sweet-almost-not scent of the boxwoods lining the front of the castle burrows into my nose. I sneeze.

Mom glides down the grey hand-hewn-brick steps. The same stones make up the exterior of the palace. She turns to her right.

"Come along, Jessamine. Do not dawdle."

"Right!" I hurry to catch up.

The front of the castle extends so far that it takes a few minutes, even at my mom's quick pace, to make it to the end. Wrought iron arcs and curls edge every window. Vines wend their way up the various stretches of the castle exterior, some reaching as high as the fourth floor.

We step off the cobblestone and onto short, freshly cut grass and make our way through the well-tended gardens overflowing with flowers, shrubs, trees, vegetables, fruits, herbs and more. The air is slightly cooler in the massive garden from all the moisture, plants, and grass. It's a favorite place for me to get lost in. Not that I can *really* get lost; I know it like the back of my own hand, but it's fun to try.

Mom doesn't wait for me as I cup a lavender colored leek blossom the size of my head in both hands and breathe deep. Sweet from the blossom and sharp from the leek below blend to make a unique aroma. Instead, she marches into the meadow that stretches for ages behind our castle home where the tall grasses and wildflowers rustle in the

3

breeze.

"Hcy, Mom. Have you thought anymore about my idea that I told you about?" I say a little out of breath as I rush to catch up.

"Which one, Jessamine? You have so many." She winks at me, but she's not wrong.

"I just told you about it yesterday. How we should ban eating animals?"

A bright yellow goldfinch swoops between us, then lands on Mom's shoulder. She pays it no attention and keeps walking.

My mom shakes her head. "I love that you have such high hopes for the world and want everything to be fair all the time for everyone. But, trust me, this is a dream I am afraid would be too difficult to accomplish."

"I still don't get it. Why not?" A garter snake slithers up my hand and wraps around my wrist. "We shouldn't be using animals or animal products for food."

My mom stops walking and places her hands on my shoulders. "Every creature serves a purpose. Some animals purpose is to be, well, food."

The snake looks at me and flicks his tongue as if to say, *"You're not buying that, are you?"*

"Nope." I shake my head at both the snake and my mom. "Not good enough. There must be a way. And I'm going to be the one to figure it out."

Mom starts walking again. "Like you figured out how to outlaw hunting?"

"Dad told you? That was supposed to be a secret!" I match her pace, even though she's slightly taller than me. "What did he say?"

My mom chuckles, the goldfinch trilling in unison. Now the bird is laughing at me, too? "Only that you are an idealistic young woman who will accomplish much good in this world." Mom glances at me sideways. "And that you need just a little bit more training in the ways of humans." Her mouth twitches. She's trying not to smile!

"But Mom, he's the King!" My little snake friend nods in agreement. "He should be able to make a law like that and the people should have to obey! It's not like he's trying to do anything bad. He'd be protecting the animals. And isn't that, like, OUR purpose in this world?" I gesture between the two of us.

"The line between what is right and what is best… and sometimes even what is possible, can be gray and fuzzy sometimes. It is an important lesson that you still need to learn."

"But I just want everyone to be happy. And the animals cannot be happy if they must worry about hunters." I stroke the snake's head. He closes his eyes and enjoys the attention.

"The *hunters* would not be happy if you outlaw hunting, though…"

I groan. She's not being argumentative; this is one way she teaches me. By poking holes in every. Single. One. Of my ideas. It does make me think harder about the solutions, though.

"Well, when I'm Queen in two years, I'm going to try these ideas out. Maybe… maybe the people will be more receptive to someone younger…" My mom gives me a little glare. "Not that you're not young or anything!" I add in a hurry.

Mom pokes me in the side which makes me flinch. "You will be a great Queen, Jessamine." She smiles. "The people won't know what hit them," she mumbles.

I pretend not to hear the last part. Instead, I bow at the waist with a flourish. "Yes, Your Majesty."

"Oh you…" She tickles me, and I run away from her.

The snake slithers out of my hand and drops to the ground. The goldfinch takes flight.

We're both laughing hard as she chases me through the meadow. I shriek when she gets close. Several rabbits and a fox stick their heads up out of the grass, and a conspiracy of ravens encourage us with loud, melodic croaks from the tops of the nearby trees.

Mom has trouble catching her breath by the time we reach our destination for today's lessons. "I'm getting too old for this." She bends over, holding her side with both hands. When I get close enough, she drops the wicker picnic basket and wraps both arms around me in a bear hug. "Gotcha! I win!"

"Hey! You tricked me!"

5

She releases me and we both take a minute to catch our breath. Our animal audience returns to their tasks.

"Alright, silly goose. Now it's time to get to work."

She lets out a soft whistle. In unison we both turn toward the wood that spans the edge of the meadow. The smooth-barked beech and towering aspen trees are in full summer leaf. All the green dances in the breeze, casting shimmering shadows on the ground below. Before too long, a cute little grey wolf pup sneaks from between the trees.

"Oh my goodness! He's soooo cute!"

Mom shoots me a gentle glare. She's afraid I'll startle the little guy.

"Call him over as you normally would." She guides me through the lesson in a soft, calm voice.

"Hey cutie. Wanna come a little closer?" I squat and wait for the wolf pup's response.

His ears perk at my voice. He understands.

With my hand stretched toward him in invitation, he wobbles toward me on his tiny little legs. My heart melts in my chest. He's so stinking adorable!

"Focus, Jessamine." Mom pulls me out of my inner gushing.

The wolf sits on his tiny haunches right in front of me. One of his ears is still bent at the top. He tips his head sideways. I want to squeal but manage to stay calm.

Mom instructs, "Place your hand on his head. No, do not rub him behind the ears, he is not a pet! Just, gently rest your hand on his head. Good."

I follow my mom's instructions even though I want to bury my fingers in his downy fur.

"Close your eyes and try to reach him with your mind." My mom stays as still as the dragon statue.

I do as she says, only I'm not exactly sure how to "reach him with my mind."

Hello little guy, how are you today? Aren't you just the cutest little thing! Do you have any brothers and sisters?

Nothing happens. I sigh and pull my eyebrows together.

The pup whimpers.

My mom places her hand on my arm, and I remove my hand from

6

the pup and open my eyes. The wolf pup skitters away from me with his tail between his legs.

"What happened?"

My eyes follow him as the baby wolf disappears into the tree line again.

"He could feel your frustration. It startled him. You must learn to keep your mind clear if you are to connect with an animal."

"How am I supposed to keep my mind clear if I'm trying to talk to the animal? Couldn't I just use my voice? The animals understand me perfectly well, even when I'm not speaking their language. And I can always understand them…"

"You are not trying to talk to them," Mom reminds me. "You are right, we already can do that with ease. This is a different kind of connection. When you have mastered this skill, you will be able to share feelings, memories, even see into their minds."

Shaking my head, a sigh pushes its way from my lungs. One by one my fingers pick the petals off a blue starshaped aster flower and watch them flutter to my feet. "That seems… impossible. I don't think I'll *ever* be able to do that." I toss the stem aside when all the petals are gone.

"But you *know* it is possible. You just need to practice. And commit."

"I tried." My shoulders lift and fall in a shrug.

"You must try harder. And you cannot afford to make *any* mistakes. A baby wolf is one thing. But if you are to ever learn to connect with something larger, or more dangerous, you cannot let your own emotions transfer to the animal. It could hurt you, or someone else. You must keep your fear, or anxiety, or frustration at bay."

"I know. It's just… really really hard."

But she's done it. Several times. I don't think anyone besides me and my dad even really knows about the connections she has made.

I stop fidgeting and face her. "Can you tell me about your experience with the kelpies again? Maybe that will help me understand better."

She nods. "I think you just like hearing about horses that look like their hair is seaweed, and can hide in the swampiest places…"

A protest forms in my mouth.

She holds up her hand to stop me. "But it never hurts to repeat a lesson. The more times you hear it, the more it will sink in."

Excellent.

Chapter Two

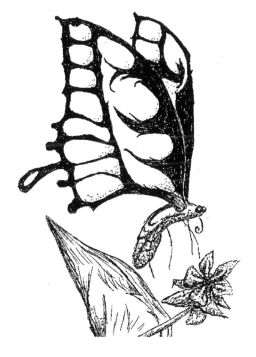

My mom clasps her hands behind her back and paces in front of me.

"I have brokered several treaties with the creatures living in and around our kingdom. They have come to trust me. Some of my agreements are with dangerous creatures. Like the family of kelpies who live in the swamps. We, as in the humans, will leave them alone if they leave us alone. They can be dangerous. Trick people into following them… and drown them. Many fear them, which keeps them safe. But I have promised to protect them from those who would cause them harm. In return, they have agreed to leave humans alone… for the most part."

"I know all of that." My hand waves in the air to push the words aside. "But, like… *how* did you do it?"

"That, my dear, is what I am trying to guide you to be able to do." She bops my nose with one finger.

My eyes blink involuntarily.

"You must clear your mind. Reach out with the very desires of your heart. Give yourself over to the creatures. They will trust you and allow you to connect with their own deepest parts of themselves. Once you have made such a connection, then you will know how you can help one another."

"So, can you, like, *make* them do stuff?"

"No." She shakes her head and frowns. "We must only use this ability to protect the animals. It is why we have this gift. When I married your father, I agreed to try to use my abilities to forge connections between the animal kingdom and our own human kingdom."

"Right. And it's what's expected of me, too." I guess I really do need to learn this stuff.

I try to call the baby wolf back to me, but he's too scared to return.

My mom can see my disappointment. "We should take a break for a bit and have some lunch."

We settle in a patch of clover that hums with honeybees. Mom politely asks the bees to clear a spot for us and promises we won't stay too long. They willingly oblige, and we thank them.

Mom opens the pale wicker basket and lays out a red and white gingham cloth on the sweet, thick clover that covers the meadow like a plush carpet. She pulls out some cucumber sandwiches, a bunch of grapes, and a small, corked bottle of lemonade that has elder blossoms and lemon slices floating in it.

I pop a pair of purple grapes into my mouth and let the juice run down my throat. Then I bite the cucumber sandwich with a crunch. "Mmmmm…" my eyes roll back.

Mom talks to me more about my future responsibilities.

My mind starts to wander. Whenever I hear the word "responsibility" it reminds me of my cousin, Juliette. She's sixteen, like me. We were as close as sisters when we were younger.

We spent our days training with our moms and had the best time playing together and encouraging each other to try new things.

But then, one day, it kind of all changed. We were young, thirteen, playing by a stream together. I practiced with a fish, and she got all mad at me. She told me that we have a *responsibility* to protect the animals, not use them for entertainment.

I told her that I wasn't trying to do anything to that fish. I was honestly just practicing. But then she acted like she was better than me, more important. I mean, yeah, she's a princess, but so am I. And I'm going to be Queen one day. She'll only ever be a princess, and only of the Forest People, which is barely even a real kingdom, anyway. How are her responsibilities any more important than mine?

Since then, I haven't talked to her much. My mom and I do our training without them now. I like it better that way anyway.

My mom snaps me out of my daydreaming. "You must learn to focus, Jessamine."

How does she always know?

She bores her eyes into mine. "Be in the here and now. You have greater power than the others of our kind. If you can master your abilities, you will be the most powerful in all the land. When you are Queen, you will be able to do so much good. You have ties to both this realm, and that of the Forest People. Your influence will be unique."

She's right. And I do try.

We pack up our lunch and walk back to the castle. By the time we reach the manicured hedges that surround the gardens, a black and orange striped caterpillar climbs up my arm, a swallow tail butterfly rests on my dark brown curls, and a ground squirrel with its funny stripes and polka dots jogs along beside me. A pair of bright red cardinals hop behind me among the blue aster flowers and bunches of milkweed, and a green ruby-throated hummingbird buzzes in my ear.

"Alright, little friends. You must be on your way." I wave goodbye to the creatures, setting the caterpillar on a hydrangea bush bursting with huge balls of lavender blossoms that look like they are glowing.

11

My mom tells me to change clothes and I hurry to my suite in the royal residences wing of the castle.

All the doors and trim are deep mahogany, like the dining room. Each suite has a theme. Mine is animals… what else? Hand-carved little birds, critters, and insects decorate the huge outer double doors, all the inner doors, the window frames, the furniture, and some of the trim work around the space.

Inside the massive walk-in closet my outfit changes from my flowy yellow day dress into a simple gray work dress with long fitted sleeves and a high collar and apron. My mom waits at the bottom of the grand marble staircase.

The sun shines onto the cobblestone street that leads us toward the capital. Fluffy white clouds move across the sky and the breeze lifts my loose curls away from my face. We both constantly, but gently, shoo animals away from us. They want to accompany us everywhere we go. In the garden or meadow, it's not that big of a deal, but in the city it's best not to draw too much attention to ourselves that way. We don't want to stand out more than we already do.

Mom reminds me, "It's important for the nobles to spend time with those less fortunate, so as to not forget our privilege and responsibility."

This is easily my favorite part of being a princess. Better than living in a castle that looks like it came straight out of a fairy tale, pointy towers, and all; or wearing custom ball gowns made from luxury materials that swish and sparkle when I move.

The merchant district is filled with delicious aromas from the different bakeries. Cinnamon, yeast, sugar… chocolate! My mouth waters and my tummy grumbles.

"You can't be hungry already," my mom admonishes.

"I am a growing girl, like you always say…" I grin wide.

We keep walking though. I'll eat at the palace. As much as I want. Any time that I want. I can't complain.

A metalsmith drops a tool and the clanging echoes off the brick exteriors of the buildings that line the street. My hand covers my heart to slow it's beating. A pungent scent wafts out the door of the apothecary; too many herbs and spices being cooked and blended at the same time.

The carpenters have left their doors and windows wide open to allow airflow through their workshops. My feet match the rhythm of the saws cutting through wood and hammers setting nails, and my eyes water from the dust in the air.

People recognize us as we make our way through, but they don't crowd us or call to us or anything. We spend enough time here that the sight of us has become as normal as it can be.

We arrive at the food sharing store and get right to work. This is another of my mother's accomplishments, creating a place where farmers, harvesters, butchers, and bakers can donate any surplus they may have, and those in need can procure food to feed their families. The staff is mostly volunteers. Many who have benefited from this charity previously and want to return the favor.

"Jessamine, why don't you help package the food, and I'll unload the new cartload of barley that has just arrived." She makes her way to the back of the building. Before she disappears through the opening, she turns to me and says, "Jessamine."

I meet her eyes. "Yes?"

"Remember who you are."

"I know, Mom." I smile at her.

She says this to me every day. Sometimes more than once. She wants me to remember that I have special abilities that are important. That I am born into privilege, from which comes certain responsibilities to use my influence for good. That I am the future Queen. It's so ingrained that whenever she says it those thoughts cycle through my head.

Her voice is muffled as she greets the other volunteers and gears them up for the work ahead.

Standing behind a low, narrow rustic table I patiently wait for customers to arrive. One of the legs is a little shorter than the other, and it wobbles when I bump against it. The surface is rough, plenty of nicks and divots after years of use. A sliver of wood embeds itself into one of my fingers, and I pick it out with my other hand.

A woman takes a tentative step through the opening at the front of the space. Her clothes are ill-fitting and tattered at the edges. Her dirty blonde hair is tied in a neat bun at the base of her head, and she carries a canvas bag of sorts in her shaky hands. She eyes the banged-up floor, peeling walls, and mismatched shelves lined with a wide variety of random food items. Fortunately, the aroma of fresh bread and dirt that clings to the vegetables masks the musty smell of the building. She hasn't spotted me; my drab clothes and dark hair blend in with my surroundings.

She's about to slink away. She doesn't want to come in any further.

Before she escapes, I smile and address her. "Welcome. What can I prepare for you today?"

She meets my eyes and startles when she recognizes me. I pretend not to notice, however, and she plays along. She retrieves a paper from her sack. It's a list of a few things she could use. It looks as though she must have a handful of children at home.

"Coming right up!" I say as cheerfully as I can.

My heart aches, though, at the circumstances she must be in to have come here today.

If I could, I would invite everyone in need to eat at the palace every night; and sleep there, too. We have enough space, after all!

The woman's eyes dart around while she waits for me to fetch her items.

To fill the woman's request, I gather a couple of day-old loaves of bread, a tightly wrapped beef bone that she can use to make a hearty stew, along with some potent onions, misshapen potatoes, and soft carrots.

"They don't look pretty, but they are still full of nutrition," I tell her with a smile.

Beside the bread loaves sits tray of sticky buns loaded with molasses and cinnamon. I wrap half a dozen in paper for her and tie the twine around it in a pretty bow.

When I hand her the items, I wink at her. "All be well with you, friend."

She can smell the sticky buns. Her eyes go wide. "Thank you, m'lady." She dips into a quick awkward curtsy, then hurries out the door. Her children are going to love those treats.

As if they can sense my presence, a pair of tiny dormice sneak onto the table in front of me.

"Oh, you were hoping for a treat, too, were you?"

They twitch their whiskers at me and give me sad eyes.

"No need to look so sorry. I know you must eat well if you live around here…" I give them a stern look.

They dip their heads, then peek at me once more.

"I suppose I can make an exception, just for today." I smile at them and scoop them into my hands.

They chatter their thanks as I carry them around the shop. They indicate with their cute little noses that they want a taste of the sticky buns, too. I hold them both in one hand and pick up as many crumbs from the tray as I can, dropping them beside the mice.

I fully expected them to gorge themselves on the sweets, but they load up their arms.

"Oh, you have children that would enjoy these, as well? How many?"

One of the mice chitters at me.

"A dozen! Well, that is quite the large family, isn't it? In that case, let's find some more." I break off the tiniest chunk from one of the buns, but big enough for the mice to feast upon. "There you go."

When we return to the table, I set the mice onto the floor and watch them scurry through a hole in the wall.

Mom and I serve many more families that day, making sure to hand out the food that needs to be eaten right away first, and saving the rest for the morrow.

Chapter Three

The next week passes much the same. Training with either my mom or dad every morning, and then service of some sort in the afternoon. It's a comfortable routine that keeps me busy and fulfilled.

After we finish our breakfast one morning, Mom clears her throat. "It's time to prepare for your birthday celebration."

"Ugh." I set down my shiny fork and drop the burgundy cloth napkin on the dark table. "Do we have to? It's such a waste. All those resources would be much better spent on the people. You know, if we're going to change the way we want the farming to take place, there are going to be certain expenses…"

My parents share a look. "Jessamine, that's a discussion for another time." My father attempts to keep the conversation on the topic they want.

Darn. Often, I can change the course of a conversation quite easily. I find if I just keep talking, polite people won't interrupt. Before I know it, I'm having the conversation that I want, instead. But it's not working this time. My shoulders slump.

My father continues. "At the very least we need to have some kind of coming-of-age celebration. You are turning seventeen in a few months. You are less than two years away from becoming Queen. You will be eligible to be courted, and perhaps even wed. What is it you would like to see?" My father looks so serious.

I squirm in my seat.

My mom brightens. "We could have a ball and invite people from all stations to attend. It would give you an opportunity to mingle with the young men that are eligible…"

"No." My hands shoot out to stop my mom's words. "No! As much as I love parties and dancing, I'm not thinking about, much less planning on, being courted by anyone anytime soon. I'm only sixteen! Give a girl a break, why don't you?"

My parents chuckle.

My mom answers, "Alright, alright! No ball. How about at least a parade? We can mingle the celebration with charity."

It's a better idea than trying to set me up with a bunch of immature boys who only want to make googly eyes at me, but... I have a different idea. "Actually, I've been thinking about something special for my birthday." I hold my hands still on the table.

"Oh? Do tell." Father leans forward, both hands supporting his bearded chin.

Butterflies erupt in my stomach. This is it. I've been thinking about this for ages but have been too afraid to ask. But if they want to know what I want for my birthday, this is the best chance I have. It's now or never.

"I would like to donate all the palace books into a new public building in town." The words rush out, as if a dam has broken. The rest of my thoughts spill out like flowing water. "I want the people to have a library. It's not fair that so many do not have access to the written word. Imagine how it would benefit everyone. People could borrow the books they like and then return them when they have finished them. We can have volunteers teach reading classes. And have fun story-time for the children. I can picture every last detail!" I'm practically bouncing in my seat as I talk, my words tumbling out faster the longer I go on.

My father looks surprised. My mom has tears in her eyes. Did I say something wrong?

"What?" I look back and forth between my parents.

My dad nods at my mom. She smiles and chokes on her words. "That sounds like a wonderful idea, Jessamine. And we can hold a charity dinner when the library opens, inviting anyone in the city to attend regardless of social standing."

That sounds more like it. A party, fancy clothes, *and* service all wrapped into one event? Yes, please!

"We will begin working on the details at once," Father announces.

"I have some things written down in my room, I'll go get them!" I jump from the table and dash for the door.

My dad's hand shoots out and grabs my arm. He pulls me to his side and wraps me in the tightest hug.

Giggles fill the air when his scratchy beard rubs against my cheek.

"I love you, Jessamine. You are growing up way too fast."

"Daaad," I draw the word out, sounding annoyed. But secretly, and I think he knows this too, I love it when he does this. My heart fills to the brim.

This is going to be the best birthday ever.

I hurry to my room, retrieve the notebook with the library notes, and return to the dining hall to present my ideas.

"You've really given this some thought!" Father peruses my notes.

He may not have thought it, but I do pay attention to what he says. To what they both say. And I take my job seriously.

My parents give me the day off from schooling and training and tell me to go have fun. We have a meeting with the leaders of the Forest People later that afternoon, so I'm not totally in the clear, but half a day off is better than none!

19

By midafternoon I've already spent the day in the forest talking to the animals and exploring. I even managed to connect with a squirrel for a little bit. I could see into her mind where she has hidden her nut stash. My mother's instructions are starting to make a little more sense now that I have experienced it for myself. I can't wait to tell her!

When the hour draws near for the meeting, I hurry inside and clean myself up. I change into my favorite lavender dress with an empire waist and half-sleeves that are a little flowy, then rush downstairs to the large sitting room.

Skidding to a halt outside the tearoom doors, the proper voices from within fill my ears. It's that kind of meeting, then. You never can tell when the Forest People come to visit. With a tall posture and slow, steady breaths, I smooth the front of my dress and push the doors open.

"Jessamine, dear, it is so nice to see you. Come give your Elder Blossom a hug." My grandma grins at me, her eyes crinkling at the corner. My mom's parents have the silliest nicknames for themselves: Elder Berry and Elder Blossom.

Grandma stands up from her seat on the brocade settee beside Grandpa. She wraps her arms around me. I bend down a little since I'm taller than her. She smells like sunshine and greenery.

She returns to her seat. Her posture is perfect, her nature-toned linen tunic style dress fits her exactly right, and her silver hair shines in the low light, almost like it's glowing. Neither of my grandparents wear shoes in the forest, but when they visit, they wear these really thin, really soft slippers that allow them to still feel every part of the ground beneath their feet.

Grandpa reaches for my hand and gives it a squeeze. His skin is cool and rough. "Growing up too fast, as usual, I see?" He winks at me.

"I love you too, Grandpa."

Making my way around the room and greeting each of the visitors with a touch on the arm, a polite squeeze of the hand, or a simple nod in some cases, takes nearly a quarter of an hour.

Uncle Henry, my dad's younger -and only- brother, and Aunt Dahlia, my mom's younger sister, are seated beside one another in a pair of wingback chairs near my grandparents. They met because of my parents, obviously. They like to tell the story and bat their eyelashes at each other, but I try to ignore it when that happens. They're the relatives I know the best out of my mom's enormous family. Seriously, she has twelve siblings! Since Henry is from the human kingdom, he and Dahlia live close by, instead of in the forest.

My cousins, Juliette and her older sister, Amelie, sit on either side of their parents. Amelie and Juliette are spitting images of one another, and their father. They both have long wavy blonde hair, pale skin, perfect red lips, and bright blue eyes. They are both part-human-part-Forest Person, just like me, but only Juliette inherited the ability to speak with the animals. Amelie, as far as anyone can tell, is a perfectly ordinary human. I have a few other cousins, some much older than me who did not attend this meeting because they have important work to do in the natural realm, and some too young to be here.

My last greeting is for Juliette. My stomach tightens. I don't know why I can't get over everything with her. It just feels so competitive. Like, yeah, she's a princess of the Forest People, but so am I. *And* I'm the princess of the humans, but who cares? We're supposed to be equals; friends- like sisters. But she edges around me as much as I her.

My eyes meet hers, but her bright blue ones look away as fast as they can. I sigh and settle beside my own mother.

"Let us begin," Grandpa says.

They were just waiting for me? I blush a little, but Mom pats my knee to reassure me.

"The rainy season has brought massive flooding in the valleys to the east. Many villages have been heavily damaged, and the people are suffering."

The others nod. We have heard about the flooding.

"It is time we use our influence and step in to assist." Grandma addresses my parents. "We need volunteers to remove mud from homes and shops, help reconstruct the roads, and provide food and clothing. The damage is on the borders of your lands, which is why we have come to officially ask for your aid."

I pay close attention. These are the things that I must know and understand.

Amelie looks a little bored and tired. Juliette has a smile plastered on her face.

My father is prepared for this meeting, already knowing what aid he will provide. "We are prepared to send enough food to last the village for several weeks, making regular deliveries, as necessary. We can also provide temporary housing for anyone who has been displaced from their homes, in the form of small, family-sized canvas tents. And we can donate tools. I have already arranged with the metalsmiths to each prepare a dozen tools, to be paid for by the royal family."

My heart swells. My dad never hesitates to help anyone he can.

"That is well," Grandpa replies. A secretary stands just behind his shoulder, making notes of the conversation.

"The Forest People will send workers to assist in the labor, and care for the animals and plants that have been displaced or damaged."

That seems fair. But what if…

I tug on my mom's sleeve and whisper into her ear. "What about the animals? Can't they do something to help? Like, a dragon could use his flames to dry out the homes, griffins could help deliver supplies…"

My mom shakes her head. "We can talk about those ideas later," she whispers.

Why are they so averse to my ideas of the animals helping more? Maybe they've already tried some of these things before? I make a mental note to make sure she explains this to me as soon as possible.

Official agreements are made between both parties. Then everyone stops acting all formal. It morphs into an almost party-like atmosphere. A low-key party, no music, dancing, punch, or anything. But fun, just the same.

"What do you want for your birthday, Jessamine?" one of my mom's sisters, Edelweiss asks me. "I can send you a rare flower for your garden. Or would you prefer a book? I know you like to read."

"Oh, you don't have to send me anything, Auntie. You can just… donate whatever the gift is to some little girl in your care that would enjoy it."

"How noble of you…" Edelweiss says. I can't tell if she's saying it sarcastically or not, but I don't care. I only ever see some of these relatives once or twice a year. And I already have everything I could ever want.

Each aunt or uncle hugs me at least twice. Only six of mom's siblings are here today. They all treat me like I'm still a kid. Except for Dahlia, who *actually* knows me.

After making polite conversation with the adults for what feels like a long time, Anthony enters the room and announces dinner. The whole group crowds into the dining room. The massive table is full, for a change. Dinner is served. It takes for-e-ver.

The menu tonight does not feature any animal protein, to be respectful to the Forest People. Instead, the cooks have prepared a vegetable dish with hints of nutty spices and tangy herbs, piles of warm flatbreads that fill the room with a yeasty smell, bowls of fluffy couscous laden with pomegranate seeds, a dozen different raw vegetables blended with spinach and lettuce, and lemony herbed roasted red potatoes that melt in my mouth. After a dessert of fruit tarts made with almond flour and raspberry syrup, my stomach feels like it might burst.

The conversation holds as much variety as the meal, and my mind is as full as my stomach by the time dinner finally ends and I say good-bye to my extended family.

Christine Marshall

Chapter Four

My grandparents, aunts, and uncles from the forest leave for home to begin the flood relief plans by the time the sun comes up the following morning. Dahlia, Henry, Amelie, and Juliette have returned to their own estate a day's journey beyond the city.

My eyes are bleary and feet clumsy when I join my parents for breakfast.

"Did you sleep well, Jessamine?" Mom asks.

I yawn, stretch, and nod.

"Cover your mouth when you yawn, dear," my mom reminds me.

"Sorry," I say behind my hand as I stifle a second yawn.

"Today the visitors from the other realms will be arriving," my father says between bites of fresh fruit and toast with nut-butter melting into it.

It smells so good that I quickly take a big bite of my own toast. The gooey nut-butter smears on my lips. I use my tongue to clean them before taking another bite.

"A large group of Forest People came with the royal family and stayed when your Grandparents and the others returned home." He drinks from his goblet filled with cranberry juice. "Much of our staff have been up through the night making final preparations in the guest wing."

I sip on my own juice and munch on a piece of cantaloupe that's probably too big to even be on my fork. My brain takes a minute to catch up.

The festival! I had totally forgotten!

"Is there anything I can do to help?" I sit up straight in my chair. My eyes feel suddenly bright, and all my sleepiness has vanished.

"I believe the Forest People, as well as others from the visiting realms, are in the meadow preparing for tomorrow's festivities. Feel free to see if there is any assistance you can provide." Mom smiles at me.

"Would it be alright if... if *I* prepare something for the festival? If this is an opportunity to show off our skills, then I have some pretty amazing skills to show off..." I grin with all my teeth showing.

My father, sensing the seriousness behind my sarcasm, nods. "I have to say it, just so *I* know that *you* know, that this is not an opportunity to show off. This is a chance for the realms to demonstrate what we can do, so that we all know what help is available in times of need."

I giggle. "I know, I know." I switch to a silly imitation of his deep voice. "This is a multi-cultural event to foster better inter-realm relations and aide in the ongoing peace of our world." He's said it to me so many times lately, that I get it. "But," I return to my own voice, "I do have a fun idea for the festival. Well, several but since it's only supposed to last three days, I'll have to narrow it down, I suppose."

He chuckles and nods. "Very well. If you need any assistance, I am sure any of the Forest People would be willing to help."

"Yes," Mom gets all excited. "In fact, I believe I saw several boys around your age among the group staying here. They looked cute to me. You should see if they want to help." My mom's eyes gleam.

I roll my eyes back at her. "I'll be fine on my own, Mom."

I hop up from the table and skip away, my second piece of nut-butter toast in one hand. I nibble on it and talk to myself as I make my way through the gardens toward the meadow. "I need to focus and come up with just one thing to do. I don't care what Father says, it *is* a chance to show off…"

A little vole pokes his head out of one of the garden boxes as I walk by. He wiggles his whiskers at me.

"You're right… I don't have to narrow it down." I shove the last bite of food in my mouth and pick up the vole. "You really think the others will agree?" I ask him.

He nods.

"Very well, let's give it a try, shall we?" I continue my walk.

He spins in an excited circle in the palm of my hand.

"Do you wish to return to the garden?" I pause just beyond the squared off hedges between the garden and the meadow.

He shakes his head.

"Great, let's go!"

We wander together across the meadow that gently slopes away from the castle and into the forest. Monarch butterflies abandon their milkweed and flutter along, like a wake in water. A spider strings herself from her web to land on the folds of my cotton day dress. A few ladybugs flit and land on my hair, decorating the braid that swoops from the base of my neck over my shoulder and rests on my chest.

Once in the woods, we proceed deeper into the understory. The beech and alder branches block a lot of the sunlight, creating the perfect environment for large, lacy ferns and huckleberry bushes to grow. Moss stretches up the north sides of the trees in some areas. In other places, the trees grow further apart, and patches of creeping thyme fills the little clearings. The almost minty smell of the thyme creates a pleasant perfume; and a fallen log overgrown with moss provides a cushioned place to sit. Near one of the beech trunks a circle of smooth white button mushrooms marks the home of a group of chanterelle pixies. I'm careful not to disturb their habitat; I'm only here to speak with the animals.

A sweet, lively tune expresses my desire for the animals to join me. Before long, the clearing is full. A pair of foxes, a swarm of yellowjackets, a single racoon, and a dozen other forest animals emerge from the trees. Soon blue birds, house finches, cardinals, and chickadees line the tree branches. Squirrels, chipmunks, and even a great horned owl descend from above. One chipmunk approaches me, not sure if she should come closer. I wave her forward and she settles in my lap.

"Welcome, friends! I have some exciting news, and I am hoping you will be willing to assist me."

The animals chirp, chatter, and buzz at my words.

I tell the animals my idea for the festival, giving the vole due credit for his encouragement. Most of the animals agree to help.

When I return to the castle, I ask my father if I can present my contribution during the opening celebration of the festival, which is to take place this evening.

"I don't see why not. What do you have up your sleeves, Jessamine?" He tugs on my long, flowy sleeve, as if he can glance up it and actually see what I'm planning.

"Oh, you'll see!" I answer in a sing-song voice. "I'll see you tonight!" I holler over my shoulder as I take the stairs two at a time to my suite.

A chamber maid brings me a plate full of cold sandwiches that disappear into my stomach in no time.

A dress made from a thick fabric that keeps one cool in the summer and warm in the winter, hand-woven by the Forest People themselves seems like the perfect choice for tonight. The grassy green color helps a Forest Person blend in when they do not wish to be seen by anyone. The scoop neck and loose sleeves are designed for comfort and function, but they are pretty, too. A bright gold sash around my waist, tied to one side with the ends dangling down to my knees, helps me stand out just a little bit. My hair remains loose. Only the front sections pulled back to either side with two sparkly clips resembling the jessamine flower: yellow star-shaped with green viny tendrils swirling around them.

"Perfect!"

Leaning out my floor-to-ceiling windows that remain open most of the time, my voice carries over the meadow and into the woods. A raven answers. They have received my message.

It's nearly time. Fireflies below dance in the late summer moonlight. People and creatures from many different races and realms gather at the far end of the meadow. The sounds of laughter echo back to me.

"No time to waste, Jessamine," I admonish myself, and hurry through the palace to join the others outside.

The air is warm and sweet with summer blooms. Not too sticky, not too cool. As if nature itself is joining us for our celebration.

The meadow fills in no time. I fidget beside my parents. My mom rests her hand on top of mine to still my fingers. I grin at her.

"I'm just excited."

She winks at me. "Me, too."

"Friends, welcome to the kingdom of Dragovalon! And to the first of its kind inter-realm festival!" My father calls to our guests.

Cheers, hoots, and hollers erupt from the crowd.

"We are honored to be joined tonight by the Forest People, of whom my wife is a proud member."

The Forest People, myself and Mom included, cheer.

"Next, welcome to the dwarves from the northlands!"

The dwarves stomp their feet and clap their hands. Their gruff voices muffled by their hairy faces call out some chant that I can't understand.

My mom shrugs her shoulders and smiles at me. Her eyes look just as excited as mine.

"We extend a warm welcome to the wood nymphs."

The tall, tree-looking people have grouped together near the edge of the forest. I suppose that's where they're most comfortable. They shake their leafy heads.

The rest of the crowd laughs at their greeting, and the nymphs bow as if they have put on a performance.

"Representing the sky realms, we have several pegasus." The winged horses whinny and flap their wings. "Thunderbirds." Two enormous birds the color of a stormy sky with lightning dancing on their wings fly a circle overhead. "And, of course, the family of dragons." The regal looking dragons, behind everyone else, make no noise, and only move their heads to dip them in greeting.

Plenty of the humans from my own kingdom ooh and ahh at the fantastic display.

"We are expecting to be joined tomorrow by several representatives from the sea. Because at present there is no body of water just beside the castle, they will not be joining us this evening. Lastly," my father squints out across the crowd as if he's looking for someone. "We invited… oh yes, there they are. Thank you for joining us tonight those from the Anastos Clan of centaurs."

Father is looking beyond even the dragons, squinting against the darkness.

"Where are they?" I whisper to my mom.

"They are wary creatures. I do not know how close they will come to such a large crowd. You will see them tomorrow, in the daytime," she whispers to me behind her hand.

My mind replays the serious conversation my parents had with me when they told me about all of this. Even though many of those in attendance are animal-*like*, they are not animals, and I am not to treat them as such.

I understand the gravity of that reminder. I don't want to be the single reason a war breaks out between the humans and one of the other realms!

"Thank you all for being here!" Father resumes his speech. Everyone quiets down once more. "We have several days of festivities ahead of us! We hope you will each take this opportunity to foster relationships with those not of your realm, building a community of friendship and trust."

The crowd cheers.

"To open our celebration, I'd like to introduce you to my daughter, Jessamine, Princess of Dragovalon."

More cheers.

I stand and wave, blushing. A mockingbird swoops toward me from the forest. He lands on my outstretched arm. I tell him to gather the others.

"My friends and I have prepared a little performance for you all. I hope you enjoy it!" I can't stop smiling.

The animals that want to participate, most of the ones from the clearing earlier, and a few more, make their way to my side in front of the audience. The birds sing a song they have practiced, while the other animals do little tricks. Flips, wiggles, hops. The owl hoots in a steady rhythm to keep the beat. The swarm of yellowjackets moves fluidly above the animals as one to make patterns that reflect the mood of the birdsong. I perform a dance that tells a story about the Forest People. I move my arms, turn, dip, and twirl. Most of those here tonight won't understand the true meaning behind the dance, but they can at least enjoy the feel of it.

When our performance is complete, the crowd erupts with applause. The animals and I beam at each other. The animals hang around for a little longer to soak up the praise of their admirers.

"That was beautiful, darling," my mom says as she wipes tears from her eyes.

"And with that," Father announces, "the festival has officially begun! Please, make yourselves at home. If you need anything, we have staff that will attend to your desires. Mingle, make friends, have fun!"

The party-like atmosphere lasts long into the night. Even after I retire to my bed, I can hear dwarves, humans, and others from my window. I listen until I can't keep my eyes open any longer.

31

Christine Marshall

Chapter Five

The palace staff has prepared the ball room, the gardens, and the meadow behind the castle for the festivities. The guest wing of the castle bustles with activity. Servants scurry all over the place like mice in a hurry, or ants in an anthill preparing for winter. Plenty are from our own staff, but many came with the groups that are visiting.

Staying in the castle are the dozens and dozens of dwarves and at least as many Forest People. The thunderbirds have prepared a temporary home in a cave not far from the palace, the centaurs are staying deep in the forest, and I'm assuming the woodnymphs are doing the same. I have no idea where the dragons are sleeping. The stable-hands have prepared a series of guest stalls for the pegasus.

Before heading to breakfast, I peek into the ball room. Large circular tables with long white tablecloths and elaborate floral centerpieces dot the shiny wooden floor. A row of banquet tables line one wall, laden with bowls of fruit, sweet rolls and pats of butter, sticky buns, jars of jams and jellies of every color, stacks of toast, as well as platters of meat, cheese, vegetable spreads, and more. My stomach rumbles at the savory aromas combined with the yeasty, sweet smell of the pastries. My mouth waters. But there's so much more to look at!

I wander between the tables, admiring the huge colorful bouquets of flowers that stand in giant urns in regular intervals along the remaining three walls. Padded benches rest between each pair. I study the banners that represent the different realms that decorate the walls.

The forest one is the most recognizable since it bears the emblem of the Forest People. My mom has a special handwoven angora blanket with this emblem on it. The wool is different shades of green, and if you stretch it out you can see the design: a large tree with branches that spread out above the trunk in a half circle, lots of branches and leaves intertwining with one another. It's a straightforward design, but it represents the stewardship the Forest People have over the natural world.

The sky realm banners are pale blue and feature an image that resembles looking down on the land from high above. Just looking at it makes me dizzy. The sea banners display an abstract design incorporating shells, waves, and small sea creatures in various shades of teal and green. The banners that represent those that live underground has a treasure box full of shimmering gold coins with a pickaxe leaning against it against a dark background. The dwarves are pretty proud of their mining abilities. The last two banners are for the mountains and the tropical places, showing towering peaks and sandy beaches, respectively.

The room overflows with light from the tall windows that lines the three exterior walls, and the colors of the decorations, the enormous floral arrangements, and the food shine like a rainbow. Dust glitters in the shafts of sunlight, giving the space a magical feel.

Guests sit at a few of the tables, though I imagine most of those visiting will sleep through the morning after the late night.

I back out of the room and hurry to the dining hall for breakfast with my parents. Similar food to that which is available for our guests in the ballroom awaits me.

"Slow down Jessamine, you don't want to choke!" My mom says through a grimace followed by a short laugh of surprise.

I don't blame her. Food enters into my mouth as fast as my hands can move.

"Done!" I stand, wrap my arms around my mom's shoulders, and squeeze. My dad gives me a kiss on the head.

"See ya later!" I holler over my shoulder as I hurry outside.

The gardeners have arranged amazing floral displays all over the place. Marble benches and lavish wooden bench-swings with stunning starshaped clematis vines climbing up the sides and across the tops finish off the displays. The mulch in the garden beds has a sweet, decaying aroma that brings back memories of digging in the garden with my mom when I was little. The vast variety of flowers fill the air with so many sweet fragrances, that it's hard to pinpoint a single smell.

Several new fountains bubble around the garden. The water running over the stone animal- and flower-statues sounds like a stream, and they smell like wet rocks in a riverbed, too.

Laughter and talking ring across the gardens from the meadow, and I even hear someone giggling behind the trellis in the rose garden. I can almost picture a young couple snuggling up beneath the tall rose trees with their heady perfume. That place will make anyone feel romantic!

The grass has been cut close to the ground, and the crisp smell awakens my senses even more. It's like walking through a wonderland.

Most of the activity is located in the meadow, and for good reason. The wide-open space is necessary for the events that will be taking place.

Even though many of the guests are still slumbering in their beds, the meadow hums with activity.

An enormous makeshift water feature, something like a fabricated pool for swimming, has been erected at one end of the meadow. Another portion of the meadow is cordoned off with thick ropes and wooden stakes hammered into the ground; enormous racks of weapons are lined up along one edge. Past the sparring arena and toward the stretch closest to my wing of the castle, an oversized easel covered in black cloth has been set up near the edge of the forest.

Spectator stands along the perimeter of each section create a playing field of sorts for each event. I've never seen anything like this. The next few days will be quite exciting, that's for sure.

By early afternoon, most everyone has risen and joined the festival. The first event is the competition between the water realm and sky realm. I sit between my parents in an elevated platform near the pool. Our platform has the special green fabric of the Forest People wrapped around three sides and the top, offering shade and protection from the bright sunlight. It's a good thing it's not mid-summer, otherwise it would be boiling hot out here. But since it's nearing fall, the temperature is moderate. Just right for spending the entire day outside.

From the elevated seats that have been arranged for all the spectators, both the pool and the sky above are easily visible. An elaborate obstacle course has been set up within the pool, fully submerged in the water. An enormous artificial coral reef; at least, I think it's artificial, with spikes, tunnels, divots, and peaks takes up a third of the pool. A series of hoops arranged in an intricate pattern rests beside the reef, some of the rings above the water, and some below. Finally, at the far end of the pool, lies a collection of enormous clam shells that shimmer iridescent in the sunlight. They slowly open and close. Resting inside each one is a huge, shiny pearl.

A matching obstacle course is suspended by some kind of fancy magic... or maybe just ropes and poles... in the sky above. Instead of an ocean theme, though, it has a sky theme. Mirrored above the coral is a fake fluffy cloud with identical divots, tunnels, and spikes. Next, a matching set of rings hovers above the rings in the water. And lastly, in the place of enormous clamshells hiding precious pearls, there's moonlike orbs that open and close, revealing bright lights within that resemble stars.

I'm bouncing in my seat by the time the competition begins. Everyone else that's watching is, too, I'm sure. The air is electric with anticipation.

As if marching… swimming?... in a parade, of sorts, the competitors from the water realm emerge from a place beneath the coral. How deep does this pool go? I'm distracted by the display for the thought to linger.

"Mom, look!" I squeeze my mom's arm with both hands.

She laughs beside me. "Yes, dear. I see them."

I'm referring to the capricorn, of course. Each creature has a front that looks like a goat and hind quarters that resemble an enormous grey shrimp tail. Long, thick tentacles poke out of their goaty heads. They swim at top speed through the water, showing off their ability to move as a group with ease. I cheer along with everyone else in the audience.

A pair of creatures joins the capricorns. They look like horses swimming under the water; their manes and tails are not hair, but frothy bubbles.

"What are those ones called again?" I ask my mom.

"Hippocamps," she reminds me.

"Right!" I smack my forehead. How could I have forgotten?

The hippocamps leap up out of the water, bubbles floating away from their manes and tails as they twist in the air, before descending below the water once more, barely disturbing the surface.

Finally, three naiads, or mermaids, as my mom says the humans refer to them, swim to the surface and float there; their human heads, shoulders, and arms rest above the water, while their scaly dolphin-like tails remain below. They all have light-colored hair pulled away from their faces and secured with shells; and seaweed wrapped around their torsos like clothes. They wave at the crowd all around them, smiling from ear to ear.

The sea competitors gather at one end of the pool and look to the skies for the sky realm competitors to present themselves.

Two juvenile dragons, one ruby red and the other charcoal gray, fly out of the forest and circle around the perimeter of the obstacle course with smoke puffing out of their noses. They land on a platform that stretches higher than the tallest beech and aspen trees.

A loud crack makes the crowd jump, and a flash of light announces the arrival of the thunderbirds. I shriek and clap my hands over my ears, anticipating their piercing cry before they release it. The air suddenly smells like it might rain, though no clouds darken the sky.

"Jessamine, look." My mom is the one to squeal this time. And for good reason. Her favorite creatures are gracefully making their appearance.

Two pure white pegasus stretch their feathery wings and glide onto the platform beside the dragons and thunderbirds. They whinny like horses and bow to my father.

"Let the race begin!" my father announces through a stiff paper cone that amplifies his voice.

The crowd erupts in cheers. Feet stomp, hands clap, people and creatures bellow their support; some for the sea, some for the skies, and some, like me, for everyone.

The creatures relay-race through their respective obstacles, attempting to prove they can maneuver through their element the best. The herd of capricorn compete as one, while the other creatures all compete as individuals.

"Doesn't that seem a bit unfair?" I holler at my mom so she can hear me above the noise.

She smiles. "Not if they do not mind." She leans close and shouts in my ear so I can hear her. But both of our eyes are still glued on the race. "There is no prize, this is all in good fun. It is more an exhibition than a competition if you think about it."

Should I watch the pool or the sky? My eyes dart back and forth between the two. The capricorn maneuver through the course as a group, while the young dark dragon matches them pace for pace above. Each competitor, or group in the case of the capricorn, retrieves one pearl or star, and makes their way back through the obstacle course to the beginning. The second dragon races the same herd of capricorn again.

"Oh! They have to do it twice…"

"Do not overthink it, dear. Just enjoy yourself!" Mom hollers back.

"You're right. This is amazing!"

When the naiads, thunderbirds, hippocamps, and pegasus have all finished their races, the outcome is a near-draw. But in the end, the sky realm wins, the last pegasus crossing the beginning of her coarse mere seconds before the hippocamp.

My voice is hoarse from cheering. My hands sting from clapping so much. My face hurts from smiling for so long.

Congratulations are announced, bragging rights awarded, and the crowd disperses to enjoy the late afternoon together. The same party-like atmosphere from the day before settles over the meadow. Since the water creatures must remain in the pool, many of the other guests decide to go swimming, too.

"I didn't realize it was salt water!" I say to a man from the Forest after I've joined the swimmers in the pool.

He nods, but swims away.

Salt water is much easier to float in, so I'm not complaining.

I splash with the hippocamps. Their bubble manes are light and airy, and not exactly attached to their bodies. I scoop the bubbles with my hands and blow them to watch them float away. And the hippocamps never run out of bubbles! The mermaids try to show me some tricks, but I'm not the strongest swimmer, and I can't keep up.

The sun reflects off the surface of the water, and by the time it sets below the horizon my skin is warm and tight. I can feel the redness in my cheeks and on my nose.

Christine Marshall

Chapter Six

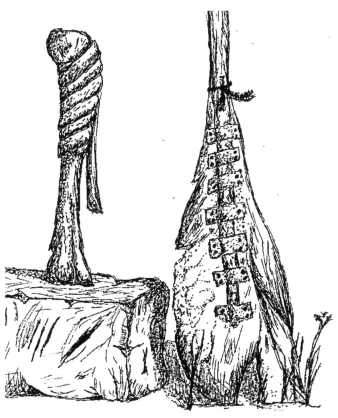

Hurrying so I don't miss a thing, I change out of my swimming clothes and back into a flowy, floral, summer-appropriate dress.

"Jessamine," my mom pokes her head into my room. "Do not forget to try to talk to as many of the guests as you can tonight. This will be a wonderful opportunity to become known as a respected leader in the eyes of the other realms."

"Yep! I'm excited! I won't forget."

"Good girl. I love you."

"I love you, too, Mom."

We head down the marble stairs arm in arm, and my dad meets us at the bottom step. The three of us enter the ballroom together.

Several more, long tables loaded with food line the furthest wall.

"There's so much food on them they look like they're going to break!" I whisper to my parents.

"Look at the variety of food. This is incredible," Mom says.

My dad nods. "Most of the visitors have brought along their own chefs, who have joined ours in the palace kitchens, and combined their skills to make some amazing fusion-style cuisine. Be sure to try a little of everything if you can."

One end of the long table is stacked high with plates. Mine fills as I make my way down the line. My parents have stopped to chat with someone from the forest, so I'm on my own.

Massive seafood platters containing lobster tails, crab legs, sardines, flying fish, shrimp, oysters, and sea anemones weigh down the first table. There's even a huge vat that I've been told contains several large whale steaks, for the dragons and thunderbirds, but I don't investigate to confirm the information. I choose to sample a few of the sea creatures, along with a couple of things from the huge, tossed salad for the herbivores of the sea. The salad is loaded with sea grapes, kelp, and seaweed, and some kind of green algae dressing. The food smells briny and some of the greens look a little slimy. But the fish and lobster have been seasoned well and the shrimp has a sweet dipping sauce to go with it. I'm not a huge fan of seafood, living so far away from the sea, but I don't mind trying a little bit of everything. Well, except the raw whale steaks.

The dwarf chefs have prepared a mushroom, potato, and rat stew; severed rat tails float on the surface. A large bowl full of toasted grubs for a crunchy topping for the stew sits beside the pair of steaming stew pots that are taller than me. A stack of bowls leans precariously between the pots, too. I scoop out enough of the stew to be polite, but the odor of the food reminds me of being underground.

"The grubs don't taste too bad," my mom whispers in my ear.

"Make sure you try at least one."

"If you say so…" I reluctantly place a couple of toasted grubs on top of my small helping of stew.

"Now this looks more appetizing," I say to Mom at the next table. An enormous non-seafood salad full of normal leafy greens, apples, cranberries, nuts, and fresh mushrooms waits for me there.

As if she can read my mind, my mom says in a low voice, "It's only 'normal' because it is what you are used to. For many here today the food that you find unusual is normal. Be aware of that."

I nod, too distracted by the salad to think too hard about how she knew I was thinking of it as "normal" food.

The table is soon surrounded by others from the forest, who will no doubt devour this salad. The dwarves, though, steer clear of the fresh fruits and vegetables.

At the last table, a large amount of beef is piled onto massive platters, and several whole roasted pigs are on display with their heads and hooves still intact. I know lots of beings eat meat. My father enjoys a rare steak from time to time. But the smell of the sizzling fat and smoky meat makes my stomach turn. I pass that portion of the buffet altogether. My mom follows close on my heals.

The ballroom-turned-banquet-hall has so many aromas from the wide variety of food and guests wafting in the air, that a lot of the guests, my family included, choose to eat our meal outside, picnic style.

Some of the guests are simply too large to eat inside, like the dragons, and thunderbirds, so the staff brings the whole roasted pigs and enormous whale steaks to the meadow for them.

The centaurs are not partaking of any of the offerings.

"Aren't they going to eat?" I ask my mom as we settle on the meadow grass.

My father joins us not two heartbeats later.

"They prefer to hunt their own food," Mom says between bites of her salad. "The men and women have taken to the forest to find their meal. They also like to eat their meat…" she tries to hide a disgusted look, "… raw."

My eyes go wide. "Gross."

"Hush, we do not wish to offend anyone," Father says quietly.

I dutifully taste the different foods that are on my plate, but fill up on the salad. When we are finished a servant collects our dishes.

As dusk turns into dark, groups of visitors explore the woods, climb trees, settle in the meadow grass, or meander through the gardens. I take my time meeting as many guests as I can, but I don't spend a lot of time with any single person or group.

A swarm of purple thistle pixies chases a pair of dwarflings out of their hiding place among the tall, flowering weeds. What were the little dwarfs even doing in there? The thistles are quite unforgiving. But the dwarves do have thick, long hair, and wear heavy clothing, even though the weather seems too warm for such attire. The young dwarfs holler at the sharp bites from the pixies which leave long thorns poking from the dwarves' thick skin.

A Forest Person tells a group of children from many of the realms a ghost story about the kelpies that live in the swamp. I settle beside the children and ooh and gasp in all the right places. When a more wise-looking Forest Person strolls by and hears the tale, she admonishes us for scaring the children.

"The children don't look scared to me." I shrug and look around.

She gives me a look that says she does not appreciate my contradiction.

I don't tell her that a couple of the young centaurs look like they may be conspiring to go on a kelpie hunt. Since they aren't human, the danger is probably not very great for them. But I warn them to be careful, just the same.

When my head finally hits my pillow after the moon has risen high and the hour grown late, it takes me no time at all to sink into sleep.

Thwack!

"Oof!"

"Arrrrgggggghhhh!"

My heart is racing in my chest.

"Go Eginhard! Smack him on the back!"

"Get up, Wyvernhelm! Before he tramples you!"

Voices ring out all around me.

Eginhard, the young centaur, gallops away from the fallen dwarf, Wyvernhelm, and tenses his muscles. He is going to charge!

Wyvernhelm struggles to his feet and grips his oversized iron sledgehammer in both grubby hands. He blinks a few times and shakes his head.

Eginhard gallops at full speed toward the dwarf, his own iron spear resting lightly in his left hand.

"Get him, Wyvernhelm!" the boy from the Forest beside me hollers, hands cupped around his mouth.

The centaur's hooves thud in the dirt. Dust clouds around him, nearly obscuring him from view.

Wyvernhelm crouches and swings his sledgehammer around him, turning in a circle.

My eyes nearly pop out of my head. As he spins, he gets faster and faster, the dust swirling around him, now, too.

"Aaaaaaarrrrrgggggghhhh!" Eginhard lets out a fierce cry just before he clashes with the dwarf. And the dwarf's sledgehammer.

All the hollers and cheers from the crowd stop in an instant, as if we are all waiting with bated breath for the result.

A sickening crunch comes from the dust cloud. As one the crowd groans. My own hands fly to my mouth.

A rough, victorious laugh from the dwarf echoes towards us, but is cut short by a snap. The dwarf cries out in pain.

The dust clears. The centaur and dwarf are a tangle of hooves, arms, tail, and beard on the ground. They grunt as they hit each other with hard fists. A steady stream of thumps and grunts comes from the mass.

Who will win?

I lean over the fence, trying desperately to get a closer look. Dust tickles my nose.

I jump when the centaur leaps to all four feet and raises his spear triumphantly.

The crowd erupts in a deafening roar of cheers, clapping, and stomping. The noise rings in my ears.

45

Am I the only one who notices that Wyvernhelm doesn't move on the ground beneath Eginhard?

"Is he…?" I grip the arm of the boy next to me.

"No," the boy shouts into my ear while still clapping his hands. "His chain mail would have prevented the spear from entering his flesh. He is knocked out, that is all."

I let out a sigh of relief.

A soldier from my own kingdom hops over the fence with ease and jogs to the centaur.

"Eginhard of the Anastos Clan claims victory!"

More cheering and hollering.

Another pair of my father's soldiers enters and carries Wyvernhelm, still unconscious, out of the arena, supporting him one under each arm. His boots drag a trench in the dirt on their way out.

"Next up," the first soldier addresses the crowd when they finally quiet down enough.

He announces the next centaur and dwarf that will battle, but I push my way through the crowd and don't hear their names.

Forest People surround my mother a little way down the meadow. Probably people she knows from growing up. I make my way over, leaving the noise, dust, and stuffiness from a couple hundred spectators behind me.

I link arms with my mom and listen to her talk to her friends for a few minutes. When there's a break in the conversation, she pats my hand.

"How was the competition?" she asks me as we walk away from the Forest People and back toward the castle.

I shake my head. "Violent."

She chuckles. "Yes, the centaurs and dwarves are both fierce in battle. And proud."

"It just seems so… barbaric. I don't know how anyone can stand to keep watching."

Mom pokes at my cheek. "No frowning, dear. The weapons are dull, and the armor is strong. No one will be gravely injured. It is all just for fun."

"Well, I don't see anything fun about it…"

"That's why you don't see me over there watching, either."

"At least the competition between the woodnymphs and Forest People tonight won't be as heated!" I pick a milkweed blossom as we walk across the meadow. I miss seeing the butterflies and critters in the meadow, but they are staying away with all the action going on. I don't blame them!

"Do not be too sure about that. The woodnymphs are a very proud race, as well."

"Yeah, but they aren't going to try to stab one of the Forest People with a spear!"

My mom tips her head back and laughs aloud.

I smile and squeeze her arm.

She's on her way to mingle with the visitors some more, but I need a break!

New foods fill the tables in the ballroom including my favorite tasty looking fruits and a lumpy cheese with blue streaks running through it.

One of the tables nearby is full of giggling girls from the Forest. They only give me a polite wave as I pass. I don't really fit in with them since I'm only half-Forest.

I sigh and slump into a chair at a table on the opposite side of the ballroom. A little mouse sneaks out from beneath the table, and I offer her a piece of the cheese. She sniffs it and shakes her whiskers, then takes it from me and scurries away.

A pair of she-dwarves enters the hall. At least, I think they are female. It can be kind of hard to tell. Their hair is so long and scraggly and hangs around their faces from beneath their iron helmets, that it looks like they have beards. But I'm pretty sure it's just hair. They hurry over to the food, then huddle together at a table to eat and talk.

The girls from the Forest stand up and exit the hall as group. I sigh. I guess I'm destined to sit here alone.

"Excuse me?" a male voice speaks politely in my ear.

Christine Marshall

Chapter Seven

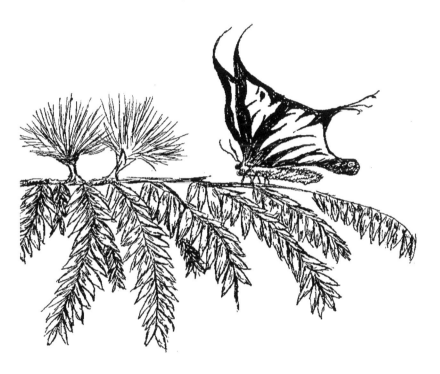

Startled, my bright red punch splashes onto the floor, sending a waft of fruity sweetness to my nose. I manage to dodge the spill and avoid getting any on my light blue dress.

The voice lets out a low chuckle. "Sorry about that. Here, let me help."

A hand reaches for my cup. I follow the bare, muscular arm with my eyes until my gaze lands on a handsome face. Blonde hair swoops across his forehead. Green eyes lined with dark lashes peer down at me. A warm smile stretches across the lower half of his face, accentuating his strong jawline and shadow of stubble.

Does he notice my gulp? He's cute. Really cute. I think my mouth might be hanging open. I snap it closed.

The visitor bows at the waist, then stands tall again. "May I join you?"

He lowers himself into the chair beside me.

"My name is Peter. Well, Prince Peter, to be precise. You must be Princess Jessamine."

My eyes are still locked with his. I nod. Again. I still haven't spoken to him.

Prince Peter. Right. I've seen him from afar before when we were both children. He's from the neighboring kingdom, but we have never properly met. The kingdoms don't intermarry for political reasons much anymore, so there was never a plan for us to court or wed or anything.

Why am I even thinking about that? At least it's warm in the ballroom so he won't notice my blush.

My nerves are twisting my insides. I swallow hard and force my voice to stay calm and clear. "You can just call me Jessamine. It's so nice to meet you, too, at last."

My brain strains to think of something to say.

"I didn't know your family would be in attendance. I haven't seen any of them these past few days." What a stupid thing to say. What is wrong with me?

Peter smiles warmly. "We have only just arrived. What did I miss so far?" He calmly waits for me to answer.

When I finally pull myself together, I talk. "Yesterday was the obstacle course race between the representatives from the sea and sky."

The more details about the close calls, and how the pegasus barely won in the end, the more excited my voice and hands become.

His eyes dance as he listens. He laughs and a dimple appears in his cheek.

My heart flutters.

"And today?" He prods me to keep talking.

"Oh, well, I'm not sure if I would exactly say you *missed* anything today…" I tell him about the barbaric showdown between the centaur and the dwarf. "I'm pretty sure the sparring is continuing, if you want to check it out."

Peter shakes his head. His blonde hair shines like strands of gold. "I'm fine right here."

Seriously, I might faint.

"I am sorry that I have missed all the festivities."

Willing myself to speak as a normal person, I assure him, "You haven't missed everything yet. There's still the competition between the woodnymphs and Forest People later today. And the ball tomorrow…"

My cheeks redden. Again. Why'd I have to bring up the ball?

His eyes twinkle. "Both events sound wonderful."

"Peter!" A woman's voice calls from the entry hall. "Oh, there you are. Come along, dear. Your father wants you to greet the King of Dragovalon."

Peter gives me a small eye roll. "Duty calls."

"I know what you mean!" My eyes don't leave his face.

He bends down and whispers in my ear. "Save me a dance…"

All on its own, with no prompting from me, my head nods.

He strides away. I can't help but take in his wide shoulders that stretch the back of his neutral-colored tunic, his tanned arms showing beneath his rolled-up sleeves, his dark brown trousers that hug his thighs, his tall leather boots, and his perfect posture as he leaves the room. He glances over his shoulder and sees me staring. He winks, and I giggle in response.

The butterflies in my stomach are performing an elaborate dance now. I hold my hand on top of my belly. "Just breathe, Jessamine."

Then I squeal only loud enough for myself to hear.

I can't wait for the ball!

On my way to the meadow for the final competition, my eyes scan the crowd for Peter.

"Looking for anyone in particular?" my mom nudges my side.

"What? No!" I answer, a little too abruptly. "I mean, no. Just…

enjoying the variety of guests and their different mannerisms and dress."

"Uh-huh…" my mom nods but doesn't meet my eyes. "Well, the King and Queen of Bennfaran are meeting with your father. They will probably be late for this event."

"Huh, interesting," I try to sound nonchalant. "Don't they have kids or something?"

My mom chuckles. "You mean, their son, Peter, who's only a year older than you?"

I shrug. "Sure…"

"Yes, Jessamine. Peter will be at the event tonight. But I'm not sure where he will be sitting. He does know some of the soldiers and guards from Dragovalon."

My heart sinks, just a teensy bit, but I try not to let my mom see.

"Do you know any of the competitors from the Forest?" I change the subject.

My mom side-eyes me but plays along. I bet she can tell I'm disappointed that she doesn't know where Peter is.

She tells me about two of the women competing. "They are twin sisters. I grew up with them. They were fun playmates as children, but since their area of stewardship is over the flora and mine fauna, we did not get to spend much time together when it came time to master our abilities. They are sweet, though. You will like them."

We settle into our seats, and I lean forward with my elbows resting on my knees.

"Posture, Jessamine."

"Right." I sit up nice and tall until my mom becomes distracted by the event, then slouch into a more comfortable position again. I smirk to myself. I have her all figured out!

Below us, two enormous circles have been marked by closely trimmed grass. A representative from the Forest People steps out and stands between the circles, in front of the large, cloth covered easel. He wears the practical style of the Forest People, and his black hair is shaved close to his head, revealing his dark skin.

"Welcome to the third and final event of the festival!"

The crowd roars. He holds out his hands for silence.

"Before you stands an easel. Beneath the covering are a series of paintings of detailed scenes from around the world.

"For tonight's competition, representatives from the wood nymphs," he gestures to a group of tree-people standing at the edge of the circle to his left. "And the Forest People," he gestures to his right. "Will each use their remarkable abilities to recreate the painting. Not with paints or oils, but with the elements themselves. You see, they will not create art. They will be creating the real thing!"

The crowd cheers again.

"Yes, yes, it is rather amazing!" He hollers with a chuckle and gestures for the crowd to calm again.

"The competition will take place in rounds, with one member of each team competing at a time. They will have several minutes to observe the painting and commit it to memory. Then they will enter their respective circle and use their abilities to recreate it down to the last detail. After thirty minutes, they will step away from their creation, and a pair of judges, one from each of their realms, will compare the work to the original painting. They will receive a score between zero and ten.

"At the end of the evening, the realm with the highest score will be declared the winner."

The dark-haired, dark-skinned man waits for a response from the crowd. He guffaws. "Now you are silent? Please, share your enthusiasm for the event!"

He leads the clapping and once the crowd is thoroughly excited, he leaves the space.

A wood nymph enters the circle to my right. It's hard to tell if it's male or female since it looks exactly like a willow tree. With arms, and legs. Sort of. It's taller than any of the humans present. The branches that droop from its head give the impression of long hair, and some wrap diagonally around its body and trail on the ground. I tip my head. It kind of looks like a dress? The face is made up of crags and bumps that resemble eyes, a nose, and a mouth, and it appears to be smiling. When the woodnymph arrives at the center of the circle, its feet -or the bottom of its trunk?- stay in one place, but the rest of it sways gently back and forth, almost like it's rocking an infant.

My mom sees me studying the figure carefully. She leans beside me and whispers in my ear, "That is Ilana. I have met her before. She is one of the few wood nymphs that does not consider humans inferior."

My mom continues. "She has been walking the woods for well-near a millennium."

I practically choke on my gasp. "You're kidding!" I turn shocked eyes onto my mother.

She shakes her head and smiles wide. "She has a very long, rich history. If you have the chance to speak with her, you should. She has many wise words to share with those of us who are not so long-lived."

Coming from my mom, that is saying something. The Forest People age differently than regular humans. They grow at a pretty normal rate until they reach adulthood. Then the aging becomes so slow that a person who looks to be middle aged could actually be several hundred years old.

"She has many talents. I am quite looking forward to seeing her performance this evening." My mom claps politely for Ilana.

My gaze returns to Ilana, seeing her through a totally different lens now that I know a little more about her.

When cheers from the Forest People erupt to my left, I'm snapped out of my wondering about Ilana.

A short, plump woman with frizzy gray hair marches to her place at the center of the circle on the left. She's wearing a green flowy sleeveless dress the same color as the meadow grass, and a floppy woven hat sits on top of her mane. She lifts her chin into the air to show that she is ready.

"Who's that?"

"That is Plum. She has been around since I was a child. She has much skill as well. This will be a close competition."

The man that introduced the competition stands beside the easel and pulls the cloth off with a flourish.

The crowd of Forest People gasps and begins to whisper to one another. The wood nymphs show no emotion whatsoever. Ilana and

Plum step closer so they can each study the painting. It is difficult to see from where I'm sitting, but my mom fills me in on the details.

"That is the julibrissin tree, or silk tree," my mom tells me. "It is native to tropical areas. They can grow very large."

"If it's just a tree, why would that be so difficult for them to recreate?"

My mom taps her chin. "That is the question, isn't it. I'm guessing that since the climate here wouldn't allow a tree like that to survive, it would be difficult to gather the required elements to make one from scratch."

Ilana nods and returns to her circle, while Plum studies the picture a little bit longer.

The willow wood nymph sways in her spot; her eyes appear to be closed. Her branch-hair swings back and forth, and a strange noise comes from within her, though her mouth is not open. As she sings and sways, brown sticks poke out of the ground. She twirls her hands in the air, as if twisting them together without touching them. In no time, a tree begins to form.

At the same time, Plum is sitting on the ground with her legs crossed beneath her. With her short stature and plump face, she reminds me of a child. She has both hands resting on the ground and is talking to the meadow floor as if chit-chatting with a friend. A tiny tree sprouts before everyone's eyes and begins to grow.

The beginnings of both trees start out very different, but soon they look nearly identical. They both have smooth brown bark on tall narrow trunks. Many, many branches stick out from all over. Ilana's even has seedlings and young versions of the tree sprouting all around the mature looking one.

Each branch on both trees is laden with a fan of smaller branches along the whole length on both sides. The smaller branches have dark-green leaves all up and down that look kind of like fern leaves, or solid looking feathers.

Time is running out when all of the sudden both trees burst with blossoms. Their perfume is carried toward the crowd on a slight breeze. Ilana and Plum are neck-in-neck with their tree growing. The blossoms on both are pink, a little deeper on Ilana's than Plum's. They look like wispy, feathery half circles sticking out of the branches all over the place.

When the horn sounds to indicate that time has run out, Ilana and Plum put the finishing touches on each of their trees, then drop their hands to their sides and stand back to observe their work.

Chapter Eight

Both look critical of their own work, but to be honest, both trees look fantastic!

The judges take the field to examine the painting and each tree. They concur for several long moments and declare Ilana the winner.

Half the crowd stands on their feet, whistles, and cheers. The Forest People look a little dejected.

But the competition isn't over. The judges touch the trees, and they both disappear in a cloud of sparkly dust, like they never even existed.

"This is seriously amazing!" I say to my mom, just as my dad joins us.

He sits beside Mom and kisses her on the cheek. She leans against him a little as the next competitors take their places.

With the arrival of my dad, I'm suddenly reminded of Peter. Where did he end up? I totally forgot to look for him with the anticipation of this event, and the spectacular display of talent.

Mom said he was friends with some of the guards and soldiers. A group of them stands close to the field in their matching red uniforms. I search the group for Peter's golden hair and neutral brown clothes. My heart leaps in my chest.

There he is! He's laughing with the other men his age as they push and tease one another. Some of the soldiers are eyeing a group of girls from the Forest. It looks like they are trying to flirt with them, but the girls are ignoring their advances.

One of the guards picks a bouquet of blue aster flowers and lavender daybells and takes it over to the girls. The girls stare at him like he's insane when he offers them the bouquet. One of the girls standing in the front tosses her long red braid over her shoulder and takes the bouquet with a raised eyebrow. The boy grins like an idiot. Until she waves her hand over the bouquet, and it wilts in an instant. She drops the limp, brown stems and dried up flower blossoms to the ground.

Peter and his friends point and guffaw at their companion as he returns with a posture of rejection.

I chuckle to myself. Those boys should have known better.

"He's cute," my mom startles me when she speaks in my ear.

My face and ears turn red, and I quickly return my eyes to the competition where one of mom's twin friends faces off with a smaller wood nymph as they try to recreate a wintry forest scene.

Mom wraps her arm around my shoulders and gives me a squeeze. "I'm sorry. I'll stop. But if you do want to talk about boys anytime, just come knocking on my door. I've been around a while and know a thing or two…"

I roll my eyes. "Moooommmm!"

I keep my attention focused on the competition. As best as I can. It's not my fault my eyes keep wandering back to Peter.

The next day drags with anticipation for the ball. And for dancing with Peter. I try to nonchalantly look for him throughout the day of mingling and picnics and palace tours and excursions into the city, but

I don't spot him anywhere. I mean, there's a LOT of people here, so I'm not that surprised. Disappointment pulls on my shoulders.

The staff transforms the ballroom from a dining hall into a magical, romantic space by the end of the day. The tables are removed, and the floor cleaned for dancing. After supper, which is eaten outside again by almost everyone, an orchestra sets up on one end of the room. The music they play is lively and inviting. Candelabras as tall as my father, full of flickering white candles have replaced the floral urns, giving the space a soft glow against the dark windows at nightfall.

Guests begin to arrive, dressed in their finest native attire. I'm practically bursting with anticipation as I take it all in.

"Go choose a dress to wear, dear, and meet us downstairs in half an hour." My mom smooths my hair behind one ear. She has a gleam in her eyes.

What does she have planned? My feet carry me to my room in a hurry to find out.

A beautiful midnight blue satin dress with a sprinkling of sparkly sapphires sewn into the bodice has been laid out on my bed. I gasp. I rush forward and scoop it up with both arms, then hurry to my huge closet to change.

The dress slides down my arms and over my head; the skirts continue around me until they reach the floor. A chamber maid joins me to lace up the back of the dress. It fits perfectly. The cap sleeves just cover my shoulders, and the sweetheart neckline rests at a modest place on my chest. The layers of tulle, satin, and organza make the skirt wider than my shoulders. And the length is exactly perfect, just brushing the floor.

The chamber maid hands me a pair of silver satin gloves that stretch up my arms past my elbows. She clasps a sapphire and pearl bracelet on my left wrist, on top of the glove. A matching necklace is placed around my neck.

Another maid pulls sections of my hair into braids of various thicknesses and pins them into a twisty pile on the back of my head. She leaves a few loose curly tendrils to frame my face on one side. Then she adds pins with sapphires and pearls into my hair.

The whole ensemble is finished off by a pair of low-heeled silver satin slippers that match my gloves.

When I look in the full-length mirror, I gasp. Now this is what a princess is supposed to look like! I love all of it. Twisting and turning to admire myself from all angles leads to heaping piles of praises onto the maids for their assistance in getting me ready.

I rush to the top of the stairs, but then pause. I must make a regal entrance. Right? What if Peter is down there? I straighten my posture and rest one hand lightly on the banister. With my other gloved hand, I carefully lift my skirts and take slow steps down the curved staircase. Half-way down, one of my silver shoes slips off my foot. I nearly stumble but manage to hold my composure. With a graceful pause my foot finds the shoe and slides back in. All without breaking my smile.

My parents wait at the bottom as I finish my descent. My dad lets out a whistle, and my mom has tears in her eyes. But no Peter. They wrap me in a group hug.

"Careful!" I admonish. I don't want them to ruin… well… any of it!

"You look absolutely perfect," my mother gushes.

"Thank you. Both of you." My own smile stretches from ear to ear.

Before the night is through, I am asked to dance by no less than three dwarves, five Forest People, and even one of the wood nymphs. Which is awkward, since they don't exactly have hands.

The dwarves, shorter than me by at least head and shoulders, speak in their gravelly voices and regale me with tales of their battles. One of them was even a competitor during the festival.

"That centaur didn't stand a chance against me. Sure, I took a few hits here and there," he flinches as he flexes his shoulders. How many bruises reside beneath his clothing? "But that cocky horse-man limped off the field with a broken leg."

My eyes go wide. Mom said they wouldn't get hurt!

The dwarf spins me away from him, and then pulls me close again.

"Not to worry, lassie." He must have caught my surprised expression. "The healers from the Forest People took care of him."

He stands on tiptoes and scans the room. "Ah, see? There he is."

Between dips and turns, my eyes follow where the dwarf is looking.

Small, female centaurs surround a young-looking half-horse half-man. They giggle at whatever he's telling them. He does look a little cocky. But he also doesn't look too worse for the wear. Although, his dark skin probably camouflages many of his injuries.

"I can't see his legs..." I say more to myself than my dancing partner.

"Aye. But there's nary a sling nor wrap on the broken one."

My attention returns to the dwarf.

We touch hands and turn in a circle, then switch hands and go the other direction.

"Did you see me defeat him, by chance?" The dwarf looks so hopeful.

I shake my head. I don't like to lie, so I don't give an excuse. The truth is, I just didn't want to watch anymore.

He shrugs and continues to give me a play-by-play of every dodge, parry, and attack between himself and the centaur as we make all the appropriate steps for the dance.

"That little filly didn't stand a chance..."

The song ends, and we stop dancing. We both face the orchestra and clap.

The dwarf gives me a low bow. "It has been a pleasure dancin' with ya' tonight, lassie."

"And you." I return the complement.

He wanders away from me and finds another pretty human girl to accompany him for the next dance.

My eyes scan the room, looking for Peter. He's with a group of young men from Dragovalon and Bennfaran. They look like they are having a fabulous time telling each other tales. When the next song begins, the group splits apart and most of them find women to pair with. Peter hasn't asked me to dance yet. Disappointment wraps around my insides, but I push it away. We only had one brief encounter yesterday. It's not like I should be expecting him to fawn all over me or anything.

61

A boy from the Forest asks me to join him for this dance. He talks about where he's from, and I ask appropriate questions to keep the conversation lively between dance steps. He's pretty cute, so I'm not complaining.

When the song is finished, I head over to sit on a bench near my parents. I am exhausted. It's been a busy, but fun, few days. My body is tired, but my eyes are happily taking in the mood of the ball. I slip my shoes off my tired feet. They are hidden beneath my gown so no one will know.

The orchestra takes a small break, for which I am relieved. I can't be asked to dance again if there's no music! I sip on some punch and watch the other people move around the room. Their gowns and robes and sashes and hats fill the room with bright colors, soft fabrics, enormous feathers, and sparkles. So many sparkles. My eyes don't know where to look.

Someone clears their throat to my left. I pay no attention, it's not like I *really* know anyone here.

"Jessamine?" the voice says in my ear.

It's Peter! Finally!

Pull yourself together, Jessamine.

I raise my eyes and keep my smile small, even though my cheeks want to pull my mouth into an enormous grin.

"I apologize for not joining you sooner," he says. He really does look regretful.

"That's alright. I have had no shortage of dance partners this evening."

He smiles, and his eyes crinkle at the corners. "I know, I've been watching."

He's been watching? I suppress a squeal and keep my composure.

"And I don't blame any of them one bit. You look…" he looks me up and down. "Breathtaking."

I blush. Hard. "Thank you," I dip my head demurely.

"Would you care to dance?" He gestures to the dance floor where couples are gathering once more.

When did the music resume?

He reaches his gloved hand out to me, and my own hand grasps it of its own accord. He gently pulls me to standing.

My shoes! I hurry to slip them back on, but only manage one.

"Oh!" My steps carry me forward, but one shoe stays behind.

Peter chuckles. "It seems you've forgotten something," he says as he bends and picks up my shoe. "May I?"

He kneels in front of me, and I lift my skirt just high enough to stick my foot out from underneath it.

Every eye in the ballroom must be on us. I sneak a peek without turning my head too far. No one pays us any attention. Whew.

"There, a perfect fit!" Peter stands. "You must be a Princess." He winks.

With my foot back in place beneath my gown, Peter leads me to the dance floor. My heart beats erratically in my chest. He smells like the outdoors. And something else. I breathe in deep. Spices. The aroma is intoxicating.

We don't take our eyes off each other as he leads me through the dance.

Is this a dream?

The music fills the hall. All other sights and sounds fade into the background. Peter spins me around with graceful movements. He leads me flawlessly through the dance, twirling me in all the right places, and never taking his eyes off me.

"I am very pleased to be sharing this dance with you, Princess Jessamine."

He maneuvers behind me and turns me to face him. We bend our knees, dipping in time to the music.

"Likewise," I answer.

Likewise? What kind of lame response is that? Peter's green eyes have me all flustered. My brain feels like mush.

As the dance continues, I can't think of a single thing to say.

Peter doesn't speak either. We are lost in each other's eyes.

Too soon the song ends.

A little out of breath, he asks, "Would you care to accompany me to the gardens?"

Does he know that's, like, the prime romantic spot for these events?

How could he? He's never been here before! Butterflies fill my stomach.

He links my hand through his bent arm, and we walk across the ballroom and through the massive doors into the night.

Chapter Nine

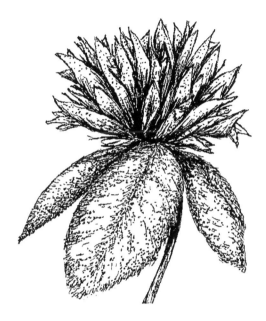

The patio has been strung with candle holders that flicker with tealight candles. Other couples mingle around the space, some sitting close together on two-person benches, others standing and sipping punch and laughing together.

The sweet scent from the floral arrangements only adds to the romantic atmosphere.

Peter leads me off the patio and into the rose gardens. "These gardens are beautiful," he says.

"I agree." I bend over to smell one of the deep red roses. The perfume fills my nose and I sigh.

Peter sets the pace slow. We meander through the maze of roses of every color and size. The scent of the roses permeates the air the further along we wander. The noises from the patio, and the ballroom within the castle, fade the further we go. The cloudless sky sparkles with starlight, and our feet make almost no noise on the manicured grassy path. As far as I can tell, we are utterly alone.

My heart races in my chest. It's a good thing I'm wearing gloves, so Peter won't be able to tell that my palms are moist.

His voice is strong and smooth as he tells me about his kingdom, his family, his friends.

"I have two brothers and a sister."

"Wow! That's a big family!" I say without thinking. "I mean," I say in a polite way. "That's wonderful, Peter."

He laughs at my outburst. "You don't have to be so formal with me. It is a big family."

I smile and relax.

He stops and faces me, grasping both of my gloved hands with his. "I would sincerely like to get to know you better. I want to hear your reactions to things. I want you to be open with me."

I gulp and nod. "Alright."

He smiles. I practically melt under his gaze. So much for being relaxed!

Looping my hand back through his arm, he takes my cue and continues to lead me on our stroll.

"I've been studying with the monks for some time, reading the ancient texts and even learning how to do that fancy writing that you see in their books. I love perusing their library and finding books to read. They have so many!"

When he starts talking about books, I light up. "I love to read, too!"

We tell each other about our favorite books.

"I love fairy tales and books of learning."

He nods. "I've been studying astronomy as of late."

"I have this plan that my parents are going to help me with." I tell him.

For the next fifteen minutes he listens to my idea for the library for my upcoming seventeenth birthday.

"I'm sorry! I've been talking your ear off!" I cover my mouth with one hand.

He chuckles. "Do not apologize. I think it sounds like a wonderful idea." He looks thoughtful. "Maybe this is something we can implement back home, as well."

All at once, out of nowhere it seems, his hand rests on the small of my back, and I'm leaning on him a little. Neither of us speaks.

We stop to gaze at the stars, extra bright due to the new moon. The air is fresh and clear. The greens from the garden, the fresh cut grass, the heady perfume of the roses, all mingle to give the perfect ambiance.

I glance at Peter. He is watching my face carefully with his deep eyes. My heart pounds in my chest.

He swallows, and in a husky voice he says, "We should probably return to the ball."

I lower my eyes and nod. I'm glad it's too dark for him to see how red my cheeks are at the moment.

We meander through the gardens and back toward the lights and sounds of the patio and ballroom. The air within the ballroom is close and sticky after the freshness of the outdoors. But Peter is a decent distraction from that, and from my tired feet, and from pretty much everything.

We share two more dances before the night ends too soon. We discover we enjoy many of the same things like charity work and the outdoors.

He is amazed when I tell him about my ability to communicate with animals, and he makes me promise to show him next time we see one another.

If only this night would never end.

While I'm lost in a dream dancing with Peter, the palace staff collects my parents' things. They load their trunks and travel bags onto the royal carriage that has been added to the caravan outside the palace.

Guests linger for as long as possible. Many seem reluctant to return to their quarters and prepare for the tour of the kingdoms and realms to continue. I, too, am reluctant to separate from Peter, but my parents are also preparing to depart.

They are joining the entourage as the tour continues to the next realm. They weren't sure they would go when the invitation was extended, but they changed their minds and have been preparing for days.

The tour had planned to leave in the morning, to give everyone time to rest up after the ball. But snow and wind are expected in the mountains. They will leave tonight in hopes that they will be able to stay ahead of the weather as they travel to the northlands.

Peter and his parents retire to their suite. They aren't going on the tour, but will return to their own home tonight, as well.

Peter wraps me in a warm embrace and waits until the last second to release me. Our eyes linger on one another as he disappears with his parents up the stairs and toward the guest wing.

I'm snapped out of my swoon when my parents come from the other direction and make their way down the stairs. They've changed out of their extravagant clothes into plain, comfortable clothing for travel.

My dad clenches his jaw a few times and rubs his eyes. "I'll miss you, Jessamine. We will return in five weeks' time. As soon as I arrive home, we will begin the plans for the library in earnest." He squeezes me in his arms again and sighs.

When he releases me it's Mom's turn.

My mom, tears in her eyes, as usual, wraps me in a hug, too. She's too choked up to speak, though.

Tears sting at my own eyes. I've never been away from them for this long before. I swallow my tears and put on a brave face. "Be safe!"

"Have fun," my mom answers, wiping the tears off her cheeks.

I scoff. "Right, like I'm going to have fun without you. I'm going to be so bored!"

My mom smiles through her tears.

"You can come out now," she calls.

I look at her like she's crazy. "What are you talking about? Come out from where?"

"Hey there, Clover Blossom!" a woman's voice says all nonchalant behind me.

I spin on my heels and barrel into the tall woman with long straight black hair and high cheekbones, who has appeared out of nowhere.

"Magnolia!!" I squeal in her ear.

"Watch it, Sunflower, you'll knock me over and then where will you be? Alone, that's where!"

My mom's best friend, Magnolia, has always called me every flower name possible, except for the one I've been given. It's kind of a standing tease between us.

She holds me at arm's length and looks me up and down. "You've grown! You're almost a head taller than you were the last time I saw you! How is that possible? And look at this get-up!" She stands back, still holding my soft silver gloves in her calloused hands. "You look like a woman! Spin around so I can see the whole deal."

I do a quick spin for Magnolia, grinning from ear to ear.

My mom laughs. "Like I said, Jessamine. Have fun!" She has a twinkle in her eye.

"Now I *will* have fun!" I grin. Magnolia is the best fake-aunt any girl could ask for. I'm kind of excited for my parents to leave now.

I hug my parents one last time. "Thank you! And have fun, too. Doing whatever it is that grown-ups even do for fun." I gesture between them, then my face goes red. "Not like that! Ew! I mean, like, read or something! Gah, never mind!"

All three of them erupt in laughter and I cover my face with both hands.

"Goodbye, my sweet Jessamine." My mom leans her forehead against mine. "Remember who you are."

She waves as they walk out the front doors.

I return the wave as the reminder of who I am echoes in my head. I have special abilities. I have been born into privilege. I am the future Queen.

As soon as the doors close, my mind returns to the present. I grab Magnolia's hand and drag her up the stairs toward my room.

"We are going to have so much fun, Magnolia! I can't believe you're here! It's been way too long. Oh my gosh, I have so much to tell you about."

Magnolia can't get a word in edgewise as I share every last detail about my recent training with my mom trying to learn to connect with the animals.

While I talk, she helps unlace my dress, and pulls off my silky gloves.

"I met the cutest little girl at the orphanage last week! When I'm the Queen I'm going to let all the orphaned children live in the castle!"

Magnolia smiles but doesn't interrupt my monologue.

The jewelry clinks into the glass bowl on my vanity as do the pins and jewels from my hair. The curls and braids fall down my back. I'm sure it looks terrible, but who even cares?

A simple pair of linen pants and loose tunic are the perfect clothes for lounging with Magnolia and staying up all night talking. My feet find a pair of soft, fluffy slippers to complete the ensemble.

"Check this out!" I wave her closer to look over my shoulder at my journal. "These are the ideas for the library that I want for my birthday. Father says we'll be able to start working on it as soon as they return. It's going to be a lot of work! We'll have to either find or construct a space to hold all the books. Then we'll have to pack and move all the books from the palace library to the new space. The palace library is going to look so empty! It'll be weird."

When I pause to take a breath, she laughs and wraps me in another hug.

"You're just trying to stop me from talking more!" I accuse her with my face buried in her shoulder. Her long hair brushes my cheek.

She just laughs some more.

"Sorry for talking your ear off. I just have so much going on right now! And I haven't seen you in so long!"

"It's wonderful, Honeysuckle. I love hearing about all these things!" She smiles at me and her eyes glow with love. "Wanna sneak down to the kitchen and whip up a midnight treat for ourselves?"

We tiptoe down the stairs and to the back of the castle. The kitchen is tidy. Plates and platters of leftover food from the celebration have been wrapped and stacked in one corner filling the space with the blended smells of all the different kinds of food. All the leftovers will be donated to the orphanage and given to those that need it. Although,

I'm not sure anyone will want the rat stew, or whale steaks…

Magnolia retrieves a bowl from a high shelf and gathers the ingredients necessary to whip together a minty pastry. She cuts chilled butter into tiny pieces. They sound like pebbles when they hit the bottom of the bowl. Next, she stirs in some flour, salt, and sugar.

"Tell me all about the festivities. And the ball!" She prods me to talk more.

She's crazy. I could literally talk to her all night long. But she asked for it!

I settle on a stool on the opposite side of the table, lean forward, and prop my face with both hands.

"Well, I danced with several dwarves. They spent most of their time bragging about their fighting skills." I roll my eyes.

Magnolia meets my eyes and grins while she mixes.

"And dancing with a wood nymph was… different."

"Any boys you have your eye on?"

I sit up and snort. "Did you even hear me? Most of my dance partners weren't even human!"

She grins sideways at me. "But at least one of them was…"

I'm sure my face is bright pink. I can feel the heat coming off it in waves. "Were you spying, or something?" I mockingly accuse.

"Or something." She keeps her eyes on her task. But a smirk rests on her face.

Christine Marshall

Chapter Ten

I huff out a breath.

"So…?" She prods me to tell her. "You've told me everything else. In great detail. You can tell me about this, too, right?"

I groan. Grown-ups!

She reaches across the table and dabs a little flour on my nose.

I sit up straight and give her a shocked look.

She laughs at me as she adds milk to the bowl and carefully stirs the mixture to form a soft dough.

"You roll, I'll mix the filling." She hands me the rolling pin and the dough.

"So… the boy…"

"I can't believe you were there the whole time and didn't join the party!" I huff as I roll the dough out.

"Not too hard or the dough won't turn out soft and flaky like we want," she reminds me.

"Right." The rolling pin rolls easier with less pressure.

"I'm not one for big parties and fancy dresses. You know that!" She answers my accusation about avoiding the ball.

"I know, but it would have been so fun to have you there!"

"Really? I think you were having enough fun without me…" Her eyes glint. "You're blushing."

A hand on my cheek leaves a streak of flour on my face. I work to brush it off.

"So, who is he?" she prods some more.

"Fine, if you must know…"

"I must!"

My eyes narrow. "His name is Peter. He's a prince from Bennfaran." My face relaxes and my grin widens. "He's not the heir or anything, he has two older brothers *and* an older sister. He likes to read, just like me, and he's going to teach me astronomy! I promised him I'd show him how I can talk to animals the next time he visits. I have no idea when that will be, though. I mean, my parents are going to be gone for five weeks! It's not like he can come visit while they're away!"

When I look at her again, she looks distracted.

"What is it, Magnolia?" I stop rolling the now flattened dough.

"Oh, I can't find the fresh mint." She turns and peers on a high shelf.

A thorough search of the kitchen produces no results.

"Is this it?" I hand her a jar from the spice rack behind me.

"That's the dried mint, but it will taste so much better with fresh mint leaves."

She makes a chattering sound.

A funny looking mouse creature appears after a few heartbeats. It's tiny, like a mouse, but has longer ears like a rabbit, and at the end of its tail is a little fluff of hair. Its back legs are impossibly long for its size, and its front legs are teeny.

"What's it called again?" I ask Magnolia.

She gives me a look. "You should know this, Lilac. I'm not giving you the answer."

I roll my eyes, but smile. What's it called… what's it called…. "A pygmy jerboa! That's right!"

74

She nods. "Very good."

Magnolia joins me on the floor, kneeling, to get a closer look. She chatters to it some more, and I understand her.

"Jerboa, would you mind at all fetching me some fresh mint from the palace garden? I would greatly appreciate it."

The little creature acknowledges her request, and hurries away at remarkable speed with its funny little hops.

I must be giving Magnolia a funny look because she asks me, "What's wrong, Sweet Pea?"

"I don't know, my mom always told me not to make the animals do stuff. I kind of got in trouble for it once, and I've always been super careful about it…" I look away, my face red.

Magnolia rests a hand on my shoulder and squeezes. We both stand. She returns to stirring the pastry filling. "Here's the thing, Buttercup. I didn't *make* the jerboa do anything. I *asked* him if he wanted to. There's a big difference."

I return to rolling out the pastry dough, even though it's probably plenty flat by now. My mind turns.

Comfortable to voice my thoughts in front of Magnolia, I speak. "I know what you're saying, but I don't think I get it. Won't the animals just do whatever we ask because we're, like, superior to them or something?"

A scurrying sound comes from the window, and Magnolia thanks the jerboa for the mint leaves. The little creature disappears back out the window.

Magnolia tears the mint into smaller pieces and smashes them with a mortar and pestle, releasing their sweet and spicy scent into the air. She drops them into the filling mixture and folds them in.

"They *don't* see us as superior. We are their caretakers, not their overlords. Most of the time, they are happy to help. And if they don't want to, I thank them anyway and move on."

She dips her finger into the filling mixture and licks it clean. "Perfect. Let's cut the dough."

She hands me a paring knife and shows me with her own how to slice the dough into large triangles. Then we scoop globs of the filling into the center, and fold them, overlapping the corners.

Magnolia brushes milk on top, then sprinkles large sugar crystals over the milk. She places the pastries on a tray and slides the whole thing into the tall brick oven that always has coals burning. They glow in the darkness. The heat reflects off my face.

A few cinders float out of the oven when she stirs the coals. They hover over my shoulder. I can't take my eyes off of them. One of the larger cinders lands on my shoulder just as the glow dissipates. When I brush it off, the air flow lights it up again.

Magnolia stands next to me. "You'll know they're done when the delicious aroma fills the kitchen."

We sit side by side on stools while we wait for our treat to finish baking.

I resume the conversation. "So, you're saying it's alright to ask animals to do things for us? Like, chores? Can I have them pick up my laundry, or make my bed?"

Magnolia laughs. The bright sound fills the space. "I guess you could ask them to do those things for you. But if you don't want to do them for yourself, why would they want to do them for you? You'd be better off just making your own bed, my little Zinnia." She rubs the top of my head.

"Hey, quit it! I'm not a little kid anymore, you know!" I laugh and rub the top of her head back.

"Don't I know it! You're almost as tall as me now. I just can't get over how fast you're growing up." She wraps her arms around me from the side and squeezes.

I roll my eyes. "Yeah, yeah, I know. You wish I could stay little forever." It's something that my mom says all the time.

"Actually, I don't." Magnolia locks her light brown eyes onto me. "I love the memories of you when you were small, and cute, and funny…"

"Are you saying I'm not cute anymore?" I raise one eyebrow at her and purse my lips. I can't hold the sassy look for long before I smile at her again.

She pokes my side. "Of course, you are. But I am also excited to watch you become a woman, a wise leader. And to fall in love and have a family of your own."

My stomach flips. It's a lot of pressure, all those things she listed. But she's right. I'm excited about those things, too.

"Mmmmm, smell that?" She turns to face the oven.

The minty, buttery, sweet smell fills my nose and makes my stomach growl. "Are they done?"

Magnolia nods, reaches for a thick cloth, and removes the tray from the oven. The tops of the pastries are golden brown. The sugar bits have melted and blended with the milk to give them a nice sheen and a little bit of a shell.

I reach for one and pull it closer to me on the worktable. It's hot but smells so good that I don't care. I break a chunk off, blow on it, and pop it into my mouth. The pastry melts on my tongue and the mint wakens my senses.

"Mmmmm…" Magnolia's eyes roll back as she savors her own pastry.

We munch in silence until we've eaten our fill, then we tidy up the space and head to my room for bed.

As we make our way up the stairs, I cover my yawn.

In a sleepy voice I ask, "Will you teach me more about what we can do with our abilities tomorrow?"

"Only if you tell me about the dance," she answers.

I stop mid-step. "I did tell you about the ball!"

She pauses beside me. "Not the ball. The Dance. With you-know-who…"

I resume my ascent. "Maybe," I tease.

"Then *maybe* I'll teach you more things tomorrow…" She hurries past me. "Race you to your room!"

"Come back here!" I chase her up the remaining stairs. I can't stop grinning.

As promised, Magnolia and I spend the day practicing some new things that I can do with my abilities.

A bright blue bird sings a sweet trill of agreement, fetches the berries I requested, lands on my outstretched hand, and drops the berries in my palm.

My eyes are wide. "Wow!" I whisper.

"Don't forget to say thank you to the bird, and offer her one of the berries," Magnolia murmurs in my ear.

"Oh, right!" I do as she says, and the bird flies off with a happy stomach.

My face must reflect my shock.

"That was…. Incredible! I don't know why my mom never taught me that before!"

Magnolia grins. "Not all of our people think we should do this. Some think it's manipulative, but I always ask politely, accept no as an answer, and offer a small reward or thank you to the animal. I don't abuse this power. It's not like I have animals do all my *chores* for me or anything." She gives me a significant look.

"What? It'd be nice, is all I meant…"

"Well, that's not their job, you know?" her words are serious, but her face is soft. "But don't you like being helpful? Being treated as an equal and given a task to do, even if your mother or father could just as easily accomplish it without you?"

I nod and pop a couple of the berries in my mouth. They are tart on my tongue.

She's right. Ever since I was young, I've always enjoyed accomplishing tasks, and being trusted with a job.

Magnolia continues. "I believe the animals feel the same way."

What she says makes sense. I could see how that power could be abused, though. Animals could be made to do things they don't want to or be punished if they refused. But Magnolia says she treats them with respect, and they want to help in return. What better way to earn the respect of the animal kingdom then to treat them like equals?

My mind fills with possibilities. "This is so amazing! I could ask a bird to sing a song for me, a fire lizard to roast a pile of nuts, a golden eagle could take me for a ride high in the clouds. I can even imagine an elephant carrying my luggage with its trunk, or a dolphin delivering a message across the sea. I can't wait to try again!"

Magnolia laughs. "Slow down, there, Lotus Blossom. Like I said, this gift should be used *sparingly*..."

"I know, I know. It's not like I'm going to do all of these things *today*. I'm just saying, like, wow!! My life is going to be so much more exciting now!" Visions of a future filled with closer animal relationships fill my mind.

"Want to try again?" she interrupts my daydreams.

"Of course!"

Searching the meadow closer to the wood for another animal to try my new skill with leads me to a mother rabbit and her half dozen fuzzy little babies hopping along the edge of the grass.

I inch closer, careful not to startle them, and speak to them in a soft voice. They all turn to look at me with their wide, watery eyes and their ears alert.

With a word of invitation, one of the little ones looks at her mother for approval, then takes several tentative hops toward me.

"Can you find me a clover blossom, please?"

She wrinkles her nose and shakes her whiskers at me, then turns to hop around and search.

I grin wide at Magnolia while I wait for the bunny to return.

When my eyes return to the bunny, she's munching on clover blossoms, stuffing them into her mouth as fast as she can.

"She's doing it!" I squeal to Magnolia.

Magnolia chuckles and covers her mouth.

I give her a questioning look, then face the baby rabbit again.

"No! Wait!" The bunny is hopping further away from me, eating more and more clover blossoms. "You're supposed to bring one back for me!" I call to the little bunny.

She ignores me.

"Well, that didn't go as planned...." I grumble.

Magnolia snickers again. "Another lesson you have learned. You can ask *any* animal to do something for you, but baby animals tend to become distracted easily and, more often than not, they will forget their task along the way."

"Oh." My shoulders slump.

"But look how cute she is with a mouthful of clover blossoms! You can't complain!" Magnolia uses baby talk to point this out.

She's right, again. The bunny is adorable. Several blossom stems stick out of her mouth.

Her mother calls to her by thumping one of her large back feet on the ground, and the little one returns to her family.

Chapter Eleven

"I think that's enough for now, what do you say?" Magnolia wraps an arm around my shoulders.

We make our way back through the gardens and into the palace. As usual, I shoo away a number of meadow insects and animals at the end of our trek. "It's good to have you back," I say to them before they can skitter, crawl, or hop away.

After lunch we spend the afternoon wandering in the woods. A large rat rides on my shoulder, wrapping his long scaly tail around my neck. I stroke his tail with two fingers as Magnolia and I collect samples of various flowers, herbs, and greens to place in my field journal when we return.

A pair of shiny blue dragonflies the length of my hand flit from plant to plant, suggesting ones for us to inspect. Magnolia teaches me about their uses, what's edible, and what's poisonous.

"I'm surprised you haven't learned these things yet, Gerbera Daisy."

"My mom has always focused on the animal stuff. And dad's preparing me to be queen. I guess we just never had the time. How do you know so much about it all?"

"Although we communicate with the fauna," she gestures between us, "it is wise to know about the flora as well. We may not be able to cause plants to grow, read the trees, or be welcomed into a meadow with a sudden burst of wildflowers; but the plants are just as useful to us anyway. I've learned as much as I can from some of the flora caretakers. It has benefited me greatly in my care for the animal kingdom."

"That's smart. I'm so excited to add these samples to my field journal and keep track of where I found them and what they are good for. What's your favorite plant?" My hands are nearly overflowing with stems, leaves, and blossoms.

"Hmm. My favorite plant…" Magnolia pauses to think. I can practically see her mind searching its depths for the one that she likes best.

After a long beat of silence, Magnolia's eyes come back into focus. "I think it would have to be the midnight caladium."

"What is that? What's it look like?"

"Well, it's a large leafy plant from the caladium family, also known as angels' wings or elephant ears. This variety is called midnight caladium, or ghost caladium, because the leaves that are normally green or pink, are pure white. Sometimes even a little translucent. The white ones grow in very dark, shady places, and will burn in direct sunlight."

"Why is your favorite plant one that grows in the dark?"

The rat squeaks the same question to Magnolia.

Magnolia smiles. "It's not my favorite because of where it grows, or even what it looks like. It's what it can do."

When she doesn't answer right away, I prod. "Well, what can it do?"

The dragonflies hover beside her, waiting to hear her answer.

Magnolia hesitates. "Not many people know this, Jessamine. Guard this information carefully." She looks so serious all of the sudden. And she has used my real name. I know to pay close attention.

Magnolia searches my face to make sure I'm taking her warning seriously. When she is satisfied that I can be trusted, she tells me.

"The midnight caladium plant is a tuber. Meaning the roots can be divided and propagated into new plants, instead of seeds. Think of a potato, for example."

"I like potatoes…"

The rat squeaks.

"Yes, I know you like potatoes, too." My finger tickles his ears.

"This plant is not food." Magnolia still sounds so serious.

I try to match her level of reverence for the plant. "So, it's a tuber…" I prod her to keep going.

"Yes. The large, arrow shaped leaves," she holds her hands out to make a triangle in the empty space between her fingers, "are poisonous, as are the stems and roots. They are not to be touched or consumed. Ever."

The rat makes a grunting noise.

"You'd better listen to her. She knows what she's talking about," I tell him.

I return my attention to Magnolia. "And…? I know that can't be all. You wouldn't be excited about some poisonous plant."

"However…" Magnolia makes her voice all mysterious.

The dragonflies huddle close together.

"…the plant has a secret."

"Tell me! Tell me!" I tug on her arm like a child begging for a sweet.

"If you *boil* the plant, any part of it, the steam can be inhaled and heal internal wounds. It has amazing healing properties when used as a steam bath. But it has to be handled with such care, that not many, besides the flora Forest People, even know about this special feature."

"That is *so* amazing!" I squeal. "We have to find one!"

"They're pretty rare, it won't be easy," she says.

"That's fine, what else are we doing today?"

I lay my stash of flora near a tree with a low branch so I can find it again.

"Want to tag along?" I ask the rat.

He does, so he remains on my shoulder.

We wander through the woods looking for midnight caladium in all the darkest shadows. We ask a fox at one point if he's seen it anywhere. He indicates that he hasn't, so we continue our search.

While we look, Magnolia asks me about the boy she saw me dance with last night. "Peter, right?"

"Yep. He's a prince from Bennfaran, but not heir."

"Yes, you mentioned that last night. You two looked like you were getting along well…"

A nervous giggle escapes me. I tell her everything about when we first met, the dance we shared, our stroll through the gardens. How nervous he looked. How nervous I felt. I blush the entire time, and gush about how sweet he is and good looking. And that he said he hoped to see me again soon.

"I have no idea what that means, or how he even plans to pull it off, since there isn't any reason for anyone from his kingdom to visit ours any time soon, but who cares? I think he likes me!"

Magnolia laughs. "You said that last night, too!" She squeezes my arm. "Even so, it's wonderful, Forget-Me-Not. And a prince! You can't beat that!" She winks at me.

The rat tickles my cheek with his whiskers.

Magnolia interrupts my daydreams of standing so close to Peter. "I was in love, once, too."

I stay quiet. I've heard that she had been in love once, but she's never talked to me about it before. I don't want to say anything and ruin the moment.

"His name was Jack. He lived in a village that I happened upon during my travels. His father was the metalsmith in the town. When I entered his workshop, Jack was there. Our eyes met. It was love at first sight."

Her eyes look dreamy. And sad. My heart aches for her.

"I spent the next week meeting him after his work was finished each day. We went on long walks, talked about everything, and made plans for a future together. I had to go, but I told him I'd be able to return soon.

"We exchanged letters via animal messengers, and I returned only a few weeks later. He declared his love for me. We were so excited to marry and never have to separate again."

She sighs.

"What happened?" I dare to ask.

A tear leaks out of one of her eyes. "The others in the village didn't trust our kind. They thought of us as evil, or witches, or worse. His father refused to allow the union."

"But he fought for you, right?"

Magnolia shakes her head.

"Oh, no," I whisper. "What did you do?"

She hangs her head. "I left." She shrugs. "He went on to marry someone else, someone his father approved of, from the village. My heart was broken. It has never fully healed."

The rat on my shoulder sighs.

Magnolia looks at me with haunted eyes, then startles.

"Jessamine! I should not have told you about that right after you tell me about Peter! I'm so sorry. Most love stories do not end this way. Besides, the humans in your kingdom and his do not have the same reservations about the Forest People. I'm sure everything will work out between you two!"

I blush. "I'm not in love with him. I just… think he's cute. That's all."

She gives me that knowing look that adults give to kids when they think they're right about something. I roll my eyes at her.

But when my thoughts turn to him, my stomach does a flip and my heart beats just a little bit faster. And my cheeks get very warm.

She grins sideways at me. Adults. Sheesh. I pretend not to notice, and we continue our search for her plant.

By the time the sun starts to sink lower in the sky, we still haven't found it. I want to keep looking, but Magnolia insists we return to the palace for the night.

"Fine," I sigh. "Even though you're, like, my favorite person in the world, you're still a grown up. You have to be responsible sometimes.

I guess."

She nudges me with her shoulder. "Don't look so glum, Sugar Plum… see what I did there?"

"Ha ha!" My words are sarcastic, but not meanspirited.

"Goodbye, friend," I say to the rat when I return him to the ground. He scampers away with a squeak.

We make our way back and eat dinner in the garden.

"Tell me more stories about the Forest People." I'm on the edge of my seat.

"You've heard a lot of this before…" she says. "Are you sure you really want to hear the stories again?"

"Yes! I love how animated you get when you talk about your home and your people. I promise that I'll keep my mouth shut… for a change, and let you do all the talking!"

"Very well, Dandelion."

"Hey! That's a weed!"

"Yes, but you are as persistent as one. I think it's fitting."

"Yeah, you're right."

Magnolia settles in her seat and folds her hands in her lap. She gets a serious look on her face, almost like she's about to make a speech. In a way, I guess she is.

"Since oral histories are one way the Forest People remember the past and learn, I will indulge your request."

"Yes!" I lean back and keep my eyes glued to her face. "I'm all ears!"

"The Forest People have a long, rich history. We live long and work hard. And we know how to have fun." She winks at me.

"Everyone has a responsibility either to the flora or fauna. Our abilities allow us to either communicate with the plants of the world of every kind, or with the animals of the sea, land, and sky."

"I wish I could talk to the plants sometimes!"

Magnolia pauses.

"Sorry," I whisper.

"We make our homes inside big trees," she continues, "or in handmade huts woven from fallen tree branches. Some groups are more nomadic, moving and migrating with the animals they watch over."

"Like you! And my mom and Aunt Dahlia. Mom told me lots of stories about the villages she's visited and how they would trade handmade items from the forest for tools and cookery that would be a lot harder to make in the forest without a forge and…"

Magnolia gives me a look, with her mouth pinched closed.

"Right, sorry. I said I'd let you do the talking…"

"Others, like many of the flora caretakers, stay in one place their whole lives.

"Every once in a while, one of the Forest People marries someone from the other kingdoms." I see a hint of sadness in her eyes. "It's always a big event but can be dividing for some families and communities. Fortunately, your kingdom does not have those prejudices. Otherwise, your mother would never have been able to marry your father."

Would Peter's family or kingdom be opposed to a union between him, and a half-Forest Person like me? Probably not. They came to the festival, after all, and mingled with many kinds of beings.

What am I thinking? I had just chewed out my mom not that long ago for trying to set me up with "eligible young men" at a ball for my seventeenth birthday. Now here I am daydreaming about the possibility of marrying Peter. What has come over me?

"We also abstain from eating animals. Some do not even eat animal products, like milk and eggs and the like." Magnolia's voice brings me back to the present.

"But you do, right?" I ask. I mean, she did put milk and butter in the pastry last night after all.

She nods. "But mostly when I'm in the human villages or cities. At home, I do not. It's not a hard and fast rule for me."

"Tell me about your favorite place you've visited."

"The sea, for sure!" She doesn't hesitate. She must have really liked it there!

"I've never been to the sea before. What did you like about it the most?"

"The smell of the salty sea air. The feel of the sand between my toes. Tide pools filled with all kinds of strange creatures that you can't find anywhere else. The wind making my hair dance." She closes her eyes, as if she can see and feel everything she describes.

"That sounds beautiful!" I sigh.

"I'll take you there sometime, Anemone!"

I giggle at the name she chose. "That's not even a flower!"

My mind is full of everything she's shared with me and taught me over the past twenty-four hours. And between the festival, Peter's magical green eyes, and Magnolia's lessons and stories, my dreams are sure to be enjoyable.

Chapter Twelve

"Remember who you are!"

My mom's voice rings in my ears. It fills my head but sounds as if it comes from far away.

My breath leaves my body and I shoot into a sitting position.

Why is my breath coming so fast? Why do I suddenly feel like a piece of me is missing?

The sky out the window is still dark, dotted with stars. It's not even morning. The blankets make no noise as I toss them away from me and spring from the bed. My footsteps echo through the quiet castle halls.

Where am I going? Am I dreaming?

The sound of a single horse galloping at top speed becomes louder as it approaches the castle. Shouts ring out. The night guard sounds some kind of alarm. Things start happening around me very fast.

A sudden hand on my shoulder makes me jump and scream. A few people glance at me, and at whoever stands behind me, and continue running all helter-skelter.

"Jessamine, come with me, love." Magnolia's voice is calm and soft in my ear.

With wide eyes I allow her to lead me away from whatever is happening into a private study off the main hall.

"Are we under attack? Should we descend to the shelter?" My voice is tight.

Magnolia has tears in her eyes.

"What's going on? What's happening?" I demand, voice shaky now.

What would make everyone act crazy like this? Why is Magnolia crying? Why does my heart feel like it has been torn in half?

"I don't know how to tell you this, Jessamine." She chokes on her tears.

She's trying to find the right words for whatever it is she needs to say.

She swallows hard and tries again. "It's… it's your parents… they're…"

"Gone." My own whisper fills the space. It fills my head. It floats around me. Somehow, I knew. She told me. My mother told me, in my dreams. How had she done it?

Before I can ask myself anymore questions, Magnolia wraps her arms around me, tight. Her chest heaves against me as she sobs.

Why am I not crying? Shouldn't I be the one sobbing?

Magnolia pulls away but keeps her hands on my shoulders. She crouches a little to meet my eyes. "I think you're in shock, Rosepetal."

I just stand there.

"Let's get you back to your room. I'll have someone bring you some cold water to drink."

She takes my hand and opens the door. She stops a servant and requests light refreshments to be brought to my room. The servant nods and hurries off to the kitchens.

"It's going to be alright, Jessamine. I'm here for you." Magnolia squeezes my hand and leads me to my room.

She tucks me into bed. Somehow, I succumb to sleep merely seconds after drinking a sip of the water.

Haunting dreams of my parents as phantoms disturb my slumber until sometime in the late morning. When I awake, Magnolia is slumped over in a chair beside my bed, lightly snoring.

So, it hadn't been a dream. My parents really are gone. What am I going to do now?

Magnolia leads me through the motions of the day. She makes all my choices about where to go, what to eat, and what to wear. I'm like a child. I am in no mental state to be able to do any of these things for myself. I barely remember getting dressed. Magnolia had the servants procure and alter a black dress for me by dawn. My choice would have been to stay in bed and never get out of it again.

Magnolia leads me down the stairs and has me sit on a padded bench outside one of the offices near my dad's study.

"Wait here." She bends down to my level and looks in my eyes. "Promise."

Where else am I going to go?

My mind and my body are numb.

Only a few minutes later, raised voices come from behind the door. Magnolia sounds really mad.

The door bangs open, startling me.

"This is ridiculous! I've never heard of anything that made less sense! There must be someone else I can speak with about this!"

She sees me sitting there and stops. Had she forgotten I was waiting for her? She has barely let me out of her sight since we both rejoined the castle midday.

Her eyes shift from angry to broken-hearted. "Come, Jessamine."

She reaches out her hand and I take it.

"Everything's going to be fine, Morning Glory. Don't worry. Everything will be just fine."

I'm pretty sure Magnolia is talking more to herself than to me. "What's happened? Why are you so upset?"

She only shakes her head, her face growing redder by the second.

"We'll talk outside," she answers through gritted teeth.

We make our way to the gardens. Butterflies land on my hair and shoulder. Magnolia finds a bench far away from the castle for us to settle onto. She's so angry that no critters or insects snuggle up to her as they usually would.

"Do you remember what I told you last night, about your parents? About the accident?"

I nod. During the night, as they traveled through the mountain range toward the northlands, their carriage had overturned and slid down a very steep, very unforgiving cliff. They had not survived.

"Are you still with me, Poppy?" Magnolia gently touches my cheek.

My eyes come back into focus. "Oh. Yes. I'm sorry."

"You have nothing to apologize for. Nothing at all."

I still don't understand why she is all upset all over again.

She takes a deep breath. "You are the Crown Princess. You are the Heir to the Throne."

"Yes…" I don't take my confused eyes off her angry ones.

"Well, apparently, this human kingdom has the most unfair, unheard-of laws of anywhere in the world. It's absolutely ridiculous!" She jumps from her seat and paces in front of me. Her hands fly in the air as if she can bat away the laws that she hates so much.

"You have prepared for the crown your entire life. I can't believe they will allow this to happen under the circumstances." She's not even speaking *to* me… more… *at* me. If she was a pepper pixie, her hair would be burning white hot by now.

"Stop, Magnolia." I place a limp hand on her arm. "I'm not following. Please, slow down. What has gotten you so angry?"

Magnolia looks me in the eye. Her face is stone. "With the death of your parents you have lost your birthright. You are no longer the Crown Princess. No longer the Heir to the Throne. As of this morning, your titles have been removed."

The garden spins. The sky is out of place. The sounds coming from the castle, and from Magnolia's hot breathing, cease to exist. Everything blurs around me.

My mother's words *"Remember who you are!"* echo in my head.

Did she know? Did she know that the kingdom she had loved and served would turn out her orphaned daughter?

My feet carry me away from the gardens and toward the wood.

"Jessamine! Wait, come back!" Magnolia's voice sounds very far away.

My pace quickens.

Bursting between the hedges that make up the perimeter of the gardens, my dress tears. Pieces of my hair come loose from the ribbon that holds half of it in a loop on the back of my head. But I ignore both things.

I run as far away from the castle as I can until I can run no longer.

Then I crumple into a heap on the ground. Tears stream down my face. The shock is gone, replaced by absolute loss.

This can't be happening. Between sobs I pinch my arm. I must be dreaming. The pinch smarts. I look around me, a stranger in a foreign land. This is supposed to be my home. My forest. My trees, and gardens, and castle. My kingdom. And now it's just... not? How can they take it all away from me?

Eventually the tears slow. I sit up. Twigs and leaves decorate my hair. I'm sure I have smudges on my face from my dirty hands wiping away the tears.

A lone silver wolf peers at me from behind one of the nearby trees.

Do I still have my abilities, or have those been stripped from me as well?

I reach out to the animal with my mind. I can *just* feel her there.

I sigh with relief. At least they can't take that away from me.

With a tight voice, I bid the wolf to come closer. I could really use the comfort of an animal right now.

She takes a few steps toward me, tentative. Then her ears prick to one side.

She turns her head, stiffens, then dashes away from me and back between the trees.

"Jessamine! Jessamine!" Several unfamiliar voices call out to me from the direction of the castle.

I don't respond.

Eventually they find me anyway. The guard who discovers me blows a whistle. Several other whistles respond. He gently pulls me to standing and escorts me across the meadow toward the castle. He doesn't say anything. Because he doesn't know what to say? Or because he doesn't serve me anymore?

My body feels heavy. The guard supports me with an arm across my back. Before we make it to the gardens my legs give out. I nearly collapse. He blows his whistle, a shorter trill this time, and a second guard joins us. The first guard lifts me into his arms and carries me back to the castle. He smells familiar, like spice. My mind can't place the scent.

One of my shoes slips off my feet. The second guard picks it up and follows close behind. My head bobs against the guard's chest. They accompany me into the entry foyer of the castle and set me on my feet, and hand me my shoe. I hold it in a limp arm by my side.

The air in the castle feels stuffy after the freshness of the forest. It only weighs me down more.

Magnolia rushes to me and enfolds me in her arms. I can tell she's angry at the way things are going, grieving the loss of her best friend, and worried about me all at the same time.

"I'm sorr…" I start to apologize again.

She stops me short. "No. Do *not* apologize. You have done nothing wrong. You have nothing to apologize for." Her words are firm.

"Alright." I drop my chin.

"Lower your eyes to no one." She lifts my face with one finger. "No matter what they say, Jessamine, you *are* a Princess. A Queen. Promise me you won't forget it." She searches my eyes for an answer.

I shrug. "Am I though?"

"Yes. You always will be." Her hands squeeze my upper arms, as if she can force me to believe it, too. "You are strong and so powerful. You will be able to accomplish *anything* you put your mind to."

"What am I to do now?" The reality of my situation drips on me like fat raindrops from the sky.

"You may return to the Forest People with me. We will take you in. Keep you as one of our own. I will take you to visit the sea. I will teach you more than you can imagine. You will be loved and respected. You are the granddaughter of royalty there."

Is that what I want? The Forest People live a very different life than the one I am used to. I don't know if that's what I want. I don't know anything anymore.

My head spins.

"You look unwell. Let's get you back to your room so you can rest." Magnolia leads me toward the stairs.

Before we can climb the bottom step, another voice calls my name.

Christine Marshall

Chapter Thirteen

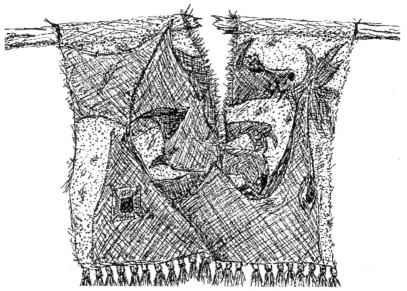

Aunt Dahlia bursts through the entrance of the castle.

Her usual bright colored dress and adornments are nowhere to be found. Instead, she is covered from head to toe in black, including her jewels.

She rushes to me and holds me tight. She whispers apologies and affirms her love repeatedly.

I melt into her arms. She feels and looks so much like my mom. She wears the same lilac perfume as my mom. I breathe deep. If I don't think too much about it, it's like hugging my mom instead of my aunt.

My eyes start to prickle again. I don't want the tears to flow anymore, so I slip out of her arms.

She turns to Magnolia and embraces her as well. They speak in low tones to one another. Words like, "gone too soon" and "it doesn't feel real."

When they break apart Aunt Dahlia faces me again. "Jessamine, you are like a daughter to me. I do not wish for you to leave the castle."

She must know about the law. She must have rushed here to make sure I don't get kicked out of my home. How come no one has ever talked about this before?

Magnolia steps to my side. She wraps her arm around my shoulders and pulls me close. "I've already invited Jessamine to return home with me." She looks down at me with sad eyes.

"Oh, I see." Aunt Dahlia looks stunned. Is she offended? "I don't want to make decisions for you, Jessamine. What would you prefer?"

They want me to choose? I don't want either choice. I want my parents back. I want *my life* back. My heart beats a little faster, but I push down these feelings of resentment that start to bubble inside of me.

They are both grieving the loss of my mom, too. They've known her their whole lives. They've loved her for so long. They only want what's best for me.

But she is, WAS, *my* mom. How am I supposed to even think about life without her? How am I supposed to choose between two people I love? Who both love me? And who both make me think of her every time I look at them?

The tears well up again. I blink them away and swallow hard.

"I… I, um…" I look back and forth between them.

"It's alright, Lily-of-the-Valley. You don't have to make any decisions just yet. Take your time." Magnolia rubs my arm that isn't leaning against her side.

Aunt Dahlia agrees and wraps her arms around Magnolia and I. We stand there in a tight embrace for a long time.

"Thank you." It's the only thing I can think to say.

Dahlia steps back, but Magnolia keeps her arm around my shoulders, making sure I don't fall over or collapse again.

"Juliette, Amelie, and Henry will be joining us this evening." Dahlia places both her hands on the sides of my face. "I just needed to arrive as quickly as possible. I needed to be sure that you were all right." Her hands are cold against my cheeks that burn with emotion.

Her eyes shine with tears. She looks so sad, so broken. Is that how I look right now, too?

All of this just feels so…. Not real. Like a dream. Like a terrible, never-ending dream from which I will never awake.

The next three days are filled with sad, sorry looks from every single person around me. Everyone tiptoes around me like I might snap or burst into tears if they do or say the wrong thing. But I won't do either of those things. I'm still stuck in a daze.

Gardeners cut huge bunches of flowers from the gardens; there won't be any left if they take many more. Bouquets are arranged all over the palace and the palace grounds, black fabric draped around the vases and planters. More black is strung along the main cobblestoned road of the capital city, just down the hill from the castle.

The street is visible from the upper windows on the front of the palace. As are the banners with the crest of my father- a golden bejeweled crown with a red dragon against a black backdrop- on poles and hanging from balconies and shop fronts. I avoid those windows.

Even the stables are bustling with activity. Apparently when the reigning royals pass away, a huge procession of carriages and staff travel quickly throughout the kingdom on a tour, of sorts, to memorialize the King and Queen. And to invite anyone who wishes to attend the funeral to return to the capital in a massive caravan. The stone masons in town are busy gathering materials and building stone monuments to be erected on each of the stops on the funeral tour as well. There will be a whole entourage.

Funeral. I'm only sixteen. I shouldn't be having a funeral for my parents.

Magnolia takes me outside to walk in the meadow for fresh air a few times each day.

Dahlia visits my room to check on me frequently, too.

"I don't want you to worry about any of the details, dear. Henry and I will take care of everything." Aunt Dahlia sits on the edge of my bed.

She stares at me a little too long. I squirm beneath her gaze.

"You look so much like her." She brushes my hair with her fingers. "You do, too." Dahlia and my mom have a strong family resemblance.

We stare at each other for a few long moments. Then she wraps her arms around me. "Let me know if you need anything. Anything at all." "Thank you."

Juliette comes to my room a little later. "I'm so sorry for your loss, Jessamine."

Her words sound sincere. She has a very sad look on her face. "Thanks. I just... miss them..." Tears well up in my eyes again.

She sits beside me and rubs my back.

"Amelie spends all her time crying in her room, too. It's alright."

That stabs my heart. Why is Amelie so upset? I shake my head. It doesn't matter.

"Do you have any friends you would like me to reach out to? To spend time with you?" Juliette offers with a sweet smile.

She doesn't know me anymore. Otherwise, she would know that I don't really have any friends. My mother was my best friend, closely followed by Father and Magnolia. And the animals.

I shake my head. "Leave me, I wish to rest."

She obeys.

Dizziness overwhelms me. It's as if the whole world is spinning around me, and I'm stuck in the eye of a massive storm.

The next time Magnolia takes me on a walk in the meadow, she tells me that the Forest People handle death very differently than the humans.

"We choose to celebrate the passing from this mortal realm to be reunited with the natural world once again."

I cry. Again. "I don't want to hear about it. Any of it. I want to pretend none of this is even happening." My pace increases so I can escape the conversation.

Before I make it even two steps, she grasps my arm and pulls me to a stop. "I understand." She doesn't look angry or upset. "I will make the arrangements myself. I won't bring it up again unless you ask me to."

Can she hold herself to that, though? If the way of the Forest People is to celebrate, why wouldn't she want to talk about it more?

I spend the rest of the day in the garden and forest, hiding from Juliette every time she tries to tag along. Hiding from Magnolia and all her questions about what my mother would have wanted. Hiding from my aunt and uncle as they try to balance their own grief with the job at hand. Hiding from… everyone.

My abilities are all over the place. Sometimes I can communicate with the animals, and other times they can barely understand me even in their own languages. I ask a bobcat to sit with me, for comfort, but it just scurries away. I had no idea emotion had so much to do with my connection to them before.

I've learned a lot about the abilities of the Forest People these last few weeks. What Magnolia taught me about inviting the animals to be helpful. My mom teaching me to connect with their minds… somehow. And the dream or communication from my mother, whatever that was. And now learning that my emotions affect my abilities. I should probably take notes. But I kind of just want to sit out here, alone, and not think about anything at all.

At dinner on the fourth night, Henry announces the details of the upcoming events.

"The funeral tour will last for ten days." He sounds so business-like. As if he's reading off a standard agenda, not discussing the deaths of my parents. "Dahlia and I will participate in the tour, as is customary for the new reigning monarch."

My stomach clenches. *I should be the new reigning monarch.*

"Amelie does not wish to attend, and Juliette has decided to stay behind to keep her company," Henry continues.

Amelie hasn't joined the family for any meals or anything since she got here.

He finally turns to look at me. "Magnolia will stay longer to keep an eye on you, Jessamine."

Keep an eye on me? Am I a child? And why haven't I been invited to go on the tour?

I guess I'm not on the guest list. Not that I'd want to go anyway, but it's just more proof that I have been reduced to a nobody.

"When we return, the funeral will be held in the gathering hall adjacent to the palace grounds and the citizenry will be invited to attend."

Dahlia stares at her hands in her lap. I can tell she's trying to hold back tears. Maybe she doesn't like the matter-of-fact way Henry speaks, either.

In the morning, I stand alongside Juliette and Magnolia on the main front balcony. The carriages and wagons leave the castle in a cacophony of horse hooves clopping on the cobblestones, squeaky wheels turning on the various conveyances, and farewell shouts from some of the staff who have family or friends leaving for the journey. By the time the caravan makes it onto the main road that leads through the city center, the tower bells are ringing. And my ears are ringing, too.

I'm being left behind. Again. With Magnolia staying behind as my guardian. Maybe I should take her up on her offer to live with the Forest People.

My stomach twists. That's not what I want. Not at all.

The library makes the best hiding place for the next week and a half. The dark shadows and smell of old paper comforts me.

Magnolia finds me, of course. She has a knack for that.

"You've been spending a lot of time in here lately, Daffodil." She strokes my hair and searches my face for some kind of emotion. "Do you wish to talk?"

I shrug.

"What are you reading?" She looks on the bench beside me for a book.

"I'm not reading anything." My gaze returns out the window and I sigh.

"Would you like me to choose something for you to read? I can find something that will take your mind off of… everything. Maybe an encyclopedia on plants?" She begins to stand.

I pull her arm and she sits again.

"No. I don't want to read anything. I just…" I choke on my words. "What if… My library idea. Will it even happen now? Father said we would begin upon his return. And now…"

I gesture around the space. "Who's going to help me with it? There's just so … much."

Magnolia ponders and her eyes wander the room that towers two stories high, bookshelves lining every single wall. The only places not covered in books are the windows. Tall ladders on wheels are attached to the shelves, and benches and tables are scattered around the space to allow places to read or study.

"It does seem like a big job," she agrees. "Have you talked to your aunt yet?"

A single tear drips down my cheek.

Magnolia pats my knee. "Well, maybe you should. Perhaps this is something that she and you can bond over. It will help you both heal."

My eyes scan her face. Should I talk to Aunt Dahlia? The idea seems good, but I just don't know.

The butler, Anthony, approaches me and Magnolia. He holds out a silver platter. An envelope sealed with a red wax blob rests on the platter.

With a polite thank you from Magnolia he leaves without a word.

"Who would be writing to me? I barely even know anyone," I say.

"Maybe it's from your aunt!" Magnolia says in a cheerful voice.

My name is scrawled in curvy letters on the front. My finger slides beneath the folds to break the wax seal. A folded parchment falls onto my lap.

A quick glance at the bottom reveals who has signed the letter.

My heart leaps. Peter! I had forgotten all about him in my grief.

My eyes fill with tears.

"Well?" Magnolia asks. I can tell she wants to peer over my shoulder but is holding herself back.

Turning the parchment so she can see Peter's name invites a smile from Magnolia. A twinkle of relief shines in her eyes.

"I'll let you read alone. Come get me if you need anything." She kisses the top of my head and leaves me alone with my letter.

It's difficult to read the kind words of comfort that he has written to me through my tears. He promises to come to the funeral and comfort me in person. Fat teardrops fall to the parchment, smearing the words. I hug the letter to my chest. It smells like spice. That was the familiar smell from the guard! In my grief my mind could not make the connection to Peter. Maybe I'm not so alone.

Chapter Fourteen

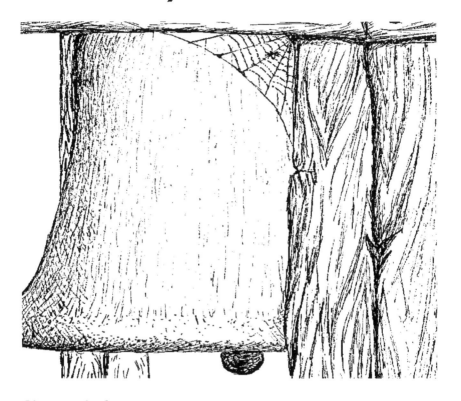

Sleep eludes me. Every night my mother's admonition to *"Remember who you are!"* rings in my head. What was she trying to tell me? Was it real?

Dreams about my aunt and uncle perishing while they are away interrupt my sleep, as well. If my parents' deaths had been anything other than an accident, my aunt and uncle probably wouldn't have gone on the tour. But there has been no indication of a conspiracy or a play for the throne. My family is safe.

On the tenth day the tower bells chime at daybreak, pulling me from a fitful sleep. I force myself out of bed and join Magnolia on the oversized balcony on the front of the palace. Juliette comes out, too, but Amelie remains inside. Juliette looks scared. Maybe she has been worried about her parents, too. A little twinge of guilt gnaws at my stomach. I send her a small wave. She smiles back.

The procession enters the capital.

"I can't believe how many people there are. Thousands and thousands of your parents' subjects have returned to honor them." Magnolia isn't exactly talking *to* me, but her words are meant for my ears.

My eyes well and my throat closes. My parents were good people. They were loved. It's not fair that they had to die.

Tears stream down my face. Magnolia wraps her arms around me from the side and cries with me. Neither of us says anything.

The city fills with visitors. Shop keepers sell commemorative flags with the King's crest. Hotels and homes fill with guests. I don't see how there will be room for everyone.

The procession ends at the massive gathering hall. The city is alive with activity. It feels too much like a celebration.

A sob escapes my lips and I flee back to my room.

Magnolia follows close on my heals.

Before I can even throw myself on my bed and bury my face in my pillow, she wraps her arms around me.

"Shhh, shhh. It's alright. Everything will be alright." She strokes my hair and rocks me back and forth.

I cry on her shoulder. Harder than I have since the day I lost them.

We stay that way for a long time.

Eventually my tears slow, and she pulls away from me. She wipes the wetness from my face and tucks my hair behind my ears. Without speaking, she leads me to my bed, removes my slippers, and tucks my mother's blanket around me.

"Where did you get this?" I croak between sobs.

She sits on the bed beside me. "I found it on your mother's bed. I thought you would want to have it."

"Thank you," I whisper.

She hums a lullaby that the Forest People sing to their children and strokes my hair.

My eyes are so dry and swollen, that I can barely keep them open. In no time I return to a dreamless slumber.

A hand gently strokes my cheek. I can smell my mother. It must have all been a dream. I pry my eyes open.

Aunt Dahlia sits beside me with red, puffy eyes.

I throw my arms around her. "You're back." I breathe.

I'm so relieved that she's home. But my heart breaks anew with the reality that my parents are truly gone.

She holds my chin and kisses my forehead. "Join us for lunch?" she asks.

I nod and force myself out of bed. I'm still wearing my sleeping clothes, so she helps me don another black dress and holds my hand as we make our way to the dining room.

When I enter the dining hall, Uncle Henry sits where my father used to sit. It leaves me frozen in place. Aunt Dahlia settles into my mother's chair. Amelie, who has finally come out of hibernation, sits in my old chair.

I guess it's not that big of a deal. It's just a chair after all.

"Sit by me!" Juliette pats the chair beside her. She sits next to Amelie.

I drag my feet and lower myself into the chair.

This just feels… wrong.

Magnolia comes in a few minutes later. She sits beside Dahlia, across the table from Juliette. No one faces me.

Henry tells stories from their travels.

Magnolia glances at me from time to time. Probably expecting me to burst into tears at any second. She's not wrong to do so. I'm barely holding myself together.

As soon as I finish my meal, I ask to be excused.

"Are you sure you wouldn't like to stay longer, darling?" Dahlia asks. Worry lines wrinkle her forehead.

"I'm sure."

"Jessamine…" Uncle Henry begins in a scolding kind of voice. "It's not polite…"

Dahlia places her hand over his and shakes her head.

"You may be excused, dear." She smiles at me.

"Thank you." I hurry from the room and head outside.

Not too much later, Juliette enters the meadow. "Jessamine? Jessamine!" She calls my name.

My shoulders slump.

Sitting from where I've been laying in the tall meadow grasses and flowers reveals my location. She sees me and waves, then hurries over to join me.

"Remember when we used to roll around in the meadow when we were supposed to be doing our lessons?" She laughs and plops down beside me.

"Yeah, I remember." I'm not trying to sound annoyed, but I must because Juliette gives me a funny look.

"Everything will work out, you know," she says in a sweet voice. She lowers her head to the soft meadow floor. She folds her hands under her hair and gazes at the clouds. "Ooh! That one looks like an alligator! Have you ever seen one in person before? Mother says…"

I stand and walk away from her.

She props herself on one elbow. "Jessamine? Where are you going?"

I stop and turn around. I search for the right words. I don't want to be rude, but I also need to be honest about how I'm feeling. I return to where she is sitting upright now.

"I'm sorry, Juliette. I just… I don't feel like talking right now."

"Oh! Alright! I didn't know. We don't have to talk." She gestures for me to join her again.

I reluctantly agree and sit on the ground once more.

It only takes a few minutes before words tumble out of her mouth.

"I want us to be friends again, you know. Now that we're sort of like sisters? I miss spending time with you. Do you want that?"

I knew she wouldn't be able to go very long without talking. But the question burning in my mind is: do I want that?

"I don't know. I mean… maybe under different circumstances…"

"What do you mean?" She looks genuinely hurt and confused.

"Juliette, don't you get it? The only reason you're here and that we're 'practically sisters' is because my parents DIED."

"I know. But when you are finished grieving…"

"I'm never going to be 'finished grieving.' Would you ever stop grieving if your parents were the ones who were dead?' I take a deep breath and will myself to calm down. "I'm sorry, Juliette. I don't want to be your sister. I just want my parents back."

She stares at me with mouth agape.

I groan and roll my eyes. "Never mind. You just can't understand."

My feet carry me toward the woods. A quick glance over my shoulder halfway to the edge of the tree line proves that she doesn't follow. She's just sitting there in the grass staring at my back.

I didn't want to hurt her feelings. She must understand that.

A small voice in my head tells me that maybe I *did* want to hurt her feelings. Maybe I want her to hurt because I'm hurting. Maybe I should apologize.

"No," I say out loud. "Magnolia was right. I don't owe anyone an apology."

A black bird swoops down from the trees and lands at my feet. He pecks at the ground, then stares at me with one beady eye.

"What?" I ask him.

He caws.

"She'll get over it," I insist.

He caws again, a little longer, then wings away.

"You don't understand, either." I call to him as he disappears in the canopy.

"No one does," I whisper to myself.

By the time night falls, I've returned to the castle. I decide to skip dinner, though, and remain in my room.

A book about plants rests in my lap. Magnolia must have left it on my bed. It has many colorful drawings and copious notes about the

109

different plants from around the world.

"I see you like the book," Magnolia says as she slides through the doors and closes them with a click.

"Yeah, it's pretty great." The book snaps shut and ends up on the bed beside me.

"How are you doing?" she asks. "Do you feel better?

"I don't know. I kind of had a fight with Juliette. It feels like she wants me to just get over my parents' deaths and move on. She says we can be like sisters now."

Magnolia listens but doesn't speak.

"And then this crow totally chewed me out in the woods afterwards! I mean, what would a bird know about all of this, anyway?"

"I know this is hard, Snapdragon."

I glare at her choice of flower names. She gives me a sly grin.

"But things will change. You will never stop feeling sad. You'll never stop missing your parents. But eventually you will be able to feel joy again. Little by little. Just take things one day at a time."

"Sure."

"And... maybe don't be so hard on Juliette?"

I start to protest but she holds up a hand to silence me.

"I mean it. She probably just doesn't know how to talk to you about all of this."

"You're right," I mumble.

"I know. I usually am." She grins at me.

I roll my eyes.

She stands. "Good night, Moonflower."

"Goodnight."

Before she leaves, she pokes her head back around the door. "And maybe be nicer to the crow next time, too!"

"Hey!" I holler, but she scurries away.

I can feel my mouth twitch, as if it wants to smile.

A vision of my mother's beautiful smile flashes before my eyes.

Your mother will never smile again, something whispers in the back of my head. *Why should you?*

All the grief comes crashing back down. I cry myself to sleep.

Magnolia returns in the morning before the sun even starts to rise. I grumble at her about the early hour.

She crawls under the covers and tucks me close, so my head rests on her shoulder and her arm circles around me.

I listen to her heartbeat.

"The funeral is this afternoon." Magnolia's voice is quiet and tight. "I can't believe it's already been two weeks."

I nod, but don't say anything. I didn't think I had any tears left, but my eyes well up again.

"Do you want to talk about it?" she asks.

I sigh. Do I? My mom always said that talking about what you're feeling can help you process your thoughts and help you feel better.

My throat is so tight, only a croak comes out.

"Me, too," Magnolia answers.

I chuckle, but without a smile.

"You know I will stay for as long as you need me to, right? Your mom's memorial celebration back home can wait. It does not need to take place right away."

My body stiffens. "I don't know if I even want to go…" I whisper. "Is that bad?"

"No, Bluebell. You don't have to go. Your mom knew you loved her. She would understand."

I swallow the lump in my throat and squeeze Magnolia tight. "Thank you."

"Are you ready for this, Jessamine?" Her voice is quiet.

"I don't think anyone can be ready to attend their own parents' funeral. Especially someone my age." I pause and take a deep breath. "But I must."

"You are so brave." She squeezes me one last time.

She pulls me out of bed and helps me prepare for one of the worst days of my life.

Christine Marshall

Chapter Fifteen

It seems half the kingdom has come to honor my parents. People huddle in crowds around the outside of the gathering hall and all the way down the cobblestone road beneath the gloomy sky that promises rain. Everyone is dressed in black, or as dark other colors as the people own. Shocked faces and endless gossip surround the carriage that takes me and Magnolia to the funeral.

The carriage drops us off in the rear of the building. There are a lot of people in the back, too.

My face is all puffy from not sleeping well and crying all the time. My hair is in a simple braid down my back. The humidity is giving me a halo of frizz, no doubt.

People point at me and whisper.

"Ignore them," Magnolia says in my ear. She shields me from them as we hurry into the building.

The gathering hall is full to overflowing. The air is thick and the constant hum of people talking presses on my ears. People mill around the rows and rows of benches that have been arranged facing the front of the building. A stage has a single wooden podium standing right in the middle. Two large flower arrangements frame the podium on either side. My mom's favorite flower, gerbera daisies are arranged with my dad's favorite, chrysanthemums. I wince when I see yellow star-shaped jessamine flowers sprinkled in as well.

The first several rows of benches are cordoned off for the royal family and any visiting dignitaries. Because the leaders of the other realms have already visited recently, just before the accident, many have not returned themselves, but have sent representatives in their places.

All twelve of my mom's siblings are in attendance, along with their spouses, children, and even grandchildren. They take up a dozen additional rows just by themselves. My grandparents have not made the trip. They will grieve their daughter at home.

The hard wooden bench right at the front where everyone can see us has been reserved for my family. The only ones sitting here besides me are Uncle Henry, Aunt Dahlia, Amelie, Juliette, and Magnolia. There's easily room for five or six more people on the bench. But people give us space; to be respectful.

Magnolia grips my hand tight.

"I don't want to be here," I murmur only loud enough for her to hear.

"I know, Pumpkin Flower. It will all be over soon. Hang on just a little longer."

My tears threaten to spill.

"What's taking so long?"

"They're just giving everyone time to settle in their seats." Magnolia squeezes my shoulder.

I tap my foot, making my knee bounce.

One of my dad's close friends and trusted advisors approaches the podium.

"Finally," I breathe out.

Magnolia gives my hand another squeeze.

"Welcome, valued citizens of Dragovalon. Welcome honored guests from far and wide."

"It's not a party," I mumble.

"Shhh," Magnolia hisses in my ear.

"Sorry," I whisper back.

"We are very sorry to have to meet under such tragic circumstances…"

He drones on and on about how wonderful my parents are and how much they will be missed.

"I don't need some guy telling me stuff I already know," I mumble to myself and shift in my seat.

Rain begins to tap a slow rhythm on the tall narrow windows and slanted roof. By the time the advisor is finished with his long, drawn-out speech, the rain is coming down in sheets. It's like a gift. It's much easier to tune out his words with the deluge of sound from the windows and roof.

"Thank you all for attending this memorial service today," the man finally says.

"Good, it's over," I murmur.

"I have invited a few who knew the King and Queen well to show their reverence by sharing a few words."

I groan.

"You can do this, Jessamine. You can do hard things," Magnolia whispers in my ear, then she kisses the top of my head.

I slouch beside her.

The whole thing takes way too long. I breathe a sigh of relief when it's finally over.

About to escape the way we came, a hand wraps around my shoulder.

"Don't run off just yet, dear." Dahlia's voice sounds motherly. "We still have a receiving line for those who wish to pay their respects. And then the banquet afterwards, too, of course. The people will want to see you and offer their condolences."

"What?" My eyes go wide. I don't want to stand in a line for who knows how long with people either telling me how sorry they are for me, or how great my parents were, or how they would be so proud of me if they were still alive. How many of these people even know I'm not the heir anymore? I'm sure word has gotten out. I'm a side show at the funeral.

"I can't be here anymore." My body refuses to move.

Dahlia doesn't hear. She moves towards her place in the receiving line.

"Go, Star Aster. I'll cover for you." Magnolia is a life saver.

She stumbles when I throw my arms around her. Then her arms engulf me.

"Thank you," I whisper in her ear. "I don't know what I would do without you."

She gently pushes me toward a back exit.

The door closes before anyone can notice my absence.

The castle is at the top of the hill, just past the meadow. I trudge through the muddy grass, not caring that my dull black dress with high neck and long sleeves is getting wet and dirty at the bottom. I'm half tempted to remove my shoes and let my toes squish in the mud.

Before I can reach my shoes, someone calls my name from behind.

I've been caught. I hurry my steps, pretending not to hear.

Footsteps quicken on the damp ground.

"Jessamine!"

It's Peter!

He is by my side in an instant. "There you are. I was going to catch you in the receiving line and steal you away. But I see you beat me to it!" He grins.

"Peter," I shake my head. "What are you doing here? Your parents didn't come, did they?"

"No, they didn't. Father didn't think it was necessary." He looks annoyed.

116

Peter takes my hand. Neither of us has gloves on today. His hand swallows mine, warming my chilled fingers.

"I promised I would come." He pulls me close and wraps his arms around me.

His spiced scent mingles with dampness from the rain this time. I linger as long as is appropriate.

"I'm sure I look like a ballybog that crawled out of the swamps." I pat down my hair with one hand.

Peter keeps his hand wrapped around my other hand. "You look beautiful."

I roll my eyes, and turn to continue my climb up the muddy, grassy hill toward the castle.

Peter walks beside me, matching my quick stride.

"I'm so sorry, Jessamine." He speaks in a low voice.

He doesn't try to press me to talk, doesn't look at me with sad, pitiful eyes. He doesn't even seem bothered by the steady drizzle that dots both of our clothes with water. He just holds my hand and faces straight ahead as we make our way back to my home.

By the time we arrive at the gardens, the sky has darkened until it almost looks like night. The rain comes hard and fast, thunder rumbles overhead.

The covered porch just off the ballroom, where not that long ago we shared our first dance together, becomes our refuge from the storm. He pulls me into his arms. I lean my hands and face against his dripping wet shirt that clings to his chest.

Now the tears decide to come.

He doesn't speak, just holds me close. His steady breathing, strong arms, and solid heartbeat help my emotions settle. After what feels like a long time, I take a deep breath, and pull away ever so slightly.

He keeps his arms wrapped around me. I tip my head so I can see his eyes.

Water drips from both of our hair onto our clothes, the ground, and each other.

So many emotions swirl around inside of me. "Thank you, Peter," is all I manage to say.

"You're welcome, Jessamine. Please, reach out to me by messenger any time. I will return as often as I am able."

He leans forward and places a tender kiss on my wet forehead.

My skin tingles. My heart is like a bird flapping in my chest.

"I'm afraid I must leave you now." He looks full of regret.

I nod.

"My parents haven't accompanied me, but they sent an advisor. He will realize I am missing soon. I don't want to cause a scene."

"I understand."

He squeezes me one last time.

He jogs down the hill; turns and blows me a kiss.

Lightning flashes overhead. Like some kind of omen. The rumbling thunder matches my feelings.

By the time everyone returns from the banquet, the day is late. My aunt, uncle, and cousins head straight for bed. All the other people who had come for the funeral return home; tradition has them leave right away.

The rain continues to fall. I stay awake with my windows open, watching the sky flash and feeling the mist blow in my direction.

My mother always said I am the future Queen. She reminded me daily. Sometimes more than once a day. She reminded me in my dream when she called out to me.

My thoughts swirl like the storm outside.

"What did you mean?" I say out loud, as if perhaps she can still hear me.

Maybe she didn't mean *The Queen*. As in the ruler of a kingdom. Maybe she just meant for me to be the queen of my own life. To not let things happen *to* me. To take control of my own destiny.

"Why did everything have to change?" I speak to the wind. "What else will be taken from me? How do I become attached to anything, or anyone, ever again?"

Images of Peter flash before my eyes. The skin on my forehead where he kissed me tingles. My back feels warm where his hands rested earlier.

"Will I lose Peter, too? How do I do this without you, Mom? Did you know that my life would turn out this way? That I would need your words when things became difficult?"

Thunder cracks open the sky and lightning blinds me for a moment.

"How do I take back my life?" I yell at the dark clouds. "How am I to still be the Queen?"

I don't expect an answer, but I wait and listen just the same.

Something deep inside ignites, like a spark in a dying fire.

The wind howls through the trees in the forest. Water droplets coat me from head to toe. I wait until I can no longer keep my eyes open, then I curl into a ball beside my open window and fall into a fitful sleep.

Sometime during the night I'm vaguely aware of my shivering frame being hoisted off the floor and tucked into my bed. The sheets become damp, and my wet hair soaks my pillow.

A gentle hand strokes my hair and warm arms wrap around me.

"You are never alone." The soft words bury themselves into my sleepy mind.

"Mom?" I whisper.

I sigh deeply, snuggle into the blanket that still smells like her, and sink into a more restful sleep.

Christine Marshall

Chapter Sixteen

I must have dreamt about my mother during the night. Or she answered my cries into the storm. That's not possible. It was probably Magnolia who tucked me into bed. But it felt so real. So much like my mother reaching out to me. Reminding me to stand up for myself.

My thoughts turn to Dahlia. If I can't talk to my mother, then her sister seems like the next best thing. And as much as I hate to admit it, she is my family now. Like, a stepmother, in a way.

The door to Aunt Dahlia's suite matches all the trim work inside: a deep mahogany with hand carved floral details. I wait a breath, then knock.

Footsteps pad closer across the plush rugs. Dahlia opens the door, her eyes red from tears. She wears a pale blue night robe that probably covers a night gown, very similar to the yellow one I wear.

"Jessamine, dear, come in." She opens the door wide. "I am so sorry for the way everything has turned out for you. I never would have wished this on anyone, let alone my own family. Please know that we love you and are here for you for whatever you need. Always."

A velvety crimson ottoman in the middle of the space is an appropriate place for me to stop. I sit on my hands to keep them still. "Aunt Dahlia, can I ask you something?"

She settles beside me and wraps an arm around my shoulders. "Of course."

I lean my head onto her shoulder. "Nothing feels the same anymore. Will my life ever feel like my own again?"

She sighs. "I do not know, darling. This is all new territory for me, as well." She pauses.

I wait to hear what she'll say to comfort me. I need some words of wisdom, or something.

"We all must face difficulties in our lives, I suppose. This is your challenge to bear."

Somehow, her words make me feel worse. *More* alone.

"But you have a family who loves you. And you never need to want for anything. I promise."

She means what she says, but she's wrong. I do want for something. I want for my parents. And my crown.

"I had so many plans for my future." My voice is just barely above a whisper.

"I know, dear." She lays her cheek on my head.

"I don't know if you knew, but… my parents and I had been planning a project together. We were to begin upon their return." My chin trembles. I take a deep breath. "I was wondering… well. I don't know."

She waits for me to continue. When I don't, she prods. "It's alright, dear. Tell me what you are thinking."

"Well, we were going to create a library in the city. And move all the books from the castle library there for the people to be able to borrow and use as they wish."

Dahlia stays still.

What does she think? Why isn't she saying anything? My parents loved the idea. Peter said he thought it sounded so good that he wanted to try it in his own kingdom.

Dahlia's silence makes my stomach clench.

"Do you think… Will we still be able to do the library project? It's really important to me."

She strokes my hair. "I am not sure how everything will work now. I do not have a very clear understanding of the laws and procedures of this kingdom. I will need to speak with Henry, and we can figure this out together. I promise."

I whisper, "It's just not fair, any of this."

"I know, sweetheart. I know. Always remember who you are…"

I tear myself away from her arms and rush out of the room.

How dare she say my mother's words to me? She's not my mother! She can never replace her!

Their mother used to say the same thing to them.

Part of me knows the truth: Dahlia isn't trying to replace my mother. She's only comforting me the way she knows how.

But another part of me just doesn't care. She tells me that I can have what I want, but then rejects my library plans. She tells me I'm not alone, but then reminds me of what I've lost.

Down the stairs and out one of the side doors of the castle, my feet carry me across the meadow as fast as they can.

The rain has left the meadow muddy. The mud squishes between my bare toes. The underlayer of the forest will be drier.

My head spins. And my heart aches. I'm so angry. And so sad. I'm broken. A shell of myself. How could everything have gone so wrong so fast? I went to bed one night happy with a bright future. Now, I'm nobody. Nothing. With no home and no one to turn to.

As my feelings of anger and hurt war within me, a wolf emerges from the trees and edges closer. He's big, like, the biggest wolf I've ever seen before. The alpha of his pack, for sure. His silver fur shines in the dappled sunlight of the wood.

He's just out of reach. He steps closer but hesitates. He looks directly into my eyes, as if he's trying to understand me, but can't.

"Don't be afraid." My voice manages to stay steady.

He cocks his head. Does he understand?

Frustration burns inside of me. I can't lose this ability, too. I can't!
My hand reaches for him.

The wolf yipes and takes three steps closer. Like he's being pulled.
He bares his teeth and growls.

His actions startle me. My hand drops to my side.

He hurries away.

What just happened?

Did I just *make* him come closer? I wasn't trying to. I just wanted a
little comfort. But he left angry and scared.

A shiver runs down my spine. I feel a little guilty, but also…
something else. Like, satisfaction.

I've connected with animals, and asked them to do things for me,
but I've never been able to *make* an animal do something that it didn't
want to do before.

Part of me kind of wants to try again.

"Is that wrong?" I say out loud, even though there is no one around.

I swear I can feel my mother standing beside me, encouraging me.

My muddy nightgown clings to my legs as I stand and listen. Birds
chirp and squirrels chatter. Snuffling sounds from the underbrush
could be any number of different creatures. But the wolves are quiet.
I won't be able to hear them.

The wolf leaves no trace of his flight. I am no tracker, and the forest
floor looks the same everywhere. I frown but continue.

A young buck with fuzzy antlers that barely stick out a hand's length
from the top of his head lifts his head to study my presence. He
watches me with a wary eye but doesn't respond to my words like he
usually would. His eyes widen and his nostrils flair, then he bounds
away from me.

I sense an owl in a nearby tree. Instead of trying to talk to it, I try
to command it. I reach out with my hand… and my mind. The owl's
feathers ruffle and he turns his wide eyes on me. He hoots,
admonishing me for interrupting his sleep. But he doesn't budge from
his hiding hole in the tree trunk.

My brow furrows.

After an hour in the woods trying to find animals and control them with no success, I finally give up and head back toward the palace.

But I won't give up on whatever this is.

Back in my room I pull out a parchment and pen a letter to Peter. I tell him everything that happened with my aunt and the wolf in the woods. My pen fills up almost two pages with all my innermost thoughts and feelings about loss, and control, and hearing my mother. I sound like a crazy person. There's no way I can send this to Peter. It would scare him off for sure. Instead, I fold the parchment and stick it in one of my many notebooks on the desk.

Maybe one day, when we know each other better, I'll show it to him.

Magnolia enters my room with a soft knock, interrupting my daydreaming about a sunny future with Peter.

"You're not even dressed yet? And what happened to your nightgown! Did you sleep in the woods or something?" Her words are accusing but her eyes are filled with laughter.

How she can be happy at all anymore. Except... *I* feel happy... a little bit... when I'm with Peter, right?

She stands with her hands on her hips and surveys my closet. "It's time to clean out this mess."

"Isn't that the servants' job?" I groan.

She glares at me. "You are perfectly capable of cleaning up your own mess, Jessamine."

I duck my head and blush. "I know."

"Besides, when your life is messy, sometimes cleaning up an actual mess can help you feel just a little bit better."

"That... doesn't make any sense." I fold my arms and wait for her to explain.

She doesn't. Instead, she finds a member of the staff to bring us lunch in my room.

"Eat quickly, and then let's get to work."

My night gown that now resembles rags goes in the bin for dirty laundry. She chooses a dark blue dress for me to wear, instead.

"Shouldn't I still wear black? The mourning period hasn't officially ended."

"Do you *want* to wear black?"

"No."

"Then, don't! What's the worst that will happen. They were *your* parents after all. *You* should get to decide when the 'mourning period' has ended."

We stuff all the fancy party dresses to the rear of the space.

"I can't imagine I'll have any reason to wear those again." All those fluttery, happy feelings that used to come when my hands ran over those dresses have vanished. Without my parents, there is no such thing as a party.

"You never know, Purple Pansy. You might want to, eventually."

We inspect what remains. There's a lot of what I used to consider simpler dresses, but they are covered in lacy trims. They don't really feel that simple anymore.

"I don't want to wear these anymore, either, Magnolia." I can't even bring myself to lift my arms to pull them off their hangers. "I want things even more simple. To match who I am now."

Magnolia scoffs. "That's ridiculous. You are still the Princess." She continues folding items of clothing and doesn't pause to look at me.

"No. I'm not THE Princess anymore. I'm *a* princess. Or, more accurately, the niece of the king and queen. That's all. I don't want all these reminders of what my life used to be like. I want a fresh start."

"I don't know exactly how you feel, Goldenrod. I can't. Our lives have been so very different. But I believe you. And I think if I was in your position, I would probably feel the same way."

Almost everything gets shoved into the back of the closet.

"It's time to go shopping," she says, hands on her hips as her eyes wander around the empty shelves and racks.

"Shopping?"

Magnolia chuckles. "Yes, *shopping*. That's how most people find clothes to wear."

She marches out of the space. "Get your shoes on. And a cloak. It looks like it might rain again."

Clothes of every shape and color surround me in one of the clothing shops in the merchant's district.

"I don't even know where to start." My eyes are wide trying to take it all in.

"I think you should try these." Magnolia holds up a blouse that buttons up the front and a pair of loose-fitting men's trousers.

"Are you sure?" I squint at the outfit.

"Just try them on." She pushes me into a small closet with a curtain that's used by people to try on the clothes they wish to purchase.

"I feel a little scandalous wearing trousers," I say when I emerge. They hug my hips, but the legs are wide on my petite frame.

"Nonsense. The women of the Forest People wear the same kinds of clothes as the men. When I'm at home, I dress much like that, too." Magnolia tucks the pale blue blouse into the grey pants and takes a step back to survey her work.

"I know. But when you're visiting you dress like the other women in the kingdom." I gesture at the pale pink day dress that floats over her hips and brushes the tops of her shoes.

"Doesn't matter. There is nothing scandalous about it. Trust me. Now, turn around so I can see how the back looks."

"I have to admit, this does feel more practical than skirts and dresses." I twist and turn to admire my look in a tall mirror.

Magnolia holds a finger on her chin and squints at my feet. "Your riding boots will work well. You can even tuck the pants into them when you're out in the forest, to keep the hems clean."

I stare in the mirror trying to picture what she sees. "You're right." I turn back toward her. "I love it. I'll take enough for every day of the week!"

She laughs. "You should probably replace some of your day dresses, too, I suppose. You wouldn't want to wear clothes like that when you take meals with the royal family. Or if you have guests, or anything."

"Yeah, I guess."

I choose simple designs, without excessive adornments, that would be fitting to wear around royals. We don't actually pay for anything; the shop keepers know to bill the castle and my aunt and uncle will reimburse them. They are all more than happy to have my business. For a second I think it's because they still see me as their beloved Princess, but then I realize it's just because I'm a well-paying customer. Nothing more.

I have the sudden urge to donate the clothing I no longer want to the less fortunate.

"Giving away things while you're grieving is not a smart idea. Give it some time. At least two seasons," Magnolia advises me.

Her words prick my heart. "It seems like getting rid of all of it would help me move on…"

"You may regret it at a later time, though."

"I doubt I'll regret any decisions I'm making today. Besides, I can always just buy new things…"

She raises one eyebrow. "Well that just seems wasteful, doesn't it?"

"Fine." I agree to wait.

Magnolia hands some coin to a delivery boy. He takes all our purchases wrapped in brown paper and places them in a hand-trolly which he drives back to the castle.

Chapter Seventeen

"How do you feel?" Magnolia asks.

I ponder the question for a moment before answering. "To be honest, the process has been cleansing. But now that it's over, I'm afraid of letting my mind wander again. I need something else to distract me."

"I will help distract you today, but soon you will need to deal with all these emotions. You can't keep distracting yourself forever. They will catch up with you eventually and hit much harder the next time."

I brush off her comments. I know she's trying to help, but for me, distraction is the best coping mechanism.

"I know what would make me feel better! Let me show you the orphanage. The kids there are the best. You'll love it, trust me!"

I tug Magnolia's arm and pull her in the direction of the orphanage.

We walk through the tall double doors, and I wave at the orphanage director through her window. She nods us through. We head into an open space that acts as a playroom and a school room.

When the children see me come through the doors, many of them gasp and run to me. They encircle me and engulf my legs with their little arms. My heart instantly soars.

"Princess! Princess!" One little girl tries to get my attention.

"Over here, Princess!" An even younger boy pulls my hand.

"All right everyone, settle down." One of the volunteers claps her hands. She crosses the room and joins us. "Children, I know we are excited to have visitors, but remember your manners. One at a time, please."

"Yes, ma'am," comes the chorus of young voices. As a group they take a step back.

"Now, who has a question for the Princess?" The woman addresses the children in a formal manner.

I want to tell her that I'm not the princess anymore, but I don't know how. My throat tightens a little.

Five or six little arms stretch hands as high into the air as they can go. Fingers wiggle and lips are pinched tight.

The teacher points to a girl with a pair of light brown braids resting on her shoulders and a smattering of matching freckles across her cute little turned up nose. She looks to be eight or nine years old.

"I heard about what happened with your parents. Are you sad?" she asks in a shy voice.

The teacher clicks her tongue, about to admonish the girl for her inappropriate question.

I rest my hand on her arm and speak in a low voice. "It's alright."

I walk to an old rocking chair on one side of the room and sit down. Magnolia stays behind the children as an observer.

The children gather at my feet and sit on knees or bottoms, their hands folded in their laps. No one makes a peep. All their eyes are wide as they wait for my answer.

"Yes. I am very sad. I miss my parents a lot." I keep my voice calm and steady.

Another girl raises her hand and speaks before being chosen. The other children don't seem to mind. "I am reawwy sowwy they died." Her words are adorable. And sincere.

"Thank you."

"I remember my parents. I miss them a lot, too," a boy near the back says loud enough for everyone to hear. Some of the children turn to look at him. His face turns red, and he ducks his head down.

This is all so heavy. I wasn't expecting this when I decided to visit.

So much for a distraction. But, also, this is good. I can relate to these kids differently than I could before. Many of them remember their parents. They are grieving in their own ways as well, and probably always will.

"Princess?" A four-year old boy stands and takes my hand. "Since you don't have a mommy and daddy anymore, does that mean you're an orphan, too?"

"Of course, she is!" an older girl says a little too know-it-all-y. I don't blame her. I'm sure this has all been a lot for them to process as well.

I nod, my eyes stinging.

Before I can answer, the little boy at my side says, "Will you come live here with us now?"

The children murmur with excitement.

A vice squeezes my heart. It drops into my stomach. I don't know how to answer them.

To my relief, Magnolia steps to my other side and places a hand on my shoulder. "As much as the Princess would love to come live with all you wonderful children, she still does have a family at the palace. She will be remaining with her aunt and uncle, the new King and Queen, for the time being."

A lot of "Oh"s and sighs echo through the room.

"Don't worry." I squeeze the little boy's hand. "I'll still come visit you as much as I can."

He smiles at me and wraps his arms around my waist in a tight hug.

"Let's play a game, shall we?" The teacher catches the children's attention and organizes a game with a ball and some laundry baskets scattered around the room. We pass the ball back and forth, toss it into the baskets, shout and laugh.

By the time the afternoon is over, I am worn out. In a good way for the first time in a long time.

Magnolia helps me unpack all my new clothing and organize my closet again.

"It still feels big and empty, like there's not enough to fill it. But how many clothes does one person really need, anyway? Maybe the space is just… too big."

Magnolia agrees. "But it's better now, right?"

"Oh, yes. Much. Thank you."

She helps me pull out the things I'm pretty sure I don't want from the pile in the back. I fold the items and place them in a stack to one side. "I promise I'll wait at least a season before making any decisions on keeping them or not."

Magnolia rubs my back. "Good girl. That's a very wise decision."

I poke her side and smile. "You sound like my father."

My breath leaves my body. I hear my father's voice. *"You are a wise young woman, Jessamine. You will make a great Queen one day."* I can feel his heavy hand on my shoulder and see his pale blue eyes peering down at me.

I clutch my chest and stumble against the door frame.

"The hurt will ease in time," Magnolia promises as she wraps me in a hug.

She helps me to my bed. On my desk beyond my bed rests a letter.

Magnolia notices that I'm staring and retrieves it for me. "It's likely from Peter. Do you wish to read it alone?"

"Yes. Thank you, Magnolia. For everything. I love you."

"I love you too much."

When Magnolia has left my room, I take a deep breath and open the letter. It is from Peter! How did he know that I would need to hear from him today? My heart lifts back into place in my chest.

Dear Jessamine,

I just wanted you to know that I am thinking of you and your beautiful brown eyes every day. I look forward to being able to gaze into them again soon.

Here in Bennfaran, we have a saying about those we have lost.

"Those who have passed are never gone. They walk

beside us."
  I hope these words can bring you comfort.
  Ever yours, Peter

Aunt Dahlia and Uncle Henry exchange a worried look when I join the family for dinner wearing one of my new, unadorned not-black dresses. Amelie avoids eye contact, as usual.

Juliette, however, quickly covers up her surprise. "You look lovely tonight, Jessamine!" Her voice is soft and sweet.

"Thank you," I whisper.

I take my seat, with Magnolia close beside me, and don't speak for the rest of the meal.

Will I ever feel like I fit in here again? I keep my mind on the sweet words in Peter's letter.

Uncle Henry addresses me when the meal is almost through. "I hear you went to the orphanage today…"

My eyes snap to his face. How did he know? And why does he sound all weird about it?

"The children care for you. And you have a part of your life that they can relate to now," the king continues.

His words sting. Does he have to rub it in? I clench my jaw and keep my eyes on my plate.

"You may continue the work you have been doing there," he finishes.

Do I need his permission to volunteer at the orphanage? Who does he think he is, anyway?

Magnolia must sense my temper begin to flare. She rests a hand on my leg beneath the table and whispers, "Breathe," into my ear.

I breathe in through my nose and out through my mouth. Subtly, so no one else will notice.

"Thank you." I address the new king but keep my eyes on my plate. "May I be excused, please?"

I hold still as a statue while I wait for permission to leave the table.

"Yes, I suppose…" Henry says, sounding thoroughly confused.

Without making eye contact with the others, I place my napkin beside my plate and walk out of the room with my fists clenched.

Outside the door I lean against the wall and take several deep breaths. The conversation continues after I've departed.

"Did I say something wrong?" Henry asks the others.

"No, dear," Dahlia answers. "You did fine."

Does he even realize how rude that whole thing had just been? Probably not.

The door to my room shuts a little harder than necessary. My dinner dress gets kicked into a corner of the closet. The slacks and blouse from Magnolia are all I want to wear right now. With my field journal, shoulder bag, and riding boots in place, I stare out the window.

I want to escape. To anywhere. But I do not want to face anyone again tonight.

With a huff I drop onto my bed. If only there was a way to get to the outdoors without having to go through the castle. Then I could come and go as I please, and not have everyone breathing down my neck about where I've been or what I've been doing. I would have just a tiny bit of control over my disaster of a life.

My pencil scratches images in my journal. It wouldn't take much to fashion a hanging ladder of sorts, just a long stretch of rope, wood slats or sticks, and a couple of hooks. Anchoring it below my window would allow me to climb right down the side of the castle. Good thing I'm not scared of heights, since my window is three stories off the ground.

Gathering the necessary supplies shouldn't be difficult. No one will even know what I'm up to. No questions. No explanations. No permission.

Gah. Uncle Henry can be so obtuse.

My eyes peruse some of the notes from my lessons with Magnolia that are carefully recorded in my field journal. I touch the pressed leaves and flowers with a gentle finger. There's so much I still wish to learn. The library would have plenty of information. My stomach twists. The *palace* library. Will my idea for a public library ever materialize?

My thoughts wander to that dream about my mother on the night of the accident. It was so real. Like she was speaking to me.

134

Was it just a dream? Or was it something more?

My hand writes *"Remember to ask Magnolia about dreams"* across the top of one of the pages. Tossing the book aside I retrieve the letter from Peter.

Stretched out on my bed I reread it over and over.

Still in my foresty clothes, with his letter resting on my chest, I fall into a deep sleep.

Chapter Eighteen

The following weeks pass as a blur. A slow, nightmarish, blur.

Aunt Dahlia and Uncle Henry move into my parent's suites. My heart and jaw clench as the servants carry all my parents' things to some storage space below the castle somewhere. The new king and queen task even more staff with redecorating the adjoining suites to their own tastes. Like they are trying to forget my parents ever lived. It makes my stomach turn.

Juliette and Amelie take over two of the other suites in the royal residences wing, just down the hall from my own. Amelie redecorates, bringing in many of her furniture and items from their previous home, including window treatments, artwork, rugs, and even some door handles. Juliette, ever the accommodating one, says no changes are necessary and she likes hers just the way it is. I roll my eyes when I hear her mother praise her for being so easy to please.

Dahlia insists I stay where I've always been, but it feels… wrong, somehow. I'm not a princess anymore, even though the family pretends I am. Shouldn't I be in the servants quarters? Or thrown out of the castle altogether? She says I can stay as long as I want. I don't even know what I want. But where else would I even go?

Maybe I do want to redecorate my room. After the castle stills for the night, I follow the path the servants took over and over again today as they put my parents' things in storage.

The storage room feels cold and spooky. Cobwebs hang from the ceiling. A large black spider lowers herself from the ceiling and rests on my shoulder. She points me to boxes filled with my parents' belongings stacked on dusty shelves. Some of the bigger items have been set in a corner. It looks like the staff has treated my parents' things with respect. Many of them probably miss the old King and Queen, too.

The flickering firelight from the candle resting on a crate creates menacing shadows around the room.

My mother's clothing hangs on a rack in the back of the space.

"I can remember every time she wore each of the dresses." My fingers caress every garment.

Pieces of art she painted lean in a stack against the wall. "She was so talented."

My eyes stop on the painting she made of my father a few years ago. I set it by the doorway.

Beside her art, facing the wall, I discover the painting from their wedding. They look so young, and so happy. I choose to claim this, as well.

In a box of knick-knacks, I rescue a blown glass flower that had been a gift from my father to my mother. It always stood on her bedside table.

A book catches my eye.

"My mother's field journal!" The worn-out leather is soft and pliable in my hands. My nose breathes in the scents of old leaves and dried flowers and old paper and ink and leather. "It's perfect." When I lift it out of the box, I spot another book that I haven't seen before.

"*The Keeping.* Huh." I flip through the pages. It's an encyclopedia or something.

What's this? The spider whispers in my ear. She crawls down my arm and settles on my hand to get a closer look.

"Part of the book is... sealed?"

What could it mean?

"I don't know. I'll have to investigate it further. Feel free to stop by my room to ask me about it sometime."

She returns to her place on my shoulder.

My father's pillow is the next thing added to my pile of treasures. It smells like him. I recover a little hand carved donkey from his youth that he kept on his own bedside table, as well as his favorite book of poems with a worn-out spine and frayed edges.

The assorted items are difficult to carry, but they all make it to my room in one piece. The portrait of the two of them finds its home on the wall opposite my bed, so they will be the first thing I see each morning. The painting of my father now hangs just beside my bed. The other items are arranged on my bedside table within reach. My father's pillow rests beneath my mother's blanket on the bed. My head sinks into his pillow and my mother's blanket wraps me in a warm hug as I drift to sleep.

They fill my dreams. I awake with a hole in my chest that feels like it will never heal.

Staffing changes are made; some servants choose to leave the employ of the new royals. Menus are altered, introducing more meat into the meals. Schedules are shifted creating a sort of rift between some of the staff.

The castle used to run perfectly smooth under the guidance of my parents, who delegated much of these details to Anthony the butler; Gilda, the head of the staff; Bertha, who oversees the kitchens; and Jonathan, captain of the guard. Henry and Dahlia make so many changes, though, until one day, it just doesn't feel like home anymore.

I write long rambling letters to Peter about it all, ranting about Henry's dimwittedness and Dahlia's lack of spine when it comes to her husband. I don't send any of them; just stuff them in the notebook until I have quite the collection.

A good chunk of my time is spent trying to distract myself.

The fresh air from my open windows flutters the pages of the book in my lap as I sit cross-legged on the floor. My mother's journal mostly has drawings and notes about a million different kinds of animals, but there are a few pressed leaves and flowers scattered here and there. Mostly things that have to do with a specific animal. Or pixies. She knew things about pixies? She never told me much since they are outside our sphere of responsibility.

There are notes about where she saw each animal in her field journal. She went on so many adventures! I don't travel much, but it might be a good idea to do the same in mine, just in case I ever do travel and want to remember where I've seen or learned something. She's even written quotes or advice from what I'm assuming were her teachers and mentors.

Combined with my own field journal full of things Magnolia has taught me about plants, I have quite the encyclopedia right at my fingertips. Pencil in hand, I add things from my mother's work to my own, and things Magnolia taught me that vary from what my mother had written down. It feels weird to correct some of her information, now that she's gone, but she always insisted on accuracy in my work and would expect nothing less.

When I've made as many notes and changes as seem necessary, I set the two books side by side on my desk. The other book from my mother's things, *The Keeping*, rests beneath my notebook now stuffed with letters to Peter that I'll probably never send. With everything else going on, and my feelings that my life is falling apart, I had kind of forgotten about this book. I settle into my desk chair, clear the surface of papers and notebooks, and center the mystery book in front of me.

"What is this. Why is part of it sealed? And… why did you never show this to me?" I speak out loud to the memory of my mother.

"The Keeping" is written in large, loopy letters on the first page inside the thick binding. Whoever did write the book was careful; the words on the pages are neat and easy to read. Not a journal, then. Something that has been copied from another work. And not by my mother, the handwriting is not hers.

The table of contents shows four different sections: common creatures, unusual creatures, dangerous creatures, and a fourth title that has been smudged out. On purpose?

I flip to that section in the book. A thick paper has been installed, blocking any words from being read. It's not sealed in such a way that I *can't* open it, just wrapped in the thick parchment, and glued inside the pages.

Why not just take the pages out completely? The information they contain must be valuable or important. Was my mother trying to stop herself from opening it? Or was it like this when she obtained the book?

I flip through the first two sections. "Common creatures" refers to non-magical, non-sentient creatures from all over the world. Listed beside each animal and simple drawing are facts about where the animals originated, where they live now, what value they provide to the world, and so on. It's all very dry. Not like a field journal with personal observations about what the animal might smell like or sound like. "Unusual creatures" follows the same pattern with less easy to find creatures or ones considered magical or somewhat sentient.

The third section intrigues me the most: dangerous creatures. There's similar factual information about hydras, dragons, sirens, and more.

"Sirens? I guess they're dangerous, to human men, at least. It seems like some of the pixies should be in this section, too, but they're not. And I don't see anything about kelpies, either."

I flip back to the page about pixies in the "Unusual Creatures" section.

"The information is so general. Maybe that's why mom always encouraged me to keep my own field journal. This book is seriously lacking."

What's in the back, though? My inner voice whispers in my ear.

It's probably sealed for a reason.

But it wouldn't hurt to look…

My letter opener makes the perfect tool for slicing through the thick parchment that seals the last section. Except, it doesn't feel like parchment.

"Is this… animal skin?" My fingers rub the parchment, inspecting the texture. "That's strange."

The skin-parchment peels easily away from the chunk of pages

141

beneath.

"The section heading is missing here, too. I wonder what this section is about?"

The drawings on the pages are like the entries in the previous sections. Only, these drawings look older, and from a different artist, perhaps? The handwriting on each page matches the rest of the book. The headings catch me off guard.

"*Locating dangerous creatures. Using plants to enhance your abilities. Transformation. Enhancements. Hybrids. Subduing the mind of the reckless animal. Harnessing pixie magic.* Is this, like, dark magic or something? Maybe this should have stayed sealed."

I close the book and let my hand rest on the front for a long minute, then shove it into one of the deeper drawers in my desk.

"I think I'll stick to Mom's field journal." My voice sounds nervous even to my own ears.

For now.

Magnolia enters the room on quick feet. I jump.

"Let's get some fresh air, shall we? Grab your boots. We're going to the swamp." She stomps out of my room.

I don't even know if she saw me, but I do as she says and hurry down the stairs to catch up with her.

She's been doing this a lot lately, dragging me into the woods for hours on end. We communicate with the animals, explore new areas, and she tells me stories about the creatures she has seen in other parts of the world. In truth, she's seething inside at the changes being made by my aunt and uncle, and spends time away from the castle with me just as much for her own sake as for mine.

On our way to explore the swamp far from the castle, I finally remember to ask her about dreams.

Chapter Nineteen

"Magnolia... are dreams... real?"

A young deer that still has his spots sidles up beside me. I rest my hand on his head and he keeps my pace.

"What do you mean by 'real'?" Magnolia asks. A squirrel follows behind her, it's fluffy tail standing tall.

"I mean... can people, like, talk to each other in their dreams?"

The deer looks up at me with worried eyes. He can sense my anxiety.

"Has something happened to you, Cattail? Why are you asking about dreams all of the sudden?"

The squirrel clings to her day dress and scurries up her back to sit on her shoulder.

"This is hard to talk about. And to explain. But I'll try. On the night of my parent's accident, I heard my mother's voice. But I was asleep. I wasn't really dreaming exactly. She called out to me from far away and said, 'Remember who you are.' It's something she said to me all the time."

Magnolia nods. "Yes, I remember her saying that to you. Are you sure it wasn't just a dream?"

My fingers rub the fawn behind one of his ears. He leans into me a little, and I change my gait so as not to fall over.

"The thing is it pulled me out of a deep sleep. And when I woke up, I felt like a part of me was missing. Like... somehow, I knew she was gone?"

Magnolia purses her lips.

The squirrel scurries around the back of her shoulders to sit on her other shoulder, the one closer to me. He gives me a questioning look.

We pick our way through curtains of moss hanging from creepy looking trees. She points to the left, indicating for me to follow.

"I have heard about dreams such as these," Magnolia says with a thoughtful sound to her voice.

"So... was it real?" My throat feels tight.

We reach the edge of the smelly swamp, and the fawn bounds away from me. The squirrel abandons us as well. I guess they don't like this place.

Magnolia gestures for me to sit on a fallen log, overgrown with moss and decorated with glowing blue mushrooms. The air is thick here. And sour. The canopy blocks a lot of the light. No wonder my mother never brought me here. A shiver runs down my spine.

Magnolia lowers herself next to me and links her arm with mine. I rest my head on her shoulder and stare out across the goopy, green water.

"I don't know, Water Hyacinth. It is supposed to be a rare gift to be able to connect with others through dreams. I have personally never known anyone able to do it." Magnolia's eyes are focused on the enormous lily pads that float on the algae covered surface of the swamp.

Several bullfrogs croak back and forth to one another, talking about us like they don't know we can understand them.

My eyes study her face. "Then how did I hear her voice? How did I somehow *know* that she was gone?" My eyes absently follow a pair of metallic blue dragonflies dance across the water over Magnolia's shoulder.

Magnolia's face scrunches as she puzzles this out. I'm glad she's here with me to help.

After a long wait, she speaks. "Well, your mother had begun to teach you to reach your mind out to the minds of other animals, correct?"

"Yeah, but I have to touch them…" I shake my head and frown.

"Right. But even the fact that that connection is *possible* is something of fairy tales, isn't it? I mean, who else other than the Forest People can do that? And even then, not many can. It's huge."

"But she was so far away from me…" I'm struggling to see the logic in Magnolia's theory.

"I've heard rumors of very powerful Forest People being able to connect with, even control, animals *without touching them*. Sometimes even from great distances. Perhaps…. Perhaps your mother was more powerful than she let on."

Magnolia's brow is furrowed, and her mouth turned down.

My thoughts spin. My mother always told me I had more power than the others. She told me that Juliette was not learning the same skills that she taught to me. Maybe it's because Aunt Dahlia doesn't have those abilities?

My breath catches. Magnolia just said that some could control animals without touch. Is that what had happened with the alpha-wolf before? Had I somehow controlled him? It doesn't make sense. I can barely connect my mind with that of a young pup. How would I have been able to connect with let alone control an alpha male?

Magnolia speaks again. "I think your mother may have been able to reach you because her emotions were high. We know their carriage crashed. It slid off the edge…"

Neither of us wants to think about the details. She skips past the speculation. "In that final moment of realization and fear, her feelings for you were strong. Strong enough to reach your mind even from a great distance."

I had been feeling really strong emotions when I had made that wolf step closer; anger, fear, grief, and frustration.

"I will need to do further research on this." Magnolia's voice startles me back to the present. "I will let you know what I discover."

We both sit in silence for a few moments. Should I tell her about what happened with the wolf? She seems upset, even disturbed, by the possibility of my mother reaching out to me. I don't want her to think there is something wrong with me, too. I decide to wait until she tells me what she finds.

"Well, enough of that," Magnolia stands suddenly. She turns and pulls me up by the hand, smiling. "Let's explore!"

We make our way around the edge of the swamp, staying on the semi-solid layer of moss and tree roots that keeps us from sinking into the stinky water. Our boots protect our skin from leeches and poisonous water snakes, and I catch a glimpse of a giant green salamander with mottled skin to match the surface of the water. A frog plunks into the swamp to get out of our way, and I hear a beaver slap the surface a bit farther away with his large, flat tail. Although I haven't explored the swamp myself before, I have learned about many of the creatures that live here.

"Do you think we will see any of the water pixies?" I ask Magnolia as we squat to inspect a pitcher plant. A few dead flies float in the water within its petals.

Magnolia shakes her head. "They are nocturnal. And they have the appearance of translucence. They look like they're made of water. So even if there were any around, we probably wouldn't notice them."

We avoid a patch of poison sumac and continue our discovery.

Magnolia shows me many of the plants that live in and around the swamp, and explains that as the water level changes, so does the habitat for plants and wildlife. "You could come here multiple times throughout the year, and you would see different things thriving each time."

"I know there's kelpies that live here somewhere," I tell her. "Because of the connection my mother made with them, they'll stay hidden. I would love to see one up close, though. And maybe even try to connect with one myself."

Magnolia stops.

"What?"

"Your mother did what?"

"She made an agreement with the kelpies…" Why does Magnolia look so confused?

"She was able to do that?"

"Yeah, so?"

"I have never heard of anyone from our kind able to reach the minds of beings of darkness before."

Why would my mother have kept that a secret from Magnolia? Should I not have said anything about it? But I trust Magnolia. Still, I tell myself to be more careful with how much of my own abilities I divulge to anyone else in the future, too.

I wonder what that other book says about communicating with animals like kelpies? The thought comes out of nowhere. I shove it aside and follow Magnolia through the swamp.

When our boots are caked with mud, and our stomachs grumble, Magnolia is ready to return to the castle.

"We could forage, and stay here longer?"

Magnolia dabs stinky mud on my nose. I flinch and wipe it off with the back of my hand.

"You need a proper meal. And some rest. You can't avoid all the changes in your life forever."

Magnolia and I get cleaned up, put on "proper" clothing, and join the others for dinner. I keep my eyes on my plate and my mouth shut. I try to tune out the conversation Dahlia is having with her daughters about their schedules for the following week. It doesn't work.

"You will resume your lessons once again. Juliette, you will study with me and the animals. There are new families of animals here that we do not know. It will be the perfect opportunity to practice your communication skills."

Juliette looks excited, and a little nervous.

Dahlia turns to Amelie. "Amelie, you will work with your father and his advisors for your royal training. You have much to learn if you are to wear the crown."

My cheeks burn. They could at least have this conversation after I've left the table. They must be able to tell how hurtful it is. Right? But they carry on as if this is a normal family dinner discussing normal family things.

Magnolia chews her own food quietly beside me. She doesn't join the conversation, either. I wonder if it bothers her, too.

When Dahlia and Henry begin to discuss the upcoming coronation, I can't take it anymore.

"May I be excused, please?" I interrupt Dahlia's long to-do list.

She gives me a shocked look.

I don't wait for an answer this time. I just stand and leave.

"Excuse me," Magnolia says before I can take three steps.

She follows me out of the dining room.

I thought she was going to comfort me or give me another pep-talk or something. But she just hugs me.

"Goodnight, Jessamine." Her eyes are red.

My own lip trembles. She squeezes me tight.

"Hang in there, Cala Lily." She tweaks my chin. "This will all be over soon…"

She doesn't sound like she even believes her own words anymore.

Chapter Twenty

Exactly two weeks after the funeral, the tower bells echo through the city.

The mourning period has officially ended. All the black is removed from everywhere within the castle, across the capital, and probably all the other cities and villages in the kingdom, too.

Life will return to normal. At least, for everyone but me.

I've been dreading this day.

Uncle Henry and Aunt Dahlia, the new king and queen, are being coronated today.

Magnolia has stayed so I don't have to endure it alone.

"Why do I even have to go?" I ask as she does an upside-down braid up the back of my head and piles my brown curls on top. She pins the curls in place.

"Your aunt and uncle are being generous by letting you stay. They love you, but they are not obligated to have you here. It is likely difficult for them to balance their new duties with wanting to respect your feelings."

I huff. "Well, then, I can just leave."

Magnolia chuckles. "I've already offered that. Several times. You clearly would prefer to stay."

She's right. But still.

Magnolia laces up the back of my teal dress. I slip my feet into a pair of matching shoes. She hands me a pair of long grey gloves.

"Do I have to wear these?"

"We do live in a society, Hyacinth."

"Whatever that even means…"

I barely look at my reflection in the mirror. This is one of the dresses that I don't want anymore. That I wanted to donate. And here I am, wearing it. Again.

"This is the last thing you'll have to endure. Then you can move on from all of this. Live your life. Find joy. Will Peter be there?"

"I know what you're trying to do. Change the subject by asking about Peter?"

"I can see your lips trying not to smile, Jessamine."

I meet her eyes in the reflection in the mirror.

I allow the smile. "Yes, he'll be there."

She squeezes my shoulders. "Wonderful. Focus on that. Ignore the rest. You'll be fine."

The new king and queen are coronated in a long, drawn-out ceremony filled with lots of speeches, and talking, and why do we even do this anyway? In the end, they are going to promise to be good leaders, and the people will clap. Can't we just skip to that part? My knee bounces and I press my hands on it to hold it still.

After my aunt and uncle swear their loyalty to the people of the kingdom comes the part I'm dreading the most. My chest tightens. My face flushes. I'm sure everyone is looking at me. I glance at the people around me without moving my head. All eyes are on Amelie. Her own face is red, and her hands squeeze each other so tight her knuckles are as white as her fancy dress. She is given the title Crown Princess, Heir to the Throne. A scarlet sash is draped across her body from shoulder to hip. My crown… no. THE crown is placed upon her blonde curls. Why doesn't *she* have to wear gloves?

I laugh at myself. Then pinch my lips. I'm going to make people think I'm a lunatic with this erratic behavior.

Calm down, Jessamine. It's almost over.

I paste a smile that probably resembles a grimace more than anything on my face. I allow my eyes to blur so I can't see anything. I focus on the sounds of feet shuffling on the floor, fabric from all the fancy clothing rustling as people shift in their seats. And the gasps and oohs from the crowd. Well, that didn't work.

"Amelie, Crown Princess of Dragovalon, although already of age at twenty years old, will assume the title of Queen when she has had sufficient time to prepare," the officiant announces.

The audience claps politely, the sound muffled by so many hands wearing gloves.

"In the meantime, her father will be our reigning monarch, King of Dragovalon. Long live the King!"

"Long live the King!" The crowd shouts in unison.

My heart squeezes in my chest. My skin is clammy. That feeling of unfairness washes over me again. I want to scream.

But I don't.

In my seat beside Juliette, my hands folded properly in my lap, I bite my tongue to hold in the tears. And anger. My head aches from grinding my teeth by the time the ceremony is over. I keep my eyes glued to the floor.

There is a celebration afterwards, of course, in the palace ballroom. This time the decorations consist of red everything, since the dragon on the King's crest is red. Henry has a red velvet cape draped over his shoulders… my father's cape, to be precise. And Dahlia wears a shiny red dress. Fortunately, one I've never seen before. Not my mother's then. Amelie is wearing white, of course, and Juliette's simpler but still fancy gown is a royal blue.

Hah. *Royal* blue. Bitterness bites at my insides.

Magnolia joins me in a dark corner, away from all the partygoers.

"This is way too elaborate if you ask me." I murmur as she settles beside me. "All the food and decorations and favors are a waste. The money would have been much better spent feeding the hungry and caring for the sick," I complain.

"Don't let that cloud linger, Jessamine. It will do you no good in the long term." Magnolia bumps my shoulder with hers. "Try to enjoy yourself, at least a little."

After too long of a silence, she leaves me to mingle. I guess there are people here she probably knows.

My mood stays sour. I spend the next hour avoiding eye contact with anyone, biding my time until I can sneak out of here. I'm so wrapped up in planning my escape, that I jump when a male voice speaks my name in my ear.

Peter lowers himself beside me. I had been so wrapped up in my own pain, and, let's be honest, jealousy, that I had forgotten he would be here. Again. I want to smack myself on the head for being such an idiot, but I refrain.

He reaches for my hand. The gloves are back on, for both of us. I wish I could feel the warmth of his skin on mine.

I look up at him and he smiles.

"This must be difficult for you." His eyes are sympathetic.

I nod. Then sigh. I'm more angry than sad right now, but he doesn't need to know that. "Yeah," is all I manage to say.

"Let's get out of here." He pulls me to standing and we slip out a side door.

"Can I take these off now?" I pull at the gloves that suffocate my arms.

"Of course!" Peter helps remove my gloves and he dangles them over the shoulder of his own very proper, very uncomfortable looking suit. He shoves his own gloves into an inside pocket on his blazer.

We stroll hand in hand, skin to skin, through the gardens once more, only this time through the zinnia boxes. The jewel toned blossoms with layers upon layers of petals are nearly as tall as me. Their green stems bend in graceful arches from the weight of the flowers.

The feel of his hand engulfing mine chases away much of my bitterness.

The sky is clear, and the stars twinkle just like the night of the ball.

We meander through an opening in the squared hedgerow and find ourselves in the meadow.

Peter breathes in deep. "It smells so good out here! The flowers, the grasses, the moisture. I wish I could come out here every day."

"I do come out here every day. Sometimes I spend all day out here. I didn't used to, but now…"

My voice trails off and my smile fades.

Peter squeezes my hand. "Well, let's see if you can keep both of your shoes on this time." He chuckles.

"Not a chance. In fact…" I pull my skirts up and kick my shoes off my feet. They go flying into the air.

His laugh booms from his chest. "You'll never be able to find them in the dark!"

"Who cares? The damp grass and soft clover feel so good between my toes… You should try it!"

"The gloves are one thing. But shoes? You can hide your bare feet beneath your dress. Me on the other hand…"

I grin.

"What do you want to talk about?" Peter asks.

"You. Talk about what you've been doing lately. I just want to listen."

He nods and regales me of tales of his funny dog, Boy, a fawn-colored mastiff that weighs more than Peter and follows him around like a puppy.

"He's probably waiting at the door for me as we speak," Peter chuckles.

The corners of my mouth turn up. I haven't felt like smiling in a long time. "Keep going, I love this." I squeeze Peter's arm.

He tells me the story of when Boy caught sight of a jack rabbit and tried to chase it.

"He ended up disturbing a ground nest of hornets. He had been the hunter, but suddenly became the hunted. He raced back to the castle at full speed, barking."

Peter imitates Boy's deep bark. I laugh out loud.

"I heard his barks and thought for sure something terrible had happened. I rushed to open the door, and he barreled into me, knocking me onto my backside."

He mimes falling over, letting go of my hand. He keeps himself from falling all the way to the ground, though.

"He continued to bark." He takes my hand again. "I looked outside. The swarm was headed straight for us! I lunged for the door from the floor, and slammed it shut."

He acts out slamming the door closed. "Then I leaned against it, panting. Boy whimpered. I crouched to the floor to check on him. He had been stung a few times, and his face was a little swollen. But he was more worried about me then himself. He licked my face and tried to climb in my lap."

The longer Peter talks, gesturing with his hands and laughing at his dog's antics, the better my mood. When he's not using his hands to tell his story, one of them always returns to hold mine. Contentment begins to settle around my heart.

By the time we return to the palace, I've been able to not think about how terrible my life is going for over an hour.

I pull Peter to a stop before he leads us inside. We're still in the shadows a little, tucked in a corner of hedges.

I hold both of his hands and stand in front of him. "Peter, thank you."

He grins sideways. "Um, you're welcome. But... I didn't do anything."

I move a little closer to him.

He swallows, but he doesn't pull away.

"But you did. You've kept me distracted for a long time. I truly needed that tonight."

He chuckles and takes a tiny step closer to me. "All I did was tell stories..."

"You made me smile. And laugh! To me, right now, that's everything."

We're standing so close now. He releases my hands and wraps both of his arms around me, clasping his hands behind my back. I rest my hands on his chest.

My heart is racing. I'm lost in his green eyes. Butterflies dance in my stomach.

He leans forward and rests his forehead against mine.

"Jessamine," his voice is soft and low. He swallows again. "May I kiss you?"

I don't blink. I barely nod.

I tilt my head back a little, and his lips meet mine in a warm, sweet kiss.

I could stay in this moment forever.

He pulls me a little closer. I reach my arms up and around his neck and close the gap between us.

Christine Marshall

Chapter Twenty-one

The door opens and a swarm of giggling girls pour out of the palace.

We break apart. I'm blushing like crazy, I know, but fortunately we're still in the shadows so Peter can't tell.

I smile at him, and his own face reflects the joy I'm sure mine is emanating.

"Shall we?" He holds out his arm for me.

"As you wish," I answer with a laugh in my voice.

I hook my hand through his arm. "Oh! The gloves!"

"Right." He carefully slides my smooth gloves back up each of my arms. The sensation leaves me feeling all tingly inside.

His eyes meet mine. I can tell that he wants to kiss me again. I want him to. But we are no longer alone, and we must return to the party.

No one can tell that my feet are lacking shoes, and Peter keeps hinting at it whenever we speak to someone. I pinch his arm when he threatens to tell my aunt and uncle that I have lost my slippers. Neither of us can stop grinning like lovesick fools the entire evening. He helps me navigate the well-wishes of the celebrators. Every time I start to feel any negativity, I just replay the kiss in my head. It works wonders.

At the end of the evening, Peter kisses my gloved hand, then winks at me.

I blush and curtsy.

It's all very proper.

When I stand, he makes sure no one is paying attention and leans closer. "I'll be back soon."

"I can't wait," I whisper back.

I politely say goodnight to the new king and queen and take the stairs two at a time- very unladylike- to my room. I change into my sleeping clothes and wrap myself in my mother's blanket.

I touch my lips. That kiss! I replay it over and over as I fall asleep.

My dreams are sweet, and in the morning, I feel... happy? Am I allowed to feel happy?

Guilt crowds out the happiness. My parents are dead. My life is in shambles. I'm lost, alone.

My lips tingle.

Maybe... not entirely alone. I smile to myself.

I'm allowed to feel a little bit of happiness, right?

The week following the coronation, I try to talk to Aunt Dahlia several times about my library project.

"When everything settles down, dear," she says every time.

I'm brushed aside. Again.

I try to stay out of the way as much as possible. Most of the servants still treat me as one of the royal family, but others side eye me, like I should be *serving* the royal family, not part of them. They're probably right. I push those thoughts away whenever they try to sneak in.

"I must return to the forest soon, Jessamine." Magnolia holds her arm out and a hawk lands on it. It holds a stick in its mouth. She takes the stick and the bird flies away.

"I've been dreading this conversation. Once you leave, things will change. Again."

"You are still welcome to join me," she reminds me.

I pick at the clover blossoms. A large black and yellow garden spider crawls onto my knee.

"What would I even do? I know nothing of the life you lead."

The spider, the size of my palm, crawls onto my open hand. She circles around and around my hand as I slowly turn it.

"You would stay with me. I travel a lot; you would join me. We could go visit the sea, like we talked about before. I could teach you even more about the world, and the plants and animals that we share it with."

She sits beside me on the ground. A little bunny settles in her lap. She strokes its silky ears.

"You'd be able to meet all kinds of new people. See new places. Try new things. It would be a grand adventure."

It does sound like a grand adventure. But am I ready to live off the land? Labor for every little thing?

"I don't know," I sigh. "It's such a different lifestyle than what I'm used to."

"You would become used to it."

I don't say it out loud, but my mind turns to Peter. If I leave, I might not see him again.

"If you decide to stay here, which I would not blame you for one bit, I will come visit as often as I can. I promise." She holds out her pinky.

"A pinky promise?" I laugh.

"We used to make pinky promises all the time, remember?"

I loop my pinky around hers. "I do remember. And thank you, Magnolia."

Releasing her pinky, I wrap my arms around her.

The spider drops herself back to the ground with a silky thread.

The morning of Magnolia's departure comes too soon.

"I wish you could stay forever," I manage to squeeze out between sobs.

"Me too. But just as much as my lifestyle is foreign to you, I wouldn't be happy living in the palace." She's not doing a good job holding her own emotions in check, either.

"I hate to see you go. It's like losing a piece of my mother that I haven't realized I've been holding onto."

She squeezes me even longer. "I love you, too much, Jessamine."

"I love you too much, too." I chuckle through my tears.

Dahlia hugs Magnolia and wipes a few tears off her cheeks, as well. We stand shoulder to shoulder and wave from the front steps as Magnolia gallops away on the back of an enormous elk.

I pen a short message to Peter telling him that I miss him. I secure it in an envelope and hand it off to Anthony to send.

The rest of the day is spent in the forest, avoiding people. Again. I don't even join the family for dinner.

In my dreams, I relive the kiss with Peter. My heart feels like it's going to burst.

But this time, instead of being interrupted by a bunch of giggling girls, my mother's scream echoes around me.

The air turns sour.

Peter fades away.

I'm alone.

Ashes and sparks float in the air, like the whole world is on fire.

I reach out to touch one of the cinders.

Just as I'm about to touch it, my mother's voice echoes all around me, "*Remember who you are!*"

I jerk awake, tangled in my blankets, neck moist.

I lay there and stare at the ceiling, willing my breathing to slow.

When sleep eventually returns, I toss and turn for the rest of the night, waiting for morning to come.

Now that Magnolia is gone, I *have* to find something to distract me.

I don't want to do lessons with Dahlia and Juliette, and my aunt allows me to take a break for a while.

I expect to hear back from Peter but several days pass without a response.

Afraid that I'll miss his message, I stay in my room, so I'll know as soon as a letter arrives.

Boredom tempts me to leave, but my mother's books entice me to stay. I tell myself to leave *The Keeping* alone.

But there's valuable information in the first three sections. As long as I keep my eyes out of the last section, there's really no harm.

"This is so dull," I groan after spending nearly an hour reading the factual entries about animals. "Who would even read this book in the first place?"

Maybe the back is more interesting?

I probably shouldn't.

A peek wouldn't hurt...

Before I can talk myself out of it, I flip to a random page in the back.

I've stopped on a page that has drawings and notes about plants. Things Magnolia taught me when she was here. About the ones that are dangerous. Some are deadly poisonous, like the midnight caladium, except when you inhale the steam from the tea, of course, though the book doesn't mention that tidbit. But others are dangerous for different reasons. Non-life-threatening reasons.

There's a vine that, when touched, can give one feelings of distress. If eaten, it can cause physical illness.

A fungus that an ant eats, then it grows inside of them, causing them to explode and spread its spores. Gross. But before that, it messes with the ant's brain and makes it climb onto a high flower or something and wait for death. Creepy.

Some palm nut that will stain your teeth red when you chew it, but also gives you feelings of euphoria.

And jimsonweed which causes terrifying hallucinations that can lead to one being so scared they take their own life. That's just messed up.

For all the beauty in the world, there are equally frightful things.

161

The next page I turn to is about kelpies.

I gasp. "Mom's handwriting?" My finger caresses her slanty letters. I force my eyes away from her scribbles and read the page from top to bottom.

> *Kelpies- dangerous waterborne creatures with the insatiable appetite for drowned human flesh.*

I shiver. That just makes them sound evil, even though the picture of one is stunning.

> *Though they generally reside in swamps, kelpies have been known to leave their watery homes in search of prey, especially when humans no longer frequent their territory. Forest People are believed to be immune to their magic, but many have disappeared after encounters with the creatures.*
> *If one should come across a kelpie, the ideal result would be to extinguish its life at once.*

"What?" I read the words again: extinguish its life at once.

"What Forest Person would ever do such a thing?" My eyes instantly look in the direction of the swamp. Then I remember to look at what Mom wrote.

> *"Able to connect with the lead mare of the herd. Kelpies are misunderstood. Only protecting their families. Made agreement with them. I will keep them safe, no matter what."*

"She always said the deal was they would help us if we helped them. But she was just trying to protect them."

My eyes sting. She was such an amazing person with such a kind heart. The world is definitely worse off without her in it. Any other Forest Person would have ended the entire herd, but she went out of her way to find a way to protect them.

A tear drips on the page, blurring some of the ink.

"No!" I hurry to dab it up. Her words are still legible.

"What else is in this book that I should know? Did she make any other notes?"

A few more turns through the section looking for her handwriting turns up nothing. But I do find a few pages that pique my interest.

I can only read for so long before I feel like I'm going to go insane. My legs need to move. My lungs need to breathe in the sweet forest air. I need to connect with the animals, to feel like there's someone in my life who wants me around. I can't leave my room without either getting pity or glares. And I don't want Dahlia trying to talk to me, or Juliette to follow me around. I just need to be alone.

It's time to construct the hanging ladder to sneak out of my room whenever I want. It's the perfect distraction.

I gather a heavy coil of rope from the stables, a pair of oversized gardening sheers, an armful of thick sticks from the forest, and some hooks with loops at one end from the workshop on the palace grounds. All of it securely wrapped inside a blanket makes it easy to carry quickly to my room. If anyone notices my odd behavior, they don't say anything.

The sheers make clean cuts in the wood, sending tiny wood chunks onto the floor and the smell of green wood into my nose. Knots in the thick rope wrap snuggly around the wood for ladder rungs. With the rope threaded through the eyes of the hooks, I jam the sharp ends into the wood frame of the window with my foot while sitting on the floor.

Time to test it.

Deep breath in, then out. The pile of sticks and rope slap the brick exterior of the castle as the ladder drops nearly to the ground. I lean out the window. Good, it's long enough. My eyes scan the surrounding palace grounds. There's no one around to notice.

Sitting on the windowsill with my legs dangling out the window, my heart races. This could end very badly. But a part of me needs to take this risk. To try something daring.

Christine Marshall

Chapter Twenty-two

Laying on my stomach, my feet reach until they find the second or third rung. My weight shifts from my upper body on the window to my feet on the ladder.

The wood with the hooks stuck in it groans. It only tightens the hooks' hold. It's working. I stretch one leg, then the other, down to a further rung, and release my grip on the window frame, holding tight to the rope itself instead. The ladder is holding all my weight. It feels secure.

The ladder sways a little as I climb down rung by rung, then drop the last little bit to the ground. The landscaping around the castle walls makes a good cover. And the vines that grow up the grey bricks camouflages the ladder.

I did it! Laughter bursts out of me. *I'm free!* Imagine all the things I will be able to do with my newfound freedom. Without questions or comments or looks or reprimands. *This is going to be epic.*

For now, though, I climb back up the ladder, then pull the entire thing rung by rung through my window into a neat pile and shove the whole bundle underneath my bed, out of sight.

After gathering the leftover wood pieces, I consider throwing them out the window, but that seems weird. Instead, they end up in a pile beside my discarded clothing at the back of my closet.

Just as I come out of the closet the chamber maid arrives with a letter.

"Thank you," I nod.

She gives me an awkward curtsy then leaves as quietly as she entered.

Plopped onto my bed, the envelope tears in my haste to open it. My eyes scan the words as quickly as they can.

A squeal escapes my throat. Peter is coming for a formal visit!

I hurry to find Aunt Dahlia. She'll be so happy for me!

Dahlia peruses the short, formal letter from Prince Peter. "Well, this is… unexpected."

She's frowning. Why is she frowning?

"I met him at the festival," I wring my hands together. Why am I so nervous? "We've seen each other since then at the other… events."

I don't want to say "funeral" or "coronation." Those both bring up strong, negative feelings from deep inside. I push those thoughts back down.

She folds the letter but does not return it to me. She barely maintains eye contact. "I'm not sure this is such a good idea, Jessamine."

"I don't understand." My smile disappears. My hands drop to my sides.

"With everything going on lately…"

Now *I'm* frowning. What is she even talking about? There's NOTHING going on. All the big things are over. There's nothing new on the schedule. I know because they rub their busy schedules in my face every night at dinner.

"And Amelie is preparing herself for her new role…" Dahlia stumbles over her words.

So, this is about *Amelie?* What does she have to do with it? I'm fuming inside.

166

She sees me eyeing the letter still in her hand. She folds her other hand over the top of it. She's not going to give it back? I lock eyes with her again.

She looks sorry. But I don't see her planning to relent.

"I see," I say.

But I truly don't see. It's not like anyone would have to do anything special for him to come to visit me.

My eyes sting.

Dahlia reaches out and places a hand on my shoulder.

My body tenses beneath her touch. For the first time. Ever.

"Perhaps when things... settle down." It sounds like an offering, or promise. But she's been saying that a lot lately.

I take measured steps back to my room. Why must she try to keep Peter from me? Does she not want him to court me? Is it because I'm not a princess anymore? I'm not good enough for him?

A path is going to be carved into my rug from my incessant pacing. But I have to release this tension somehow. My temper is mounting. Something I've never really experienced before.

My mother always said, when things don't go your way serving those less fortunate helps put things back into perspective. And she was right. It always does.

I grab a cloak and a small satchel and drop the ladder out my window. I climb down quickly, then realize I have no way to hide it while I'm away. I shrug. Who even cares anymore? What are they going to do, throw me out of the castle for sneaking out? I don't really belong here anymore, anyway.

I turn away from the castle and head down the meadow hillside toward the city to spend the afternoon in the service of others.

As the afternoon blends into evening, my anger slips away replaced with little bits of joy from the smiles on the faces of the sick and afflicted whom I serve.

By the time I return home, I'm a little like my old self again. And totally empowered. Like the day I accidentally made that alpha wolf step toward me against his will.

167

I didn't ask permission; I didn't tell anyone where I was going. I just… left. The world didn't catch on fire. Nothing bad happened, only good. I like this newfound freedom. In fact…

With parchment, envelope, and ink pen splayed out on my writing desk, I write a reply to Peter.

> *Peter,*
> *Of course, you are welcome to come see me. But it will not be a formal visit.*

A simple diagram shows him where my window is from the outside of the castle.

> *Meet me there tomorrow.*
> *Love, Jessamine*

The folded letter fits snugly inside the envelope. Peter's name looks perfect scrawled in loopy letters on the front.

I stand, ready to take it to the butler.

But wait. Will Dahlia find out that I've invited Peter to come, without her permission? It's not like she'll punish me or anything. But will she allow the letter to be delivered? Or will she take it as she has done with the one from Peter to me?

A vision of Magnolia and Jack using animals as messengers flash in my mind. Then the memory of Magnolia asking that little jerboa thing to fetch the fresh mint for her.

Perhaps… perhaps I could get an animal to deliver my letter? I haven't really practiced that much over the past few weeks. But maybe if I ask nice enough?

Standing in front of my open windows, I scan the forest for the animal appropriate for the task. A large flock of ravens settles into the canopy. Their funny croaks fill the air, and they look like a shadow above the treetops.

Perfect.

I call to the birds. They respond. One flies closer and perches on my windowsill. He's nearly as tall as my torso, and his long black beak curves toward the floor. He looks at me with a sharp eye. These birds are much more intelligent than most people realize.

I greet the raven. "Please deliver this message to Prince Peter of Bennfaran. With haste."

The bird dips his head in acknowledgement and takes the letter. It dangles from his beak, but I can see that he has it pinched tight. He calls out to his flock with a loud, screechy caw, and the entire group, hundreds of them, follow him toward Peter's home. They darken the sky with their huge wings and pierce the air with their sharp cries.

The sight is ominous. They are serving me. That feeling of power twinges in my mind again. My lips stretch out into a wide smile.

"Remember who you are!" echoes around me.

Impatiently waiting for Peter's arrival, my field journal fills with sketches of plants and animals along with notes about the things Magnolia has taught me combined with information from my mother's journal. Mom's extensive abilities with the animals never ceases to amaze me. And Magnolia's vast knowledge of the flora even though she works with animals is inspiring. Combining both of their knowledge into one book will make me wiser and help me grow my abilities better than ever.

My mind hums as I draw a sketch of the massive conspiracy of ravens darkening the sky, Peter's letter visible dangling from a beak. Waiting for Peter to come feels like torture, but this is a good enough distraction.

"Jessamine?" Peter calls tentatively from below my window.

I spring from my bed and toss the books aside. They bounce on my bed and bump into one another as I hurry to the window.

Peter gazes up at me from three stories below. He's wearing brown canvas pants that hug his waist, and a loose tunic style shirt that he's left open at the top. His riding boots stretch to his knees over his pants. He pushes his messy blonde hair off his face.

When he sees me, his worried expression breaks into a huge grin.

169

His green eyes with dark lashes crinkle at the corners.

My heart skips a beat.

"Wait there," I call down, but not too loud.

I drag the ladder out from beneath my bed, install the hooks in their holes, and unfurl the rungs down the side of the castle. It clatters against the bricks.

Peter looks surprised. And worried.

With my shoulder bag slung across my torso I dangle my legs out the window from a sitting position on the sill.

"Is that such a good idea?" Peter sounds nervous.

"Yep." I roll onto my stomach and plant my feet on the fourth rung.

I climb down, faster than usual.

"Be careful!" Peter calls.

When my feet hit the ground, my mouth stretches into a grin. "See? Nothing to worry about!"

Just a few short steps closes the distance between us.

"Well, this is all very clandestine, isn't it?" He grins as he pulls me into his strong arms.

My own arms wrap themselves around his torso and my hands press into his back. Stepping so our arms are still around each other, I give him a sly look.

"I'm so glad you got my messages. I was afraid you hadn't got the first one I sent, but when I received your announcement that you wanted to visit, I was so relieved!"

"Wait," Peter interrupts. "I only received the message last night, from the birds. Which was brilliant, by the way. Your abilities never cease to amaze me!"

I'm almost too wrapped up in his adoring compliments to hear the bit about not getting my first message.

"I wrote to you the day Magnolia left…"

"Oh, has she gone? I'm sorry, Jessamine. That must have been difficult to say goodbye."

"It was, but… I wrote to you about it. Anthony was to send the message."

He shakes his head. "No, I only received the one from the birds…"

"Dahlia!" my brow furrows.

He plants a quick kiss on my wrinkled skin. "You look adorable when you're mad. But, what about Queen Dahlia?"

I bristle inside at the use of her title that used to belong to my mother, but I brush those feelings aside. Peter is proper and polite; he's not saying it for any other reason.

"Well, when I showed Dahlia the letter from you, she got all weird about you coming for a formal visit. She says they're too busy or something. I know they're not too busy. They just don't want to make time for anything in my life, that's all."

I pause. Now I just sound whiney. "Sorry. Again. I'm just so glad you came!"

I lean against his chest, and he holds me close. My anger at Dahlia for suppressing my message to Peter wars with my victory at finding my own way to communicate with him. The spite wins and a part of me wants to rub it in her face. But also… I don't want to share Peter with anyone. What we have is a secret. And the longer it stays that way, the better.

"Well," his chin rests on my head. "If we aren't going to do all the normal boring formal things, like tea, and dull conversation, and exchanging pleasantries and thin complements with the rest of the family, what *are* we going to do this afternoon?"

I shrug.

He pushes me away a teeny bit, just so I'll look up at him. "I have one idea…"

His lips meet mine in a tentative kiss.

I lean into him and kiss him back.

Christine Marshall

Chapter Twenty-three

When we finally separate, we are both grinning from ear to ear.

"I have an idea, too," I say.

I grab his hand and pull him toward the woods. His dark horse is tethered to a tree and blends in with the shadows. We run across the meadow, hand in hand. I'm giggling, he's laughing. We don't have a care in the world.

In between moments of kissing and hand holding, we stroll side by side through a grove of quaking aspens in the forest. Their leaves shimmer and rattle in the breeze.

"You know, I've never seen a woman wear trousers before." He pulls me close and wraps a hand around my waist.

"This is how the Forest People dress," I explain.

"Even the women?" he sounds surprised.

"Yes," I laugh. "Even the women. It's way more practical for the work they do then long, flowy dresses with tight bodices."

"I have to admit, I like how you look." He swings me away from him and twirls me around. He studies me carefully from head to toe.

I blush and return to his side.

"I can see more of your figure in these clothes than the dresses you usually wear." His eyes twinkle. "However… that blue ballgown from the festival?" His cheeks turn red, and he wraps his arms around me again. "That is definitely my favorite."

We share a long kiss. My heart feels like it's going to burst.

We continue our trek through the woods. I show him all my favorite places.

The rabbit family I know approaches.

"Well, aren't you just growing up so fast?" I ask the bunnies who are almost as big as their mom now. "Should we show Peter what you little ones can do?"

The bunnies do some hops and twists. They turn somersaults on the mossy floor of the woods.

Peter claps. "Bravo!" The forest rings with his laughter.

When hunger tickles the back of my throat, instead of returning to the castle, we forage for edible plants in the woods. We eat our fill of a wide variety of nuts, mushrooms, and berries. I even show him where to find wild mint to chew on as a breath freshener.

When the stars dot the night sky, we lie in the meadow side by side. My head rests on his chest and his arms wrap around me. We gaze at the stars. He points out the constellations.

"Astronomy is a subject I haven't studied before," I tell him.

"I will spend as many nights with you as it takes to teach you everything you could ever want to know about the stars." His voice is husky in my ears.

"I could stay like this forever," I sigh.

He hums in reply. "Me, too."

When my eyes get heavy, we stand. We walk arm in arm back to my ladder. We share one more long kiss, and a tight embrace. He watches as I climb back to my room.

"Be careful!" he whispers loudly.

I giggle. "I'm not scared of heights!" I dangle with one hand and one foot off the ladder.

He gasps.

"Are you??" I tease.

"What? No! I just… I don't want anything to happen to you. Ever." His voice holds no sarcasm. Only affection.

My eyes mist. I climb the rest of the way more carefully. I don't want to upset him.

When I'm safely over the sill, I stand in the tall window frame. My loose pants flap a little in the breeze, and my curls float on the air.

Peter walks backwards through the meadow toward his horse. He waves and blows kisses. I giggle and return them.

He mounts his horse, and gives me one last, longing look before he gallops away.

I don't take my eyes off him as he disappears into the woods.

Life settles into a new routine over the next two weeks. I desperately miss my old routine, but I try to live in the present instead of pining for the past. My new normal has some similarities to my old life.

Birds land on my windowsill and trill for me to wake up.

"Alright, alright, I'm up!" My muffled voice greets them.

I force myself out of bed and splash cool water on my face, comb my hair, and get dressed. All my day dresses are pretty much the same: colorful cotton fabric with elbow-length sleeves, empire waist, and long narrow skirt. Some have a simple satin ribbon around the waist, others do not. I choose one at random. I pull my hair into a low, loose bun at the base of my neck, though several of the dark curls escape and frame my face within minutes.

Parting the curtains all the way reveals the view across the meadow into the forest. My body tingles thinking about the amazing day I spent with Peter a little over a week ago. The kisses, talking, and stargazing. Feeling like someone still wants me. I sigh with content.

More birds join me, as well as a garden snake that slithers up the vines, and a beautiful brown spider who's web decorates the corner of the window.

"I'll see you all later," I wave at the creatures and leave my room.

The royal family is already gathered in the dining room for breakfast.

Juliette smiles at me as I enter, and I politely return the smile. She's given up trying to really talk to me, though. Our lives are too different now, and with our rocky relationship these past few years, our interactions are awkward at best.

Amelie is slowly accepting her new role. The advisors that formerly served my father have aided the new king in teaching his eldest daughter her responsibilities. They are preparing for her to accept the crown in the coming year.

Honestly, the sooner the better at this point. I don't even care anymore. It hurts too much to think about, so I just... don't.

After breakfast I return to my suite and change into the more comfortable trousers and blouse and my tall riding boots. The trip down the ladder takes seconds and in no time I'm in my element in the woods.

I avoid lessons with Juliette and Dahlia. Magnolia was right about my mom being more powerful than she had known. Dahlia and Juliette don't have the same ease and ability with the animals as my mother had. I'm more advanced than Juliette and have nearly surpassed Dahlia as well. I insist that I will continue the training my mother has started on my own.

Just as my mother would expect, I continue to practice connecting with the animals. The days I'm more frustrated or upset yield completely different results than when I'm not. I keep copious amounts of notes on what works and what doesn't, and hone in on the skills that are the most affective. In what feels like no time but has actually been a couple of weeks, I can now connect with every animal that I attempt to connect with by touch. They all willingly share their minds with me. The level of understanding that I gain from these experiences helps me better anticipate their needs and desires.

If I lived with the Forest People, I would surely be a leader among the animal caretakers. I have no responsibility to the animals in this realm, however.

That feeling from when I connected with, almost controlled, that alpha wolf without touching him skirts around the edge of my mind. I haven't been able to repeat the experience.

My nights are no longer haunted with dreams of my mother's voice. No more fires burn around me. No cinders float in the air. I mostly dream of the animals. And Peter. He's so handsome. And funny, and kind. I'm truly falling for him.

If I was still the crown princess, he would be formally courting me by now. But since I hold no titles and have no real station, our relationship has remained a secret. He insists he won't get into any trouble. As the fourth child and third son he has no duty to the crown when it comes to relationships or marriage.

The ravens have become our very own "carrier pigeons." Although, if they ever knew I thought of them that way, they would probably stop helping me. They willingly deliver our messages back and forth. They actually seem to like it. We've come to an understanding. They deliver our messages; we reward them with shiny things: jewels, shells, sparkly rocks, chain links, anything we can find. I've begun to collect anything shiny when I am out and about. I have quite the collection on my bedside table now.

For as normal as I try to spend my days, there is still one thing that eats at me.

My birthday project has been brushed aside over and over again. I ache for it to happen. And in time for my birthday. I doubt anyone will even remember to celebrate it this year since they're all so focused on Amelie. It's my coming-of-age birthday. My parents should be announcing a betrothal with Peter at my birthday celebration. It's exactly what my mom wanted for me.

My stomach churns. Fire builds in my veins. I stomp through the woods, anger blurring my vision. Any animals I come across scurry or flap away from me.

I can't have a party. I can't have Peter; at least, not officially. Not yet. I can't have the crown.

But there's one thing I could still have for my birthday. And if Dahlia won't help me, then I will just have to tackle the project on my

177

own. I've trained for this my whole life, after all. Why shouldn't I take matters into my own hands?

With a renewed sense of determination, and maybe a little spite, I return to my room and begin to make plans.

Over the next several days I walk up and down the streets of the city, looking through the different districts and buildings that are vacant or nearly vacant, to try to determine the best location for a library. Several places catch my eye, and I speak with the property managers. Since most of the land is owned by the reigning king and queen, and I'm still a princess to many, I don't seek out permission from my aunt and uncle. I imply to those I speak with that I already have it

A granary near the housing district turns out to be the ideal location. The two-story brick structure has a tiled roof that slants on either end. Sturdy stilts hold the structure off the ground. The floor is at my shoulder height. The lift keeps the grain from becoming moist and keeps the temperatures more neutral with the airflow. These features will be perfect for a library to protect the books from extreme temperatures and moisture. I couldn't have designed a more perfect structure. I make notes in my book and draw a crude sketch of the outside of the building.

The property manager and I arrange for them to move their operation to a nearby millhouse in exchange for additional purchases from the castle for the grain. We don't really need the surplus of grain, but my aunt and uncle can pay for it, and I'll have the granary manager donate it to the poor. Everyone wins.

A crew of the older orphan boys gladly accepts payment in exchange for cleaning out the space once the current occupants have vacated. The sweet smell of the grain gives the building an outdoorsy aroma, which, combined with the massive granary doors that can be pushed open on rollers, provides the perfect ambiance for getting lost in a book.

I draw up plans for how to organize the space, how many shelves will be needed, where to buy the wood, who to contract for the carpentry work, and how the books will be organized. After carefully perusing the catalog within the palace library I make a sort of map of where everything will go in the new public space.

My book is full of possible ideas for how the borrowing system will work, how to obtain new books, and when to donate books to the people. The more I work on it, the more excited I become. This is going to be a dream come true. Not just for me, but for my... not "my" anymore, just "the"... people. I get a hitch in my chest. They used to be my people. I still feel like they are. I am doing this for them.

Peter and I continue to send messages back and forth. I tell him every last detail as the project progresses. He promises to come see me as soon as he can so I can show him my plans.

I read myself to sleep every night; sometimes from my father's favorite poems, sometimes from my mother's field journal, and sometimes, under the covers as if someone might catch me in the act, from the now-unsealed section of the other book. Why do I feel so guilty looking at it? I only read bits at a time before my conscience tells me to stop. But these bits spark something deep inside of me. Curiosity at what rules can be broken, knowledge of things I'm not supposed to know, and a desire to see what my own abilities would allow me to do.

Christine Marshall

Chapter Twenty-four

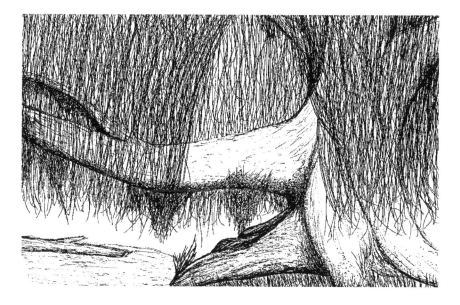

Peter finally manages to sneak away a week after his promise, though we have written to one another daily in between.

I take him to the swamp far away from the castle. The water level is low, and the muddy ground buzzes with insects. Peter has a fragrant jessamine flower pinned to his tunic to mask the sour air.

"Aren't there kelpies in this swamp? I've heard tales…"

My hand brushes away his words. "Don't worry, they won't bother us."

He gives me a skeptical look.

"Trust me!" I laugh. "It's unlikely we'll even see them. They'll stay tucked away while I'm here."

He shrugs. "If you say so."

We settle onto a low wide branch of a weeping willow tree near the edge of the swamp. Peter leans his back against the tree and stretches his legs in front of him. I snuggle my back into his chest, and he wraps his arms around me.

"Now, show me what's in that magical book of yours."

I giggle. "It's not magical."

"All of your ideas are magical. Therefore, your book is magical."

"Oh, Peter…"

I open the book and flip through the pages.

"I like the building you've chosen," he says when we reach the page with the sketch of the exterior.

"You should see it! The boys from the orphanage have done a spectacular job sprucing it up!"

"How do you plan to organize the books?" He asks after a few more pages.

I show him my ideas, and he offers a few suggestions of his own. Using the pencil attached to my book with a string, I write his ideas.

"See? Magical! Who else would have thought to attach a writing implement to their book?"

His arms tighten around me, and he kisses my neck. It sends a shiver down my spine. In a good way.

We bounce more ideas back and forth, and I take careful notes.

"Jessamine, this is incredible," he says at last. "Henry and Dahlia will have no reason to deny your request now. They'll barely even have to do anything. Only arrange to have the books moved from the palace to the library and announce a grand opening."

He pauses.

I swallow.

Before I can respond, he continues. "You are an amazing woman. This is going to change so many lives."

I shake my head. "Your feedback has been invaluable and will make the library even better. Thank you so much."

I tuck the book behind Peter's back against the tree and turn my body sideways so I can see his face. He supports my back with a bent knee and a strong arm.

I'm sure I'm glowing in the dim light from his praise.

He pulls me close so we can kiss.

In the morning, three weeks since Peter's first secret visit, I present my plans to Aunt Dahlia. My stomach is full of butterflies.

"I know you've said we'll get to it eventually, but I've taken the liberty of doing a lot of the initial legwork myself. I think you'll be pleased with what I've come up with." My words are formal.

She sets her teacup on the saucer, and places them on the side table with a little clink.

We're in her private sitting room. I should be able to sit beside her on the small settee and speak with her in a familiar way. She is supposed to be like a mother to me now.

But lately things have felt different.

I keep my posture straight and my eyes on the floor.

She hesitates, then reaches for my book of plans. She flips through the pages.

I hold my breath.

"This is…" her voice is breathy, and she meets my eyes. "…impressive."

I'm a little surprised. I was fully expecting to be rebuffed. I was planning to go ahead with it anyway, even without her approval. But it would be so much easier with Dahlia by my side. My shoulders relax and my smile is wide.

She carefully studies several of the pages. "You did this on your own?" She sounds amazed.

I nod. "Yes."

She stands and hugs me tight. "It is so good to see you smile again. I had wondered what you've been up to lately. I was a little worried that… never mind. I am so glad that you showed this to me. Thank you." She gives me another quick hug.

Her words sting. She was worried that… what? I was doing something bad? Does she even know me at all?

Before I can form a coherent thought on the subject, she reaches for my hand. "We must show your uncle at once."

My mind freezes. "Really? You… you think he'll like it?"

"Darling, I know he'll love it."

Excitement builds in my chest. My smile stretches from ear to ear. "Great! Yeah, let's show him!"

Uncle Henry is impressed by my work, just like Dahlia said. My heart swells. I can't believe they are suddenly on board with this. I can't wait to tell Peter! There's just enough time to get it finished before my birthday. I can't stop smiling.

"Well done, Jessamine." The king shuts my book with a snap. "This will be the perfect way for Amelie to introduce herself to the kingdom."

Did he just say this will be perfect for *Amelie*?

My smile freezes. Ice runs through my veins. My heart drops into my stomach.

That little spark of confidence that has been growing inside of me fizzles completely.

My uncle's next words sound like they come from far away.

"It will give her the opportunity to be part of something charitable right from the beginning, and I will guide her through the steps of seeing this through to completion. Thank you, Jessamine."

He takes the notebook and puts it on the shelf behind his desk.

Aunt Dahlia squeezes my shoulder. She shuffles me out of the room.

My smile disappears. My eyes are glossy. What just happened? *Amelie* will present this to the people? *Amelie* will get all the credit for the project?

"Well done, Jessamine. I am so proud of you!" Dahlia kisses my cheek and strides away.

Was this Dahlia's plan all along? Was this why she was so excited to show my idea to the king? Just so they could pass it along to *Amelie*?

Dahlia has disappeared around the corner. I'm standing like an idiot outside the king's office. Henry shuffles papers around and mutters things to himself in his office.

I should have stood up for myself. I should have insisted that this is *my* project. I mean, the least they could do is let me have this one thing. But they're going to just finish all my hard work and pretend it was Amelie's idea?

My blood warms. My head aches as my eyebrows pinch together. The spark returns.

It's not fair. They can't do this to me!

I turn to reenter the king's office. My hand hovers over the handle. I hesitate. Magnolia's words about how lucky I am to still be here echo in my mind.

I should just be glad they are allowing me to stay. To still wear fancy clothes and eat only the best foods. To be treated as a royal when I'm so clearly not anymore. I can't go complaining that someone else will get credit for my hard work. That wouldn't be very grateful. What would my mother say? What would she do in this situation?

"Remember who you are."

I take a deep breath. I didn't do all this work so that I would get credit for it. I did it for the people.

Didn't I?

The only thing holding me together at this point is knowing that I have Peter. Maybe we'll just run away together. Then I wouldn't have to deal with all this garbage anymore.

My feet carry me back toward an exterior door. I will escape to the woods. I will practice my connection with the animals. I will practice control.

I will be in control of my own life. I do remember who I am. I am supposed to be the Queen. And one way or another, I will heed my mother's words. I will be Queen.

As if this day couldn't get any worse, Juliette and Dahlia are in the meadow. Great. The last thing I want to do right now is talk to anyone, especially Dahlia. She just stole my biggest dream from me. What else is she going to try to take?

"Ah, Jessamine. Please, come join us." Dahlia motions me over.

Ever the obedient niece, I comply. I put a fake, albeit not very big, smile on my face. Well, I try. The best I can do right now is not frown. If only they could see the fire lighting within me.

"I was just instructing Juliette on some communication techniques to use with birds. Let me demonstrate." Dahlia whistles. A robin flies toward her from quite far away and lands on her hand. Dahlia talks to the bird, and the bird tweets back.

I inwardly roll my eyes. This is primary level stuff. Is this really what Juliette is still working on?

"Now, you girls try," Dahlia says as the bird flies back into the trees.

Juliette trills some notes that mean absolutely nothing to the birds. I can't even tell which species she's trying to call. When nothing happens, Dahlia gives her some pointers. But Juliette just keeps failing time and again.

"That's alright, dear. We'll keep trying." Dahlia rubs her daughter's back.

Juliette looks at the ground, embarrassed, probably.

Dahlia turns toward me. "It's your turn, Jessamine. Let's see what you can do." She smiles at me.

Is she trying to pit me against Juliette? Does she think I'm just as untalented as her own daughter?

I'll show her how powerful I am. Like my mother was.

I call softly.

Dahlia is about to say something to me, to give me a pointer or something. But before she can, a red-winged blackbird swoops from a treetop and lands on my shoulder.

"That's… quite impressive, dear." Dahlia sounds surprised more than impressed.

I whisper to the blackbird. He bobs his head in response. Then he wings away.

As he's flying away, I reach out my hand and use my mind to connect with his. I call him back.

At first, he doesn't comply. I push a little harder with my mind. My power flares.

As if being blown backward by a strong wind, he flaps strangely in the air. He squawks in fright, then his wings twist in an awkward way. He falls to the ground.

"Oh my!" Juliette rushes to the bird and scoops him up with both hands. She checks him for injuries. "His wings are both broken." She looks at me with a horrified expression.

Dahlia says nothing. They both just stare.

Do they think I did that on purpose? It was completely an accident!

I refuse to try to explain myself to them. They couldn't possibly understand the power I am trying to harness and control. Accidents happen. It was a mistake.

Juliette, at least, should know me enough to know I wouldn't harm anyone or anything on purpose.

I storm into the woods. They don't try to stop me.

After a few minutes my race turns into a brisk walk. Away from Juliette's accusing glare. Away from Dahlia's haughty attitude. Away from the castle.

I plop onto the ground beneath a wide beech tree and lean against the mossy trunk.

The fire inside me burns. I close my eyes. I must calm myself.

A she-wolf pads toward me. I feel her presence more than hear her steps.

I open my eyes. She stops, just beyond my reach.

I'm afraid to try to connect with her just in case I mess up again.

Instead, I just speak to her.

"Hello, friend."

When my emotions are under control, she approaches, unafraid, and sits beside me. I lean into her and stroke her thick, soft silver fur. Her presence soothes me. She licks the tears from my face.

"It was an accident, I swear," I whisper to the wolf.

She doesn't know of what I speak but noses me to tell me that she believes me.

"Thank you." I hug her until she no longer wishes to stay, then watch her lope away.

Christine Marshall

Chapter Twenty-five

I write to Peter and tell him what happened, pouring all my emotions into the letter. Fear of my abilities, guilt for the injured bird, embarrassment of my mistake, disbelief that my family could look at me like I was some kind of villain.

I wish I could speak to you in person. Having to wait for a response is difficult. But I know you have your own duties to attend to.

Things I used to be able to relate to. Now, I just try to fill my time as best I can. I'm counting down the days until the stupid library project is over. Maybe then things will get better.

The raven carries my message to Peter. It could be hours before I receive a response. Maybe not even until tomorrow.

My eyes locked on the ceiling are heavy. So is my heart. As sleep overtakes me, the page about the kelpies from that book fills my mind. Where my mother went against the advice, and things actually turned out better for the kelpies and for us. What other good things might happen if the words of warning were not heeded, but pushed against?

Peter's reply is delivered to my bedroom window during supper the following day. I can hear the ravens through the open window, down the halls and stairs, and into the dining room. Or maybe I can sense them? I excuse myself from the table and leave before I receive permission. With quick steps, I return to my bedroom.

Once the raven has his shiny trinket, he flies away.

Wasting no time, I pour over Peter's words:

> *Sweet Jessamine,*
>
> *I am heartbroken at the treatment you are receiving from your aunt. I would do anything to be able to rescue you.*
>
> *My father is insisting I accompany him on a tour of our kingdom for the next several weeks. I have tried to have myself excused, but I have been unsuccessful.*
>
> *I will write as much as I am able, but I am afraid I will not be able to send you the messages until I return.*
>
> *In the meantime, please know that I think of you constantly and will be counting the days until I may hold you in my arms once more.*
>
> *Ever yours, Peter*

Even though I know he won't receive it until he returns home, I pen a response.

190

Dearest Peter,

Thank you for being so kind. I think of you all the time as well.

Be safe on your journey and I, too, will await your return with eager arms. And lips.

Love, Jessamine

The castle bustles anew with activity over the next few weeks as all the books in the entire palace library are carefully cataloged, packed, and carried away for their new home in the city.

By the end of the third week, it's too painful to be around. I stay in my room, out of sight and out of the way.

Absentmindedly, I flip the pages of my field journal with the additional information recently added. It's like studying a whole new book.

How come I can connect with the animals only by touch? Except when I'm frustrated or upset, then my abilities seem amplified.

Kind of like what Magnolia said about my mom speaking to me through a dream. Her emotions had somehow amplified her already powerful abilities.

Maybe that was the key. But I can't rely on red-hot emotions to help me control the animals. I need to be able to reach them at any time. Even from very far away. My eyes wander away from my book to stare out the window.

"Feed the fire." I startle. The voice sounded like… my mother.

My eyes are drawn to where that other book sticks out from beneath my pillow. Does she want me to look at it some more?

I pull it into my lap and let the pages fall open where they will. They land on the page titled *Using plants to enhance your abilities.* My breath catches. Is this what my mom wanted me to see?

Comparing notes from the book and the now enhanced field journal, I can't believe my eyes.

"Can this really work?" Both books lay on my bed in front of me.

191

My eyes jump back and forth between the two.

There's a warning on the page about using plants to enhance abilities. *Dangerous, not to be trifled with. Unexpected outcomes may occur.*

But that other page said to kill the kelpies. And it was wrong. Mom proved that, and even made a note about it. If that was the case there, then maybe this book is wrong about this, too.

I look at the various formulas suggested for optimum results.

"Some of these things grow right in my own garden and wood…"

My stomach twists. What about the warning. Unexpected outcomes? Like what? I study the page carefully for anything that might indicate what could go wrong.

"Nothing."

Is it worth trying? I wouldn't be hurting anyone. I'd only be trying to enhance my abilities so I could serve the animals better.

If Juliette, or worse, Dahlia, found out though, they'd probably be really mad.

I'd need to try this in secret.

Besides, I swear I heard my mother's voice tell me to "feed the fire." What better way than to grow my power? Right?

If only I had a more private place to work on this. I mean, my room *is* my private place, but the staff are free to come and go for cleaning purposes, to deliver messages, and such. I'd need somewhere better. Somewhere… secret.

My finger taps my chin and my eyes narrow. It'd have to be somewhere *no one* would know about or be able to stumble upon.

I walk the perimeter of my suite. When I come to my huge closet and see all the dresses piled in the back, a spark ignites in my mind.

"That's it." Elation washes over me. My body buzzes with excitement.

If my closet was to be altered, a false wall erected closer to the front, and the unwanted dresses piled in front of it, no one would even notice the difference. I'd have my own secret workspace all to myself.

Back on my bed, I draw up a simple plan in my sketchbook.

I'll need a worktable, something tall that I can stand beside. And a tall stool would be useful. Pottery, mixing tools, maybe a mini stove. The space will need to be ventilated, so I don't smoke myself out. I can probably carve a decent sized hole through the exterior wall, and no one would ever notice from the outside

Painted boards will work for the false wall. There's an art room in the palace where my mother used to paint.

"I bet I can find the painting supplies in there. If anyone asks, I'll just tell them I'm working on a painting, like her. They'll feel so sorry for me they won't ask any further questions. As for the boards, hmmm." I'm thinking out loud, now. I tap my pencil against my cheek and try to picture where I'd be able to find boards that no one would notice missing.

The cellars. There's rows and rows of shelves down there, hundreds. If I scavenge some from throughout the cellar, instead of all from one place, it wouldn't be noticeable.

I furiously make lists and notes. I'll need a hammer, nails, a hand saw, and some hinges or something for a makeshift door. I'll have to be careful when I do my building. I don't want the noise to arouse suspicion. With all the books being swiped from the library right now, the palace is plenty noisy all day long.

I snap my book shut and smile wide. Talk about a distraction.

"What library?" I say to no one.

I've got my own plans to carry out. And no one will ever even know.

"Jessamine! Are you ready? We're leaving soon!"

My aunt's voice rings up the stairs several days later. It echoes around the two-story entrance.

"*Jessamine?*" she calls again, louder.

I sigh and roll my eyes, rest my tools on my new workbench, and push the hidden door closed. I pile the dresses against the wall, making sure it looks as messy as ever.

Satisfied that it's well-hidden, I head out to my suite and open the main door to call down the stairs.

"Coming." I don't try to sound excited. Because I'm not.

The last thing I want to do today is get all dressed up and attend another stupid royal ceremony. Especially this one. As if watching all my books, I mean the *palace* books, be whisked away for a library that was my idea that I'm not getting any credit for wasn't hard enough, I'd awoken with a headache.

My own project is nearly complete. I would much rather stay here and finish putting my secret workroom together.

But of course, I can't be so lucky. I haven't been about literally anything else in my life so far, so why this?

With gritted teeth, I grab the first gown I see in my extensive walk-in closet. It's a deep red taffeta that shimmers a little like metal. It reminds me of something I'd wear for the winter solstice.

"Whatever," I mumble to myself.

My pants and blouse end up in a puddle on the floor, and the dress now adorns my body. I loosely lace up the back by myself and glance in the mirror. The dress has wrinkles from being in a pile on the floor for so long. And since it's not laced very tight, it kind of hangs funny.

"Good enough."

Except… I lean closer to the mirror and use a handkerchief on my vanity to wipe away a smudge of dirt, then make sure there aren't any other blemishes anywhere.

"There."

The dress sparkles, even through the wrinkles. Any other girl would die to wear a dress like this. Not me. Not anymore.

I turn my eyes away before I get too choked up, snatch a pair of black satin slippers from the floor, then exit my room.

For every step that carries me to the marble entryway and massive door, I list the things I have lost.

My parents.

My home.

My birthright.

My kingdom.

It's not fair. A dark cloud settles over me.

Henry and Dahlia wait in the carriage. Juliette waits in the marble foyer.

"Jess, you look beautiful! That color is perfect for you!" she gushes.
I just nod, but don't look at her.

"Jessamine! Your shoe!"

One of my black slippers sits on the marble floor behind me.

"I'd pick it up for you but…" She gestures at her own lavender gown with its stiff bone-lined corset and wide skirt. She'd probably fall on her face if she bends too far.

"It's fine." I slip my foot back into my shoe. Peter's face fills my mind. The tingly feeling when he slipped my shoe back on my foot at the ball. And then when I flung my shoes away from me and finished the coronation party barefoot! I miss him so much.

Juliette follows a half step behind. She's trying to get me to talk to her again. She probably feels bad about what happened with the bird before, and her accusing look. I've put it behind me though. I don't really care what they think right about now. Not today.

Anthony waits beside the carriage. His hand reaches out to assist the ascent up the two collapsible wooden steps. The opening is low, and he makes sure I don't bump it with my head.

The king and queen take up one entire side of the carriage. Amelie sits with perfect posture in her shimmery silver dress in the middle of the facing bench. I climb over her massive skirts while hitching my own skirts practically to my knees.

Dahlia inspects my look. She doesn't appreciate how little effort I've put into my appearance today.

Amelie turns her body to make room and offers me a sad smile. "You look lovely, Jessamine." She speaks in a soft voice. She looks sorry. She knows that this is my project. And that she's taking all the credit for it.

I don't respond. Instead, I stare out the window and pretend the others aren't giving me pitying looks.

Juliette plops onto the bench on Amelie's other side and the king shuts the carriage door with a click.

The driver takes his cue and prods the horses to begin a gentle trot away from the castle that used to be my home but now belongs to someone else.

Someday, sooner than later, I hope, I'm going to get away from this place, join Peter in his kingdom, and never look back. I just need to get through this one day.

Chapter Twenty-six

The horses' hooves make a clip-clop sound on the cobblestone street. The carriage rattles as it bumps up and down. My headache grows.

My heart breaks a little more with every street we pass, every mass of adoring citizens waving and cheering.

And because Peter couldn't come today. The tour with his father is nearly over. He had hoped to be back by the time the library ceremony was to take place, but he's still traveling. I sink lower into my seat. Dahlia clicks her tongue at my poor posture, but I ignore her.

In what feels like no time we arrive at the new two-story public library. It's the first of its kind in our kingdom. I worked so hard to make this a reality. So much planning, organizing, bargaining. I've wanted this for such a long time. And Amelie gets all the credit.

Juliette links her arm with mine, snapping me out of my thoughts. I stiffen but don't pull away as we make our way up the steps at the front of the building. My shoe threatens to slide off my foot again, but I shuffle my feet so it will stay where it belongs.

The outside looks much the same as it did when the hired boys finished cleaning it. The red exterior bricks have been scrubbed, all the oversized windows are shiny, and a new, wider set of stone stairs with an ironwork railing stretches across the front, narrowing where they meet the door.

The inside is better than I could have imagined. The main level has been kept wide open, the ceiling reaching the roof. Every wall has brand new bookshelves custom made for the space. The shelves have a clip attached where a list of the books on that particular shelf has been posted. That was Peter's idea. My heart twinges.

And there are so many books! I knew the castle had a lot, but for some reason it looks like even more in this space.

There are intricate designs carved into the trim work, and a host of circular tables, comfortable chairs, and window seats for reading. A set of matching stairs curves up to a series of balconies that run the perimeter of the upper level, where even more books are placed neatly on shelves that are perpendicular to the walls, allowing for many more books to be housed. Each of those shelves also has a parchment that lists the titles in each row.

A reception desk is situated near the door, where patrons may ask a volunteer for assistance. And there are a couple of nooks set aside for group learning or lessons.

Along the back wall the enormous opening that had once been used to haul grain has a brand-new set of tall, wooden doors with ironwork details that match the front doors and the handrails on all the stairs. The doors are on rollers and can slide all the way open to either side on the outside, so they do not obstruct any of the shelves of books on the inside.

Many of my design ideas are featured throughout the space,

including the beautiful crystal chandelier that once hung in the castle library. They moved it here. Just as I had wanted.

But for some reason, seeing this all look so perfect, just makes everything feel worse.

Amelie and her parents step onto a temporary stage that has been constructed in the center of the massive space. I stop mid-step as I approach the platform. Four velvety cushioned chairs with high backs, plush armrests, and tons of gold-leaf detail have been placed in a perfect line. They look like they have come from the palace. Maybe they have. There's one each for the king and queen, one for Amelie, and one for Juliette.

Juliette sees it at the same moment I do. There is no chair for me. She swallows and a worried look crosses her face. She squeezes my arm and whispers, "I'll grab another chair for you. There's got to be one around here somewhere."

"It's fine, don't worry about it."

Juliette frantically searches for a fifth seat. Even if she found something, it would be rustic and out of place beside the opulent chairs arranged for the royal family.

Before she can find anything, though, the herald sounds his horn, signaling for the ceremony to begin. Citizens pour through the doors of the library and surround the platform. The library fills with excited voices pointing out all the details, the books, and the view out the back of the building. Everyone is in awe. They squeeze in as tight as they can. I can tell that they're all trying to get the best view of Amelie and her parents.

I slink away and sink to the floor behind a bookshelf. No one notices.

Amelie welcomes everyone to the new library with cheerful words and a sweet smile on her face.

I pull my knees to my chest and bury my face in the stiff red taffeta. Tears leak from my eyes. They probably ruin my dress. But it's not like it matters.

Another piece of my heart smolders and dies.

Why do I even have to come to these ceremonies? Or the balls or parties. Or fancy royal dinners. No one even notices my presence anymore. And if they do, I'm just the sad girl whose parents died, who used to be a princess. Either people pity me, or they've forgotten who I am altogether.

Taffeta crinkles in my fists. My knuckles turn white. It's just. Not. Fair.

"Why did you have to leave me?" I whisper to my very not-present parents.

"Embrace the embers," my mother's voice whispers back.

Am I going insane? I should *not* be hearing her voice like this. It was one thing to hear the words, *"Remember who you are"* in her voice. She said them to me aaalllll the time. But these new words? She's never said anything like them before.

On the way home from the library, after the feast in the city gathering hall, where once again, I did not have a place at the table with the royal family, I pretend to be asleep. I really don't want to talk to Juliette or Amelie, even though they both insisted that I sit with them for the meal. They pulled a place setting and chair from one of the other tables and I picked at my food until it was time to leave.

"You did well, my dear," the queen says to Amelie.

I can just see in my mind's eye Amelie's long eyelashes rest on her pink blushing cheeks. "Thank you," she says.

"Yes," agrees the king. "However, next time be sure you are more outgoing after the ceremony. You must be more engaging if you are to grow your trust as a leader."

I inwardly roll my eyes. That's not going to happen any time soon. Amelie is one of the most shy people I've ever met.

Not like Juliette, who flits from person to person with an innocence that endears her to anyone she meets.

People used to say that about me, too. Happy all the time, engaged with everyone around me. Smiling.

Not anymore. Except with Peter.

When we get home, I pretend to awaken and make my way to my room, denying the offers of assistance from the castle staff and ignoring the kind good-nights of my wanna-be family.

The door to my suite closes with a click. The dark wood supports my back for a moment and all the air releases from my lungs. It's over. I can move on now. Time to get out of these clothes and into something more comfortable. My pale-yellow sleeping dress has mud stains along the hem. But who cares? The only thing that I care about now is Peter. I can't wait for him to come home. To take me away from here.

The floor in front of the tall windows is cool even through the layers of the nightgown and my mother's angora blanket draped around me. The night sky is clear, and the layers and layers of stars shine bright in the sky. After a long time, the full moon rises behind the woods. It casts shadows among the castle grounds and the trees.

When the moon makes it above the tree line, the wolf pack that lives in the woods calls to one another. The long, haunting howls hang in the air. I envy the freedom of the wolves sometimes. They aren't stuck in a place they don't want to be. They can move freely through the wood, and no one bothers them.

Leaning my back against the cool window, I sketch a wolf pack in my sketchbook retrieved from beneath my pillow. The alpha stands on a hilltop howling at the full moon.

I still haven't successfully been able to connect with an animal so large. Now that my workroom is complete my experiments can begin. According to that book, the right combination of plants and herbs will help enhance my abilities.

Some of the ingredients I'll need don't grow around here, though. I'll need help. And I know just who to ask.

In the morning, after another maddening breakfast, I make my way down my ladder and into the woods. With a simple trill from my lips, a blue jay, mockingbird, and several house finches gather on a branch nearby.

"I would like you to fetch me some salvia," I address the blue jay. "You should find it growing nearby, even in this forest. I need quite a bouquet of that one. It looks like mint but smells like sage. Do not eat

201

it." He squawks at me and flies away.

"You, Mr. Mockingbird, will need to go on quite a journey to find the midnight caladium and red palm nuts. Someplace tropical for the nuts, and dark for the caladium. You may delegate if you don't want to make the journey yourself and carry enough back for my needs. But I expect to have my goods in a few days' time, no longer." He sasses me but complies. He'll probably trick some other birds or animals to do the job for him. Fine by me.

I ask the house finches to collect as many holly berries from the northlands as they can. "We're not that far from the northlands. You should be able to obtain the berries within a day's flight if you don't dawdle." I again warn the birds not to eat the berries, but to return them to me.

It will be difficult to wait two or more days for some of the ingredients.

You could have purchased a few of those things at the apothecary…

But without coin of my own, the palace would have been billed, which may have led to unwanted questions. Besides, Dahlia already thinks I'm up to no good. She doesn't need any other reasons to suspect anything.

Also, I haven't been to the city in a while. I honestly haven't been thinking about the needy or the orphans that much lately. My own life is in shambles. Even though my mother said that serving others is a good distraction. But what I'm working on seems like a pretty decent distraction. And my discoveries could change the lives of the Forest People if they succeed. That's kind of like service.

So, I will just have to wait. In the meantime, the palace gardens grow a wide variety of herbs that have medicinal benefits in addition to culinary applications.

I start with small amounts, only a stem or two of each one, until I figure out which ones work for my purposes. The formulas suggest a variety of different things that may be used as substitutes for one another. I should gather as many as I can. Many boxes grow classic herbs, like oregano, thyme, rosemary, and mint. But there are others with more unusual selections.

Pineapple sage, with its notes of sweetness, can be used as an anti-inflammatory. So can chamomile, which can also help as a de-stressor.

The waxy, heart shaped betel leaves with their bitter, peppery taste aids in the healing of wounds.

Pennywort has some of the same qualities as the others but can also be a memory enhancer.

Rigani, a member of the oregano family, in addition to being pleasing to the eye with its dark, hairy leaves and small white flowers, can aid in respiratory distress. So can the mint-like fragrance of the velvety tomentosa succulent.

My final selection is the elfdock flower. This is one I saw in the book Magnolia brought to me from the library. It's tall and bushy with bright golden yellow flowers that resemble sunflowers. Taken internally as a tea it can be used to ease respiratory ailments, aide with loss of appetite, rid the body of intestinal worms, and assist with digestive problems. I pull a few of the blossom stems close to the ground, so I gather the roots, as well.

The aroma of all the different herbs as a large bouquet in my hands is a little much. My mind spins with all the possibilities of these herbs in addition to the plants that the animals will collect for me.

When the individual herbs are sorted, tied into tiny bouquets, and hung on hooks beneath a shelf to dry in my secret room, I step back and survey my space.

It's missing something.

Right, the book.

I hurry to my bed, snatch *The Keeping* into my arms, and race back to my secret room.

"There." The book leans against the grey stone exterior wall of the palace. The sun shines through the window illuminating the cover.

"Perfect."

Christine Marshall

Chapter Twenty-seven

Dinner that evening is another wordless affair for me. The others, however, hash out every detail of the library ceremony and feast. If only I could stuff some of the rice in my ears so I wouldn't have to listen.

"The feeling of helping people is so amazing! I'm so glad I had the opportunity to present the library to the people," Amelie says in her quiet voice. But she sounds happy for the first time in a long time.

Glad I could be of assistance, Your Highness, my mind answers, though my mouth stays closed.

"Yes, dear. You are one step closer to being ready for your own coronation," Henry responds.

Amelie blushes and ducks her head. Her eyes flick to me, but quickly return to her plate.

Good, maybe she feels guilty about stealing pretty much everything from me. At least they don't know about Peter. If they did, they'd probably take him, too.

Juliette clears her throat and glances sideways at me. "How about that sunrise this morning? Wasn't it spectacular?" Her smile is tight. Is she trying to change the subject?

Her mother gives her a funny look. "Yes, dear, I suppose it was." She turns her attention back to Amelie. "Your next step toward becoming Queen will be to…"

Juliette interrupts again. "Mother, I was wondering if we could have our lessons in the forest tomorrow? There are whispers among the animals that a unicorn has made its way into our wood!"

I stop chewing. I haven't heard any such thing. What is Juliette doing? She's making stuff up to get her mother's attention? Is she jealous of Amelie, too?

She looks sideways at me again, and hurries before her mother can answer. "It would be wonderful to meet one in person and ask it questions about where it's been and…"

"Juliette," Dahlia admonishes a little harshly. "Not now. We can discuss those things at a later time. Please, do not interrupt me again."

Juliette sinks in her seat. She leans a little closer to me and whispers, "Sorry, I tried."

My fork stops halfway to my mouth. She was trying to change the conversation for me? Was my distress really that obvious? Or does she know me more than I've given her credit for?

My dark brown eyes meet her bright blue ones. We couldn't be more opposite in every way. Appearance, yes, but lately in mood and mannerisms, too. Yet, she still reaches out to me. Tries to be my friend.

I nod my thanks and return to my meal. It's a little easier to tune out the conversation after that.

During the night, the raven wakens me from a heavy sleep with several taps on my open window.

Something dangles from his beak. When my mind can focus on the bird, I spring from my bed.

It's a note from Peter!

I can just make out the words in the moonlight from my open window.

> *Jessamine,*
> *I'm back. I will be at your window first thing in the morning.*
> *Ever Yours, Peter*

"Yes!" I say out loud.

The raven squawks at me, picks up a trinket from my bedside table on his own this time, and flies out the window.

"Thank you!" I call after him.

The night drags. It's been almost four weeks since I've seen Peter, or even heard from him for that matter. But he's back! And he's coming to see me!

Peter leaves when the sky is still dark. He arrives below my window not long after sunrise. Having changed into my foresty clothes before the sun came up, I'm more than ready to meet him.

With a picnic lunch dangling over one arm, descending the ladder in the morning is tricky.

When my feet hit the ground, I drop the basket and rush into Peter's arms.

He swings me in a circle, my feet dangling in the air. I giggle and he laughs.

"I've missed you so!" he gushes.

Before I can even answer, we kiss. My feet find the ground again, and we pull each other close.

My mind swirls. What fake family? What stolen crown? I have Peter!

Dahlia assumes I spend all my time wallowing in grief in my room by myself, probably reading or drawing or something. She has no idea that I'm out with a prince today. The secret makes me grin.

We explore an area of the wood far away from the castle. The forest shifts from beech and alder to a variety of oak, maple, and elm. Some of the leaves have transitioned from deep green to paler shades of green with edges of yellow, orange, and red. Fall approaches. My favorite season.

We climb a hillside dotted with compact honeysuckle shrubs and yellow flowering mustard gone to seed.

Peter picks me a bouquet of the cute little mustard flowers surrounding a branch laden with blue-black oblong honeyberries that have a white bloom on their skin.

"Both are edible, you know," I tell him.

"I wondered but didn't know for sure. Your knowledge of nature is never ending!"

"Yes, Magnolia taught me some things while she was here, and I've been studying my notes and looking through an encyclopedia that she gave me. There's so much information!"

"I love it. Tell me everything you know!"

He squeezes my hand and I fill our climb with details about the honeysuckle and honeyberries, and the vast variety of uses, both culinary and medicinal, for the mustard plant.

We spread out our picnic at the top of the hill. The kitchen staff provided me with a plethora of food, not knowing for what purpose I requested it, of course. Fruits, toasted nuts, cubes of several different kinds of cheeses, soft flatbread, a thick dipping sauce made from chickpeas and eggplant, olives of a variety of colors and sharpness, and even a few leftover pastries from yesterday's breakfast. Peter pulls a corked bottle of deep purple grape juice for drinking from the basket, and the fabric basket liner doubles as a picnic blanket.

We lounge on the blanket, facing each other. Peter pops berries into my mouth, and we sample the different cheeses.

"The soft one with dill is my favorite!" My eyes close as I savor the sharp cheese and the grassy, citrusy dill.

Peter nods. "But the spicy jack cheese is delightful as well!"

We laugh as we try to simultaneously feed each other the cubes of white cheese dotted with either tiny lines of dill or spicy pepper seeds.

We mix and match the different options and eat until we can't eat anymore. Peter puts the leftovers back in the basket, as well as the now empty juice bottle.

He leans back and props himself with his arms. I rest my head on his shoulder, my own arms wrapped around my knees.

My eyes scan the scene below. "The view here is incredible!"

The city stretches out below us, the streets forming a crisscross pattern that fans out away from the castle. Beyond the outskirts of the city, the river winds through the valley and disappears behind the mountains.

Peter purrs in response. His chest rumbles beneath my ear.

We sit in silence for some time.

"What are you thinking about?" he asks me at last.

"That I don't know why I've never been up here before. I can see so far! I guess I've always been too busy preparing for my future. Lessons with my mom and the animals, training with Father for the crown." I swallow a lump in my throat, then grin. "At least that's one good thing about the way things are turning out for me. No responsibility means more freedom."

And more time with you. I keep that last sentence to myself.

"It is a gorgeous view." Peter's deep voice speaks right into my ear.

I glance up at him. He's not looking at the view of the city and valley beyond. His eyes are fixed on me.

He sits up a little, and I reposition so I'm no longer leaning against him.

He digs a tiny, wooden box with intricate carvings all over it from a pocket in his trousers.

"Happy birthday." He places the box on my lap.

He leans closer, one of his arms crossing behind my back. I can feel his warmth, and his nervousness.

"What? How did you know?" I touch the box gingerly and look back up into his eyes.

He smiles but doesn't answer.

I must have told him at some point that my birthday was approaching. Maybe when I was telling him about the library? Everyone else has forgotten. I've pushed it away as well. There was no point in dwelling on it. It's just another day, after all.

But Peter's surprise fills me with joy. I would've spent the day trying not to think about my parents, or all the other things, but instead I'm here with him. Tears fill my eyes.

"Open it." His breath tickles my neck.

He peers over my shoulder as I carefully remove the lid and set it beside the box. Inside the box is a bundle of deep purple silk the same color as the grape juice. I pull the corners aside.

I gasp. "Oh Peter!" My hands fly to my mouth.

He removes the simple gold ring from the folds of shiny purple. "It's not much, nothing flashy. But look."

Inscribed on the inside are the words, *"Ever Yours."*

He slips it onto my ring finger on my right hand.

He holds my hand in his, but in a way so I can see the ring.

When I finally find my voice, I can only whisper. "It's perfect."

He truly knows me. I wouldn't have wanted anything all flashy and covered with jewels. Not anymore. I like that it's simple. Discreet. No one will even notice it since they barely notice my presence most of the time.

And those words. *Ever yours.* Just like he signs his letters to me.

The tears leak from my eyes. I spring to my knees and throw my arms around his neck. "Thank you!"

He laughs and we fall over into a heap on the grass. I lay on my back, my hair spread out around my head, probably full of grass and leaves. He leans beside me, propped on one elbow. I wrap a hand around his neck and gently pull his face close until our lips meet.

As dusk turns to dark we make our way back to the castle hand in hand. I sense the wolf pack nearby. One of the lesser wolves in the pack slinks from between the trees to join us.

Peter stops mid-step. He's afraid but doesn't want to show it.

"It's alright. They aren't going to hurt us," I assure him.

I say hello to the wolf. He bows his head in response.

He comes closer, and circles Peter with a wary eye.

"What's it doing?"

"He's making sure you aren't a threat." I laugh a little.

"Peter is my friend," I tell the wolf.

He sits on his haunches in front of Peter, peering up at him with his beautiful silver eyes.

"You can touch him," I encourage Peter.

He hesitates but reaches out. The wolf leans into his hand a little. Peter strokes his fur, then crouches down to be eye to eye with the wolf.

"He's incredible!" Peter gushes.

I beam. He is so amazing. Not the wolf. Peter. I… I love him.

My heart warms inside of me.

I reach down and rub the wolf's softness as well. I connect with him and can feel that he likes Peter. I share my feelings for Peter with the wolf and he nuzzles deeper into Peter's hand.

After a few more minutes, the wolf departs.

Peter and I stand and face each other.

"Thank you, Jessamine." His eyes are full of wonder.

"Peter, there's something I need to tell you."

Peter's look changes to one of concern. He takes both of my hands. "Yes?"

"Peter… I love you." My words are thick with emotion.

Peter's eyes dance as he moves his face closer. "Jessamine, I love you."

Then our mouths meet. This kiss is different than our previous kisses. It feels more. Like, deeper, more sincere. Like we're expressing our true love for one another, not just our attraction.

My heart feels like it's going to beat right out of my chest.

I've found my future.

When we finally pause to breathe, Peter pulls me close, his arms wrapped snug around me. He rests his chin on my head. I can hear his heart pounding in his chest, too.

He clears his throat. "I've been thinking about something. I hope you will agree."

I pull back to meet his eyes.

His face is pale and his hands fidget. "I wish to ask your uncle for your hand."

He pauses and waits.

My eyes fill with tears. Is this real? Is he asking me to... marry him?

"Well... what do you think?" His hands are shaking, as if he's worried what the answer will be.

"Yes! Of course, yes!" I laugh and throw my arms around his neck.

We share a long kiss. When the kiss ends, I stare into his eyes. I have to be sure. With the way everything else has gone for me, I just have to double check.

"Are you serious? You're truly going to ask him?"

"Of course, Jessamine. As soon as I can."

His smile is so wide his teeth flash in the moonlight.

Chapter Twenty-eight

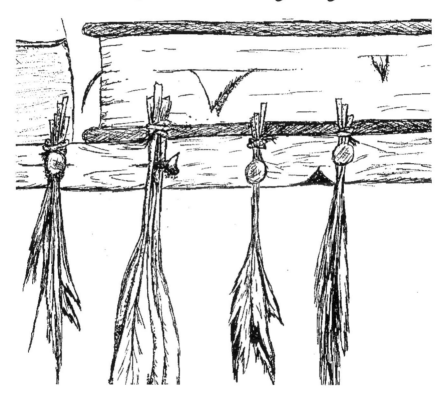

Peter's horse carries him away in the bright moonlight. When I can see him no longer, I flop myself onto my bed. I can't stop smiling. This is the best birthday I could have hoped for, with my parents gone.

Resting on my pillow I find a beautiful, exotic looking flower, along with a handwritten note.

Jessamine,
I've had the ravens leave this for you as one last

birthday surprise.

I hope your day turned out perfect. Or, as perfect as it could be.

Thank you for being a considerate, kind woman, and for teaching me so much about the forest, the animals, and myself.

I look forward to the next time I see you and kiss your beautiful face.

Until then, this flower will remind you of me.

Ever yours, Peter

My heart flutters in my chest. I could float right out the window.

I love him!

As if my mom sits on the bed next to me, I tell her everything.

"Peter came into my life at exactly the right moment. We are meant to be together. I don't think I could have survived all of this without him. I would have run away. Maybe to be with Magnolia. Maybe to be on my own. But knowing that he's going to take me away from here, and we'll be able to have our own life together makes dealing with everything else so much easier. Now I only have to wait for Uncle's approval, and then we can truly begin our lives together."

I imagine my mother wrapping me in a hug. *"That's wonderful, sweetheart,"* she would say.

Though she's not here, knowing that Peter wants me and loves me pushes some of the sorrow away.

With the window open wide and my head in the clouds, I crawl into bed, eager to dream of Peter.

Anthony, the butler, interrupts our family breakfast in the morning, with a letter resting on a tray.

Maybe it's for me!

But Anthony hands it to my uncle, then stands back to wait for a reply or dismissal.

My aunt leans over Henry's shoulder to read the letter, scrawled with loopy handwriting. She looks at Henry with surprise, then they both turn their eyes to me.

"What?" Things have been weird since the library ceremony and subsequent feast. But daily I swallow my pride and dutifully join the family for meals. They are just as formally polite in return.

"It would seem…" Henry begins to answer.

"Henry, not here," Dahlia whispers loudly to him.

He gives her a questioning look. She glances at Amelie and shakes her head at Henry ever so slightly.

What in the world is going on? I look back and forth between my aunt and uncle. They are acting so strange. I twist Peter's ring around my finger in my lap while I wait for someone to say something.

"It's fine, Dahlia," Henry pats her hand, then turns to look at me. "It seems that Prince Peter of Bennfaran wishes to formally call on you, Jessamine."

My heart skips a beat. This must be it! He must be coming to ask Henry to allow me to marry him! My time here is coming to an end. Finally. I can't wait to pack up my things. My mind races with a to do list.

"However…" Henry continues.

I snap my attention back to him.

Dahlia avoids eye contact with me, picking at the food on her plate instead. Amelie listens intently, a serious look on her face. Juliette seems unconcerned by the whole exchange, clearly out of the loop, and clearly not caring.

"With things the way they are… er. After the unfortunate turn of events…" Henry sighs. "I don't know how to say this." He turns to Dahlia.

She gives him an "I told you so" look and he frowns. Then he returns his eyes to me.

"I must refuse such a visit. It just isn't proper. Anymore. You know…" He waves his hand in the air as if that would explain what he means.

"What isn't 'proper'?" I ask, setting my fork firmly on the table and dropping my napkin onto my plate.

I have a feeling I know what he means, but I want to hear him say it. I want someone to finally admit that I'm not good enough for any of this, instead of always treating me like I'm some ornament that came with the castle.

"Well, you see… you are no longer a Pr… you no longer hold a title…" He drops his hands in his lap and stands, his chair scraping the floor. "I don't want to hurt your feelings, Jessamine." The words rush out of his mouth. "But he is a prince after all, and you, I'm afraid, are… beneath him. I'm sure his parents must feel the same. I am truly sorry."

My eyes well up. Why do they have to be so mean about it?

"Jessamine, darling," Dahlia speaks with forced smoothness. "Is everything alright?"

I look at her with a stunned expression, I'm sure. 'Is everything alright?' Of course, it isn't! But I can't get any words to leave my mouth. My throat is so tight with anger and something near despair.

"It's not as if you are attached to him in any way," Dahlia continues. "I'm sure they have just forgotten about your new… arrangements… as of late. Henry will write to Peter's father and inform him of your… situation. This is all just a misunderstanding."

She smiles at me as if she has solved everyone's problems.

My mind fogs. My legs are wobbly as I stand. My head spins. Of course they don't know about me and Peter. We've been sneaking around, and I haven't mentioned him once since the coronation. They have no idea that I'm in love with him. That WE'RE in love with each other. That we are meant to be together- prince and princess or man and woman, it doesn't matter.

"Jessamine?" Juliette has stopped eating and turns worried eyes toward me.

I rush out of the room, tears dripping down my cheeks.

"I don't understand that girl." Henry's voice booms out from the dining hall to echo in the two-story marble entry.

I don't linger to hear what any of the responses are. My feet carry me to my room.

Back pressed against my closed bedroom door, my mind races.

What's going to happen next? Peter's father will get the response from Henry in a few hours, and then Peter will hear the answer for himself. He'll write to me once he knows the situation. He'll know what to do.

But my anger at my "family" burns bright. My heart is on fire. I must tamp down the flames, somehow.

"I need a distraction."

I march into my workroom, careful to close the door behind me. The sky is blue through the small window carved through to the exterior of the castle. Birds chirp. Butterflies flit across the meadow. The sun shines on everything. It's a beautiful day out there. Not in here.

Plopping onto my stool, I flip through the pages of *The Keeping* until I find the right one.

I study the formulas, comparing my collection with the required ingredients.

The bouquets of herbs, both the ones from the castle gardens, and the ones the birds have brought to me, have dried. Even the stems of spiked holly leaves laden with holly berries have dried out a bit. The dried leaves and blossoms from the bouquets crumble in the clay mortar when smashed with the pestle. I'm more aggressive than I need to be.

When a variety of different powders have been created, jarred, and labeled, and lined up along the back of the work bench, I check the formulas carefully to make sure I've got everything.

My eyes catch on the phrase: *essence of self.*

"What does that mean?" I pour over every word on the page again, trying to figure it out.

"Essence of self... essence of self."

I flip through every page until I reach the very end. There's a glossary that I had skipped over before, since I know what all the plants and animals are thanks to my mom and Magnolia. My finger runs down the list of words in bold.

"Here! Essence of self. A prick of the finger will yield a drop of blood. Use sparingly."

My eyebrows sink over my eyes.

217

A prick of who's finger? A drop of blood? This is... weird. Maybe I shouldn't be doing this.

Then my uncle's words echo in my mind.

"But he is a prince after all, and you, I'm afraid, are... beneath him."

I'll show them who's beneath whom. I will enhance my abilities. I will be more of a "princess" then they could ever imagine.

"It's called essence of SELF. I need MY blood. Of course."

I prick my finger and squeeze a dozen drops of my blood into a small vial with a pipette attached to the inside of the lid.

A fat mouse pokes his head through my small window.

"Hello little guy, would you like to help me with my project?"

He pauses to think.

"I'll share my dessert with you tonight..." I have no idea what dessert will be, but his round tummy and chubby cheeks imply that he likes the richer things in life.

He readily agrees.

"Great! I'm going to be trying out some different things, and then I'll just try to reach you with my mind. You won't have to do anything, and it won't hurt you at all. Just make yourself comfortable nearby."

He curls his tail around his haunches and watches me from the window, basking in the midday sun.

"I'm no apothecary, but... here goes."

I mix a couple of the formulas that use dried herbs blended together with a drop of my own blood, consuming a small spoonful of each one.

I write notes in a new notebook about the tests and results:

<u>Edible blends</u>

a- Other than feeling queasy, did not provide any difference in connecting with my volunteer.

b- A little dizzy, no changes in abilities.

c- Maybe it's the combination of things, but I could feel the mouse's consciousness without touching him a little bit. That's a first.

d- Same as last time, a slight increase.

Feeling lightheaded, need to take a break.

I was hoping for more drastic results. A sudden surge of abilities, instant connection with the mouse, but other than being able to just sense him without touch, I don't feel a whole lot different. Except for nausea. I chew on a mint leaf and reread the formulas.

Maybe... eating isn't the right form of ingestion. Perhaps a tea would work better. The formulas are not specific on how to ingest the ingredients.

I light a fire in my small stove and set a pot of water over the flame. While the water heats, the carefully measured herbs find homes in the bottoms of an array of tiny clay cups. A dash of boiling water in each cup, a quick stir, and a long steep makes a wide variety of herby teas.

I sip each of the teas and I carefully note the results.

<u>Tea blends</u>
a- No queasiness, slight increase in ability to connect without touch.
b- No dizziness, no change.
c- No side effects, a little increase.
d- Slight increase, queasy again.

Overall, disappointing results. My pencil snaps in two when it slams onto the notebook.

"One of these has got to work!" I groan in frustration.

The mouse squeaks at me. He's ready for his treat.

"Sorry little guy, we've got to keep going."

The mouse sighs in response but doesn't leave.

Between brewing tea blends, trying different combinations of ingredients, and writing down every detail, the whole process takes a long time. Unfortunately, even the new blends yield the same results. Little to no change in my ability to connect. When all the combinations, and myself, if I'm being honest, become exhausted the sky is pink and the sun nears the horizon.

Well, it worked. I've distracted myself for the entire day.

Christine Marshall

My breath catches. Maybe I'll have a message from Peter!

"Gotta go, friend!"

He squeaks a sigh of relief while I scribble down the last of my notes, promise him a big slice of cake, carefully put out the tiny stove-fire, snuff out the candles, and exit the space.

Chapter Twenty-nine

My eyes scan my bed, desk, and windowsill. No note from Peter anywhere. My heart sinks.

What if my uncle was so forceful in his message that Peter decides not to follow through with his promise?

What if he is convinced by his father that I am, indeed, beneath him?

It's only been a few hours, Jessamine. Well, an entire span of daylight. But still. I can't jump to any conclusions. Not yet.

I take my supper in my room instead of joining the family. It's considered rude, but I honestly don't care. Like they said, my circumstances have *changed*. If they want to rub it in, I'll act the part of a non-titled, not-princess nobody. Maybe then they'll realize how hurtful they've been to me.

My chubby mouse friend appears to retrieve his promised dessert.

Propped in bed with my back against the headboard and eyes glued to the window, wishing for the ravens to bring me a message from Peter, I replay the previous day over and over. The picnic. The laughter. The kisses. The ring. The wolf. The proposal. We are so in love. There's no way he won't keep his promise.

But a voice in the back of my head keeps whispering, *"What if?"* It's not my mother's voice this time, but my own.

Slumber overtakes me during my long wait. In my dreams Peter dances with someone at a ball. The ballroom is unfamiliar. The people strangers. The woman in Peter's arms has pretty blonde hair topped with a sparkly tiara and wears an extravagant pale dress with a crimson sash the color of blood across her torso. Who is she?

People block my view. I skirt around the edges to get a better look. Peter seems to be searching the room for something, or someone. He's not paying attention to the woman. Is he looking for me just as I'm trying to see him? But everyone is standing in our way. I reach out a gloved hand and call his name. Just as his beautiful sorrow-filled emerald eyes meet mine, I awake.

My breathing is fast. Is he going to give up on me? Is it really over?

I roll onto my side, squeeze my eyes shut, and try to ignore the now all too familiar tears as they drip onto my pillow. When will something go right for a change?

"Jessamine!" Dahlia's voice pulls me from slumber. "It's almost time to leave!"

Ugh, here we go again.

I've had it, though. I don't want to go to another place full of people that look at Amelie with googly eyes and worship the ground she walks on. A quick scan of my room reveals that there's still no letter from Peter, either. The last thing I need right now is to be reminded of everything I've lost. Again.

"I just want to stay home for a change!" I murmur to myself.

"Jessamine? Are you coming?" Dahlia calls from the entryway, making me flinch.

Why does her voice have to be so shrill? Would it kill her to just walk up the stairs and talk to me face to face like a normal person?

I don't answer her call. Instead, I hurry to my sink to splash hot water on my face and dampen the hair on my forehead a little. Back in my bed piled high with down-filled duvets, my body curls into a ball, my breathing mimics sleep. Even though I didn't feel totally myself after consuming all those different things yesterday, I don't seem to be worse for the wear this morning. Still, illness is the best excuse.

Footsteps make their way up the stairs. Not Dahlia, though, she would never make the arduous journey. She probably sent a servant. Anthony, since he would be right there, or one of the passing maids.

Someone knocks on my door. I remain silent.

"Jessamine, m'lady," Anthony says through the door. Yep, she sent someone else! "The Queen is requesting your presence."

Silence.

The door opens a crack. Anthony is likely peering into my room, afraid of seeing something that he shouldn't. "Miss?"

I breathe deep and roll toward the door. With bleary eyes I mumble something unintelligible. On purpose.

"I'm sorry, miss. May I enter?" He pauses, and then steps into the room, leaving the door wide open.

He makes his way to my bed, sees my sweaty forehead and moist, red face and says, "I'll get the head housekeeper to check on you, dear."

"That won't be necessary. I just need to go back to sleep." My words are slurred.

"Very well," he says, a concerned look on his face. He exits my room with quiet footsteps and carefully closes the door so as not to disturb my rest.

His footsteps are steady as he makes his way back down the stairs. Muffled voices find their way to my ears. The front doors close, and the carriage rattles as it pulls away from the front of the castle.

Free at last! I don't know why I haven't tried this sooner!

Which reminds me…

After making sure the coast is clear and no one from the staff intends to check on me, I make my way to my work room. I have to get this right today.

My little mouse friend isn't around. Probably sleeping in after that hefty portion of oatmeal almond cake that he ate last night. The little guy could barely wobble to the window when he was finished. Hopefully he was able to squeeze back into his home.

"Maybe I'll find another willing participant in the meadow or woods, instead. That would get me out of the castle, too."

My thoughts war with myself as I prepare to leave the castle for the day. What if Peter sends a message? Or decides to come visit? Hope blossoms in my chest.

If I stay in this room all day, though, glancing at the window every few minutes in hopes of hearing from him or seeing him, I will go insane.

I make up my mind and hurry down the ladder outside my window. Clouds hang low. It looks like it wants to rain. But the air is sweet with blossoms and berries.

The ravens call to me from the sky as I tromp across the meadow, my notebook tucked into my bag that's slung across my shoulder. My raven friend drops a letter into my hands without landing, and the whole flock flies into the forest to settle on the treetops.

My heart races. Is this the letter where Peter will tell me it's over? That he's sorry, he loves me, but it just can't happen between us?

I don't want to open it.

And I need to with every fiber of my being.

But not here, not out in the open.

I dart into the woods and find my favorite beech tree to lean against.

With my back against the smooth bark, I sink onto the ground. Mud soaks into my trousers, but I don't take my hands or eyes off the folded parchment.

I take a deep breath.

"Come on Jessamine, you can do this. What's the worst that will happen? He tells you he doesn't love you; you'll pack your things and leave before the others even return home. You'll find Magnolia. She loves you. Everything will be fine."

A pair of squirrels stop stuffing their mouths full of seeds and freeze in place. The ravens drop lower in the trees. My letter carrier hops on the ground beside me, tilting his head as if to tell me to hurry up already. A small, wild boar edges out from between the shrubs and grunts.

Great. Now I have an audience.

My heart is in my throat. I choke on a sob and close my eyes, wishing with everything I have that my story doesn't end in heartbreak. I want a happily ever after. I want to be with my true love.

I breathe in, hold my breath, and release it as I open the stiff folds.

My sweet Jessamine...

That's a good start, right?

Unless he's easing me into the bad news...

This is a nightmare. I need to get this over with.

I skim the rest of the words as fast as I can, looking for "I'm sorry" or "it's over" or anything like that.

At the end he has signed it: "*Ever yours, Peter.*"

A cry escapes my lips and the paper crinkles between my fingers. "Ever yours!"

The squirrels skitter away. The ravens call out with menacing sounds and make a ruckus as they fly to the treetops again. The boar grunts and backs his way into the underbrush.

My head spins.

Peter's not pushing me aside. He still loves me. Still wants me.

Smile wide and face wet, I open the now crumpled parchment once more and read the words more carefully this time.

> *My sweet Jessamine,*
> *My father has insisted that I turn my attentions to another.*
> *He is a fool. He does not understand that title and position mean nothing to me.*
> *You are an amazing woman, princess or not, and*

I will find a way to be with you. No matter what.

Do not despair, no matter what rumors you may hear. This is not over. Not by a long shot.

I will come see you as soon as I am able, but I'm afraid my father is keeping a close eye on me to prevent that from happening.

In the meantime, I will continue to write to you.

I love you, Jessamine.

Ever yours, Peter

My head swirls. His father *is* a fool. So is my uncle.

But Peter! Peter is wonderful. He's perfect. And he's right, we will find a way. Love always wins.

We spend the day writing back and forth to one another. I tell him the family's outing plans, hoping he'll be able to come when they aren't here. But his father is keeping him home.

He suggests he tries to come when they *are* home, so he can corner my uncle and speak with him face to face. It's highly unusual, but he is a prince, and is allowed certain social improprieties. Like calling on a king unannounced.

We agree that he will somehow elude his father and return within the week to confront my uncle. The plans are made. Now we must wait.

"*Jessamine!*" My aunt calls my name with her piercing voice the following morning, telling me it's time to go somewhere.

I feign illness again.

After they leave, my time is filled with experiments in my secret room. A mockingbird has agreed to join me so I can tell if the experiments are working.

Day 3

More of the same results. What am I doing wrong

here? Why isn't the book more specific about how to use the various formulas? Would different ingredients help? Maybe some with the same properties that I have now would yield better results.

"Thank you for your help today, Mr. Mockingbird."

He sings a few different bird songs at me.

"Come again!" I call when he flies away.

When the messenger raven comes to my window to take my note for Peter, a thought pops into my head.

"Sir, I need ingredients for my project. Anything with rumors of enhancing abilities or improving skills in any way. If you have any thoughts on the matter, I would love to hear them."

The raven blinks at me. He'll take my letter. But what's in it for him if he does more?

"Hmm. More shiny things?"

It'd have to be something really special.

"Perhaps something from... the palace jewels?" I flinch. Are they even mine anymore? I suppose not. Technically nothing is mine anymore. My irritation simmers.

Jewels will do.

He flies away with a call to his companions.

What will he return with? It's like waiting for a birthday present. Or for my parents to come home.

My chest squeezes.

"Don't think about that, Jessamine. Think about your power. And Peter. That's all that matters now."

The book about plants from Magnolia sticks out from under the edge of my bed. Since delving deeper into my mother's books, I haven't given it much thought. Maybe it's time to give it another look.

The section about medicinal plants is massive. *"Plants have been used to treat a plethora of illnesses and maladies for as long as life has existed."*

Yeah, seeing as how I'm a Forest Person, I know that already.

227

However, I don't know everything about plants. At least, not yet.

The list is long. Many that I know about, and have samples of, already. But some I hadn't considered before. Some grow wild, like dandelion, and lavender. Others have been planted and thrive in the palace herb gardens: rosemary, parsley, and lemon balm.

"This is interesting. I've seen these in the flower beds! Marigold, primrose, echinacea! Fantastic!"

There's so much available right here at the palace.

"But I'll have to get my friends to fetch some of these other ones though. I'll make a list, so I don't forget."

Feverfew leaf, gingerroot, ginseng root, goldenseal root, and turmeric root.

"Plus, whatever the ravens come up with," I remind myself.

Chapter Thirty

Peter and I exchange letters daily, and when I'm not writing to him, I'm writing in my notebook.

<u>Day 4</u>

A grey squirrel and pygmy raccoon have agreed to join me tomorrow.

Today is for refilling my supplies.

Have gathered more plant samples and prepared a new list of edible blends and tea samples.

Raven has returned with a tuft of fur from a golden kitsune.

Note: kitsune is a shapeshifting fox with multiple tails, do more research.

Wish I had some training in apothecary work. This is

going to take forever.

Dear Peter,
Any news on when you will be able to escape your father's
watchful eye?
Miss you.
Love, Jessamine

Day 5

New blends of teas seem to have a positive effect on my ability to connect with the squirrel and racoon, but still not a lot. I've been dreading this thought, but maybe it's time I add more than just a drop of my blood? My finger is still sore from the first prick. Raccoon offers to help. With my eyes closed he pricked a different finger and refilled the vial with my blood.

Dear Jessamine,
My father is planning to receive guests in three
days.
Perhaps I will be able to slip away then? Will keep
you updated.
Ever yours, Peter

Day 6

I think I've found a good blend of herbs suggested from the book, combined with some that I have gathered from the gardens and animals. I've increased blood to two drops per mixture. The new blend includes some medicinal plants to ease some of the more uncomfortable side effects. When I swallowed the mixture, I felt my power amplify almost immediately, but faded too fast.

Raven liked the jewel. Has brought me a leech full of unicorn blood. I don't know where he got it. I don't want to know. Leech in jar. Not sure if I'll do anything with it.

Dear Peter,
I look forward to your visit.
Do you think Henry will say yes?
What will we do if he refuses?
Love, Jessamine

Day 7

I tried the same mixture as yesterday. Only, something unexpected happened.

When I leaned over the cup of steaming tea to call to an animal out the window, the steam billowed into my face. I felt the effects immediately when I inhaled the cloud. It didn't fade quickly like it did when I drank the tea. Maybe it was the steam all along?

Dear Jessamine,
Nothing will keep me from marrying you. I love you.
If all goes well, I shall declare my love for you in front of your family tomorrow.
Ever yours, Peter

Day 8

Finally, after so many trials and errors, I think I've got it right.

Sidenote- raven has brought me a leviathan tooth. Or, at least, a chunk of one. This is getting out of control...

Dear Peter,
I wait with bated breath.
Love you forever, Jessamine

Only one day to go.

In the meantime, I need to try out my theory. The results could be amazing. But the warning from the book about unexpected outcomes lingers in the back of my mind.

"Everything will be fine," I tell myself as I settle onto my stool.

The mockingbird peers at me with his beady black eyes from the windowsill. Almost like he's accusing me of something.

"What?" I ask him. "I'm not doing anything wrong. I'm making my abilities stronger so I can help all of *you* better."

He looks too smart for his own good. Like he can tell that part of me likes the feeling of the amplified power. That maybe my reasons aren't as selfless as I try to convince myself they are.

"It's time to put my idea to the test," I announce to him. "Just relax. Don't worry so much."

He blinks back at me but doesn't respond.

The terra cotta bowl thuds onto the surface of the wooden worktable. The herb bottles clink, and the crushed dried herbs make a rustling sound as they descend into the bowl. In my haste, I knock over the vials that hold the samples from the raven. The leech starts writhing on the table and doesn't settle until he's back in his jar. When the golden-reddish fur and tooth chunk are back in place, the experiment can resume.

The pestle scrapes the sides of the bowl, releasing a wide array of scents into the air. The salvia's blend of mint and fruitiness clash with the bitter smokey smell from the poppy stems and seeds. The caladium fills the space with a tangy smell that makes my nostrils flare. All the ingredients combined seem to be the perfect formula. Salvia for mind control, poppy seeds and stems for calmness, pennywort for enhanced memory, and the key- midnight caladium- to counter the effects of the other ingredients that would make me physically ill… or worse.

With the water poured over the mixture, the next step is to boil the blend over the small open flame. The hole in the bricks allows the smoke and steam to escape outside. The mockingbird wings to a high shelf, away from my worktable and the cloud of steam. He scolds me in a variety of bird languages.

"Oh hush." My brow furrows at his complaints. "I doubt it would have any effect on you anyway."

I inhale the steam deeply, then hold my breath, allowing the steam to saturate my lungs with whatever combination of plants has allowed this to work.

The menthol aroma from the tomentosa succulent opens my airways, making my nostrils flare. The midnight caladium has no smell, but I can feel the strange healing effects even as some of the other ingredients threaten my system with nausea. It passes quickly. The pennywort sharpens my mind. And my "essence" pulls everything together. I can feel my abilities amplify.

My mind stretches to the mockingbird. I can see things from his perspective. The sensation of watching myself from a high shelf behind me is disorienting.

I release my breath and take several more deep breaths. The voice of the mockingbird invades my thoughts, admonishing me for being reckless with my power and the unnaturalness of consuming one's own blood.

"It's only a couple of drops. And it's been boiled into steam, so it's not really blood anymore anyway," I tell him.

When the steam stops billowing from the bowl, I pour the contents out the window and clean up my workspace. I can continue to see things from the mockingbird's eyes.

Now I must practice controlling this newfound ability. I concentrate really hard on closing out the mind of the mockingbird. It takes a few tries, but I get the hang of it before long. Then I practice turning it on and off, like lighting and snuffing out a candle.

My body and mind are exhausted after an hour. The control over my insight into the bird's mind isn't perfect, but it's pretty close.

Day 8, continued...

It worked. I can connect with the mockingbird when I'm not looking at him, not even touching him, at will. It even works when he's in the workroom and I'm not. The effects don't seem to be diminishing with time, either. Perhaps the midnight caladium is to thank for that. Have added my formula to that page in the book. And nothing dangerous or unexpected has happened. I never imagined myself as a scientist, but this endeavor has proved fruitful.

What else could I try?

What other books might the library hold that would aid me? Maybe I'll go down to the library…. But no. The library is now located in the city. It's too painful for me to go there. I haven't been back since the ceremony. It just brings up too much resentment.

My mind continues to stew over these dark thoughts until the others return from wherever they have been all day. Probably someplace else where they could heap attention on Amelie and pretend that I don't exist.

I swallow my hurt and anger and carefully place my books beneath my pillows so I can prepare myself for dinner.

Being sullen and locking myself away from the others will not win any favors when it comes time for Peter's proposal, so I join them for dinner.

"How are you feeling, Jessamine?" Aunt Dahlia inquires of me.

Why is she asking me this? Can she tell that I've changed?

But no. I pretended to be ill so I wouldn't have to join them. Does she not believe that I was sick? I mean, I wasn't, but she shouldn't have any reason to doubt me. Can she read the irritation rolling off me in waves?

I mumble something about feeling better and take my place at the table beside Juliette.

She turns her head ever so slightly to glance at me, but I ignore her.

"Dahlia," Henry addresses his wife. He bites into his roasted chicken leg and waits for a response. Grease drips down his lips and into his beard.

My throat squeezes. I avert my eyes to my own plate filled with only vegetables and boiled amaranth seeds. I have forgone the chicken.

"Have you written to your people for advice on how to handle the hydra that has housed itself in the lake-lands to the west?"

My ears perk. I listen carefully.

Dahlia sighs. "No, Henry, I haven't."

"Dear, this is urgent business. We require their aid."

Dahlia barely manages to keep her face from looking annoyed, but then glances at her audience and plasters on a fake smile.

"I will do it first thing tomorrow…"

Before realizing I've even started to speak, I find myself suggesting something my mother would have done in the situation.

"I can contact the kelpies in the swamp and ask them to intervene with the hydra on our behalf before anything really bad happens. We don't really need any of the Forest People. This is something I can do."

With my new enhanced abilities, plus the information from my mom's books, I should have no trouble connecting with the kelpies and asking them to help. The kelpies should respect me as they did my mother.

My mood instantly lifts. This is precisely why I've been trying to enhance my abilities in the first place. And if I had become queen, I would be using these gifts in this way on a regular basis. I'd be able to do so much good for the kingdom, for the animals. It would be incredible.

Dahlia and Henry share a look.

Henry gives Dahlia a look as if to say, *"You talk to her about it."*

Dahlia's eyes widen, as if to protest.

Is it really so hard for them to even speak to me? Is my presence that difficult for them to endure?

My eyes narrow. One of them will have to say *something* to me. To treat me like a person. Eventually. Right?

Dahlia breaks first. "Jessamine, dear, I don't think…"

Juliette jumps beside me when my fork crashes onto my plate. My chair hits the ground with a thud and a crack. My fists are clenched and my face pinched.

Dahlia's eyes grow wide. Henry's bushy eyebrows lower on his face.

"You NEVER listen to my ideas. You NEVER appreciate what I have to contribute. I've been preparing to run the kingdom my ENTIRE LIFE, and yet you treat me like I'm stupid or something. What's your problem with me, anyway?" My shouts bounce off the walls. Juliette flinches with every exaggerated point.

My aunt and uncle appear to be too stunned to speak.

Amelie starts quietly crying.

"And what's *your* problem, Amelie?" I address my older cousin for the first time in a long time. "All you ever do is frown at me and avoid eye contact. Would you be happier if I just… what… went away? Then you wouldn't be reminded that you stole my life from me?"

Amelie stands from the table, face buried in her hands, and runs from the room.

"Jessamine!" Uncle Henry shoots up from his seat. "That is enough!" he barks.

I can't believe they are treating me like this. Like I'M the one who has done something wrong. Don't they see that I've lost everything?

My roar of anger is so loud that it makes my throat raw, then I storm from the room.

Chapter Thirty-one

I can just imagine them all talking about me after I go. It's not fair!

Without looking back my feet carry me out the front door, through the gardens, and into the woods. What am I to do with this rage? Throwing rocks at trees and kicking ferns, sending leaves fluttering, certainly doesn't help. A group of bats squeaks in the sky. They hurry away from me. Even *they* don't want to be around me. My anger is so hot I can't even cry.

Deeper in the woods, my hair catches on branches, as does my dress. I'm pretty sure I hear it tear a couple of times. Good! Another thing that I've ruined.

I collapse against the smooth trunk of a beech tree, pull my knees to my face, and finally the tears come.

Two wolves from my pack join me. When did I start thinking of them as *my* pack? It doesn't matter, they are. They're more of a family then those… imposters sitting in the castle right now, sleeping in my parents' beds, wearing my parents' crowns.

The she-wolf whimpers, and they both come closer. They sensed me as soon as I entered the wood. My enhanced abilities are working both ways, it seems. Maybe because I do think of them as *my pack* my mind is open to them already? They settle at my feet, flopping down on top of each other and my toes.

Their presence calms me. I touch one on the head, and I can feel her sympathy for me. She sends warm thoughts of acceptance and belonging back into my mind.

My heart and breathing slow. I stretch my legs out. The wolves slide on their bellies beside me. Sleep arrives when my breathing matches theirs; my arms wrapped around both of them tight.

I dream about the forest. Cinders float in the air again. The trees and brush glow with heat. Smoke fills the air. The flame engulfs me, and yet I do not burn. The air shimmers with heat waves. The stench of the bubbling sap and burning grass stings my nose. But there is no heat. I inspect the ground at my feet. The leaves smolder and glow. Even the edges of my dress are singed. Smoke rises into the sky.

"Embrace the cinders." My mother's voice comes from every direction. I do as she says, close my eyes, and become one with the fire.

When my eyes flutter in the morning the forest is still intact. Nothing has burned. My dress is in one piece. And my arms are still wrapped tightly around the wolves.

The last thing I want to do right now is return to the castle. Instead, my wandering in the woods is aimless. My mind reaches out to any animal that I can see, and plenty that I cannot see. Power rushes through my veins every time. I can turn it on and off with ease. Some of the animals are wary of my presence in their minds, but many reach back to comfort me when they feel my distress.

My hands shake with hunger by late morning. When I pick a handful of berries from a salmonberry bush, something orange on my hand catches my eye. I bring my hand close to my face and there, on the back of my knuckles, are a few long scraggly orangey-red hairs. My eyes dart to my other hand. Identical hairs grow there, too. I pull up my sleeves and there's more on my arms.

"What is this?" I whisper.

By the time I climb my ladder that stays out all the time now, my breath is coming fast. I don't pause to catch it, but rush toward the mirror on my vanity.

Day 9

The steam worked. I can easily connect with individual animals. And my connection to the pair of wolves last night was natural.

A strange side effect has occurred, however. I have grown a few red hairs on my arms and hands, and on my head. Where only dark brown curls were present, there are several strands of bright red.

Upon close inspection of my workspace, I can see that not all the kitsune fur made it back into the jar. Some of it must have landed in the mortar before I mixed it.

I turn to the section in the book about transformations. It's the only explanation. I would not have intentionally studied this page. The idea of changing one's physical appearance seems unpleasant and… wrong. But it looks like I've inadvertently done that already. Will this change continue? Will it get worse?

The information in the book is helpful. At least I know how it happened. The kitsune fur seems to be the catalyst for the change. Nothing else fits. But I still don't know what the long-term effects will be. As long as I don't actually turn into a kitsune, though, I can handle plucking a few red hairs now and then.

I'm dying to increase my abilities and attempt to connect with an entire group of animals at the same time. The steam from the nonkitsune-fur-infused tea fills my lungs. My power grows within me. The sensation is strange, like I can feel my "essence" change every time.

Settled at the edge of the tree line with my back to the castle, I call out to the small creatures of the forest. Before long I'm surrounded by chipmunks, squirrels, blue birds, rabbits, a pair of skunks, an entire opossum family, and a red fox. The ravens watch with keen eyes from above.

"Welcome, friends! I am so glad you have chosen to join me today. I love all of you so much. I've been working on a way to get to know you better. I'd like to try if that's alright."

The animals are curious and excited. They trust me completely.

I close my eyes, take a deep breath, and reach my mind to all the animals at the same time.

The effect on the animals is immediate. They each freeze in place. They can feel me in their heads. My influence reaches beyond just the animals in front of me. There are others out of sight that are connected to me as well. I ask them to sit or lie down. They all comply, even the ones not in my audience. I ask them to stand at attention. They do as I request. I don't control them, exactly, but my presence in their minds must be strong enough for them to not question me. A surge of joy rushes through me. The animals chitter and sing in response. They can feel what I feel.

"What are you doing?"

Juliette's words in my ear make me jump.

I turn to face her, blocking her view of the group of hypnotized creatures.

"Nothing," I snap at her.

She looks at me as if I am not to be trusted.

What makes her think this? There's no way she can tell what I've done; her abilities are too weak with the animals.

She folds her arms and gives me a sad look.

Fully expecting her to accuse me of manipulating the animals, her next words surprise me. "It's not fair how you treated Amelie, you know."

If I'm being honest, her words aren't really that accusing. More like an olive branch. Like she's trying to make amends. Again.

She's probably right. It probably wasn't fair for me to lash out at Amelie like that. But before I can even finish that thought, Juliette keeps talking.

"It's not like she asked for any of this," she says.

Any feelings of regret instantly burn away. "Are you kidding me? She didn't ask for any of what? My home, my kingdom, my title? Is this some kind of joke?"

Juliette looks stunned. Her arms drop to her sides. "No, Jess, that's not what I mean…"

My hands ball into fists.

She backs up a couple of steps, as if she's afraid of me.

My anger smolders. "Well, *I* didn't ask to have my parents ripped away from me. *I* didn't ask for her to come here and take away *everything* from me. If she doesn't want it, she doesn't have to take it. She can give it *back!*" I'm yelling by the time I finish.

"All I'm saying is, you could try to be a little more understanding," Juliette pleads with me.

I can't believe my ears. *Be more understanding?* The fire within me burns brighter.

The animals shift behind me. My emotions have reached them. I can feel their anger growing with mine.

Juliette gasps. "What is happening?" She looks around me at the animals who are responding to my emotions. "What did you do to them?" She must be able to sense their heightened emotions now, too.

She moves to step around me toward the small crowd, but I block her way.

"I haven't DONE anything. My abilities are just better than yours. The animals are connected to me." It's not the entire truth, but it is true. I haven't done anything *bad…* but is it *right?*

I brush the thought away. Who is Juliette to judge me? She has no idea what I've been through.

Juliette looks back and forth between the upset animals and my face. She leans away. "Whatever it is you're doing here," she gestures between me and the animals. "Just… be careful. Please."

I scoff. "This is none of your business, Juliette."

"Jessamine, I care about you. I don't want you to get hurt."

"Well, it's a little late for that, now, isn't it?"

"Do you hear yourself, Jessamine? You sound so bitter. This isn't like you."

Why can't she just leave me alone? She would be bitter, too, if everything had been ripped away from her.

"Just go," I tell her, and then I turn my back to her.

Her steps are hesitant, slow, like she wants to stay. To help me or accuse me? I have no idea. Either way, I don't need her company. I don't need anyone.

With that singular thought, my mind releases its connection to the animals, and they skitter away. Some of them give me accusing looks. Others just look afraid of me.

My heart twinges. I do need the animals though, in order to still feel like part of a family.

And I need Peter.

He's coming today. I must prepare.

"Goodbye friends." I hope they aren't mad at me. I didn't intend for my negativity to spread to them. It must have been unsettling for them to feel such resentment toward Juliette, one who they should be able to trust. In a way, I've betrayed them. And her. But I push those thoughts out of my head. I just need to remember this so I can be more careful next time.

The entire day passes with no sign from Peter, and no word, either. His father must have prevented him from coming. If he hadn't been so forceful about his conviction to be with me, I might worry. But his love is as strong as mine. And he's right, nothing can stand between us. Things are just… delayed.

The following afternoon, Dahlia sends a servant to insist that I join them for tea. If Peter is still going to propose, which he is, I know it, I must try to be a little bit cordial.

Wearing a traditional, albeit simple, day dress, I join the others in the front sitting room. Amelie serves tea from one of my mother's favorite sets. I grind my teeth but say nothing.

"Jessamine, dear," Dahlia addresses me.

Here it comes. She's going to scold me for what happened with Juliette yesterday. But she doesn't speak of it, asking me a polite question about how my day is going instead.

My eyes dart in Juliette's direction. She knows what I'm thinking. She ducks her head. Maybe she didn't tattle on me? That would be a first. She's such a rule follower, always trying to help even if her help is unwanted.

For the next hour I speak only when spoken to. It's apparent that Dahlia is just using me to help train Amelie on how to host guests. And I'm the "guest." Figures. I play my part and stare out the window when I'm not needed. Again, trying to keep things somewhat civil, so that when Peter is ready...

The butler knocks on the tearoom door. "You have a visitor, Ma'am."

My aunt looks confused. "I'm not expecting anyone. That is odd." She looks at Amelie. She grins. "This will be even better practice. You never know when you need to be 'on!'"

Amelie looks like an owl, the way her eyes have gone all wide. She is not cut out for this at all. Satisfaction at her discomfort stirs within me.

Dahlia stands and follows Anthony to the entry hall.

I hear a familiar voice. *Peter* is the unexpected visitor. He's come, like he promised!

I sit up a little taller. Amelie gives me a curious look, but I ignore her. My eyes and ears are glued to the door that stands open between me and my future.

This is it! My whole life is about to change again, for the better.

Christine Marshall

Chapter Thirty-two

My uncle's voice fills the entryway. He sounds irritated. I can't hear the words, but I can recognize the pleading in Peter's voice.

Rising to my feet I move closer to the door.

"Jessamine, it isn't proper…" Amelie starts to scold me.

I glare at her, and she shuts up.

From just inside the doorway, they can't see me, but I can hear everything.

"It is time for you to give up on this, Peter. It will never happen," Uncle Henry speaks to Peter as if giving him sound advice.

"But I love her," Peter counters, firmly. "If you will not give your permission, then we will elope. It is not what either you or I want."

Henry says nothing.

Would he rather I just run away and never come back? Because that can be arranged.

"You should speak with your father, Peter. This… dream… of

Jessamine, cannot be. She is too young. It is a ridiculous request. Return home. Move on."

Why do they think they can control my whole life?

I burst from the tearoom. "This has been your plan all along, hasn't it? You just want me to be miserable."

My aunt gasps, all offended when Peter puts an arm around my waist. I roll my eyes at her. Which makes her gasp again.

"Now, Jessamine, be reasonable…" Uncle Henry ignores the physical affection that affronts my aunt so badly. "You are too young…"

"I am of age! My birthday was over two weeks ago! You all forgot about it. But Peter didn't. And we *will* marry, whether you like it or not!"

"No, you won't!" Uncle Henry bellows, his face red.

Peter stiffens beside me; his hand clenches my waist tighter. His anger kindled at the way Henry has addressed me.

But what Henry says next is the last thing either of us expect.

"Peter is to wed Amelie!" Henry shouts at us.

Neither Peter nor I respond. We are both too stunned to speak.

"Excuse me?" I ask after a long pause.

"What are you speaking of?" Peter demands at the same time.

"It has all been arranged. This kingdom needs a King when Amelie takes the crown. Someone with experience. Peter is the most convenient choice. Their age difference isn't so much as to be improper, and Peter's father agrees to the plan."

My eyes sting. So now Amelie is going to take away my love, too? That's all I have left. Without Peter, I will be truly alone.

"I will refuse," Peter's whole body stiffens.

My heart wants to burst from his declaration. He will not leave me! My chest alternates between joy and anger.

"How could you do this to me?" I whisper through my glare at my uncle. "Do you not care for me at all? You claim that I am part of your family, and yet you treat me as beneath you. What do you want for me, for my future? Nothing?" I'm full on crying now.

Dahlia's eyes are misty, but Henry looks solid as a statue. Unfeeling.

"It is done. I am sorry."

"No! It is not done. And it never will be." Peter's voice is full of strength and courage. "Come, Jessamine. You do not have to stay here any longer."

"Peter, your father will hear about this. He will force your hand," Henry growls.

"I'd like to see him try," Peter responds.

Hand in hand Peter and I march out the castle doors.

After we've turned the corner, out of view of any prying eyes, Peter breaks into a sprint. I don't let go of his hand, and I run right alongside him.

When we make it beneath the orange, yellow, and golden fall foliage, he stops, and bends over his knees. His breathing is heavy. I place my hand on his arm.

The sweet aroma of decaying leaves beneath our feet blends with the anxiety that emanates from Peter.

"Peter?" I tug on his arm a little.

When he stands straight, I can't believe my eyes. He's crying. For real.

"Peter, what is it? This is what you want, right, to be with me?" Fear of rejection and heartbreak grips my chest again. My own tears flow once more.

He wraps his arms around me so fast, I barely have time to react. "It is the only thing I want, Jessamine. I only want you."

"Then, what troubles you?" I stand back so I can meet his eyes. My voice is shaky.

Peter's tears leak out again. "I am afraid your uncle is correct. My father will force my hand. He will send his soldiers to fetch me if he must. He will make me go through with it. I know I said I will refuse, and I will, but in the end, it is his decision."

This can't be how our story ends. "Let's run away." My voice is frantic. "We can leave right now; I don't have much to pack…" I swipe at the wetness on my cheeks.

Peter shakes his head. He runs his hands through his blonde hair, leaving it a crazy mess. "He'll send his trackers to find me. We will not be able to hide from them. Then he will have them kill you and bring me home if it comes to that. I cannot lose you like that, Jessamine." He covers his face with both hands. "What are we to do?"

"I don't know Peter." I rub his arms, my own head swirling. "But we'll find a way to be together."

He wraps his arms around me again and holds me close. I melt into his chest.

A wolf edges out of the woods.

An idea glows like embers at the edges of my mind. At the same moment a voice whispers, *"Embrace the cinders."* It's impossible to tell if it's my mother's voice, my voice… or maybe a blend of them both.

The wolf is wary. She can sense my emotions, and Peter's distress, and she's not sure she wants to be here.

I force my emotions under control and slip from Peter's arms.

"It's alright," my words soothe the wolf.

If this works, then maybe…

She takes a tentative step closer.

I connect with her mind and ask her to remain still. She obeys.

With confident steps I approach. She doesn't even flinch when my hand rests on her head. She doesn't move a muscle. The smaller animals obeying my requests was one thing. But the wolf? This is huge.

"I have an idea, Peter," I smile at my love.

He looks confused.

"I've enhanced my abilities to connect with the animals. They will do as I say. And the effects can last a long time if I want them to."

Peter studies my hand on the wolf. He lowers his eyebrows.

"What does this have to do with us?" Peter rests a hand on the wolf's head, too. He runs his fingers through her soft fur. It calms him.

The she-wolf moves her eyes back and forth between us. With a single thought I thank her for her assistance and remove my connection from her mind.

She stays. Unlike the other animals who felt betrayed by my invasion, she doesn't mind. Perhaps because she lives in a pack. She is already submissive to the alpha male and alpha female, as well as the betas. Relief floods over me. If she had rejected me, it would have ruined another piece of my heart. But now... now I am emboldened.

My thoughts spin almost faster than I can explain them to Peter.

"I can enhance my abilities a little bit more. Then I'll be able to influence the minds of my uncle, and your father. And their wives. Then they will agree to let us marry, and no one can question it. Don't you see, Peter? This is how we will be together!"

Peter thinks for a minute and starts to look excited, too. But then his face falls. "But if it's only temporary, eventually they would come to their senses. It wouldn't last."

His eyes plead with mine for a solution.

Oh. He's right. I can't keep their minds clouded forever. Well, I *could...* if I enhanced my abilities even more. But that wouldn't be right. Then it comes to me.

"We'll keep them confused long enough for us to escape. Really escape. I think there's a way for me to change our appearances. We'll charter a ship and sail across the seas! I've always wanted to see the ocean! By the time they realize we are gone, it will be far too late to catch up to us."

My heart beats faster. This is going to work!

Peter doesn't take his eyes from mine. His mouth stretches into a smile. "Jessamine, my love, you are brilliant."

He picks me up and twirls me in a circle. When he sets me down, he leans close. We share a long, deep kiss.

When we finally break apart, he asks, "This can truly work?"

I don't tell him that I've never tried using my abilities to connect with a person before. Or that I haven't exactly figured out the transformation stuff yet. But I don't want to let him down. And besides, there's no reason our plan won't work. I just need time to figure it all out.

Hiding any hint of hesitation from Peter, my voice sounds confident. "Yes, Peter. It will work."

It has to.

Then I kiss him again.

By the time I climb the ladder and go to bed, my mind is racing. I'll need to test the transformation, which means I need to study that section in the book further.

I stay up half the night reading and rereading every last detail about the transformations. The formulas for the transformations are different than the power enhancing ones, but they use many of the same kinds of ingredients. Plus a few things that I never would have thought of. Like a blood sample of the one being transformed, a hair sample of the thing that the subject will be transformed into, and…

"Nixie tears? Or kitsune fur!" Did the raven… know?

The formula must be ingested as a potion. The book says the process can range from mildly uncomfortable to excruciatingly painful.

And it also says that interspecies transformations are forbidden.

"Forbidden like saving the life a kelpie?" I raise one eyebrow. A lot of the "facts" in this book are to be questioned.

"What happens if an interspecies transformation is done? *Can produce unexpected results*? What does that even mean? Thanks for nothing, book." I continue my study.

As if he knew I was thinking of him, my raven friend perches on my window. *But what about people?*

"There's nothing in here about a human using this potion." I snap the book shut with frustration.

He watches me, but doesn't respond, only listens as I think out loud.

"I'm not worried about being able to cloud the minds of the two kings." I pace back and forth, the raven's dark eyes and menacing beak follow my path. "I'll practice that in the morning at breakfast."

My stomach twinges at the thought of transforming Peter and myself into something unrecognizable.

Perhaps a test?

My eyes meet the raven's. "Is there something you know but aren't telling me?"

No, just giving suggestions… He returns to the forest before I can ask him anything else.

I set the book down and return to my suite. Where did that raven go? I lean out the window searching the treetops for any sign of him.

The chamber maid slips through the doors to bring me fresh linens for the morning.

She startles when she sees me standing by the window. "Oh, excuse me, miss. I didn't know you were still awake!"

I wave away her apology. After all, I shouldn't even have servants anymore.

Her bright red hair is unusual for those from our kingdom. She must be from the northlands.

My stomach clenches.

Bright red hair. Like kitsune hair.

Christine Marshall

Chapter Thirty-three

I could use a strand of her hair and transform myself to look like her.

She's much smaller than me. And her appearance is so different from mine, it would be easy to tell if it worked.

"Thank you for bringing me the linens." I smile sweetly at her. *And for giving me a brilliant idea.*

She looks confused. As she should. It's not like I've ever behaved this way before.

"You're welcome, miss. Goodnight."

I inspect the linens for any stray hairs that may have fallen from her head.

Drat, there aren't any.

"Mouse!" I holler. There must be one within earshot.

A squeak answers back, and a pair of mice skitter toward me. They bow low. They've never done that before.

"I need a strand of that maid's hair. The red hair. By morning, please."

They've never been so quick to comply before.

My breath quickens. Dizziness begins to overwhelm me. Am I really going to transform myself to look like another person? What if the "unexpected results" are permanent? What if…

"Calm down, Jessamine. No need to worry about something that hasn't even happened."

A voice in the back of my mind whispers, *"…yet."*

My churning stomach and racing mind keep me awake most of the night.

The family looks surprised to see me at breakfast. Peter did imply that I was leaving with him. Maybe it has nothing to do with my wrinkled clothes, messy hair, and giant purple bags under my bloodshot eyes. They avoid eye contact and don't speak to me for the duration of the meal.

The mice should return with my hair at any time. Will they leave it on my vanity? Or wait for me to return?

I barely eat. I'm dreading the experiment I must do today. But if it will allow Peter and I to be together, any risk is worth it.

On my way back to my room, I realize I have forgotten to try to connect with the minds of the others at breakfast. "There's always next time."

A letter from Peter waits for me, along with the raven and his next "gift." This time he's brought me what looks like an ogre's disgusting toenail.

"Where do you find these things?" My face is twisted at the foul odor coming from the toenail.

He won't say, only that he has access to a great many things… for the right price.

"No wonder you're called a conspiracy of ravens."

He doesn't respond.

"I'll get the jewel."

When he has his prize retrieved from a hidden compartment in my writing desk, he takes flight.

"Thank you!" I call after him.

He croaks at me.

> *My love,*
> *Is there anything you need me to do to assist with our plan?*
> *Please let me know, but be careful how you word your letters, just in case.*
> *I love you and will do anything to be with you.*
> *Ever yours.*

His words are all the encouragement I need to spend the entire day working in my secret space.

Day 11

Unplanned transformation experiment.

Have obtained hair from red-head maid. Following formula, I mixed it with a strand of the kitsune fur, and the other ingredients, then boiled the mixture with water until it reduced into a thick potion.

Upon ingestion became violently ill.

Bones felt like they were compressing. Skull changed shape. Internal parts squished into smaller frame.

Transformation complete. I look exactly like the maid. My voice even sounds like her, too.

Must find a way to make the transformation less painful.

Also, what other applications might this have?

Waiting to see how long my new appearance will last. Will stay in secret room, just in case.

Also, raven has brought me an ogre toenail. Added to collection. Have no idea what I'm supposed to use it for. I'll need to research that, I suppose, but not yet.

The altered appearance lasts for a couple of hours, and the switch back is just as painful. Only this time my bones feel like they are being stretched.

After an entire day making lists, studying medicinal plants from Magnolia's book more carefully, and preparing formulas, my notebook is almost full of ideas for making the change less painful. Good thing there's a whole stack of empty notebooks in one of my desk drawers. I'm going to need them.

Day 11 continued
May have found solution to ease the transformation process.
Have skipped dinner with the family. Will try connecting in the morning.

"Mouse!" I don't even look up from my book.
The pair of mice emerge. They bow low, again.
"What's this all about?"
Your Highness... how may we be of service?
Your Highness? Since when do they think of me in that way?
My mother's voice rings in my ears. *"Remember who you are!"*
I can communicate with the animals. They obey me. I have power. I am the future Queen.
Is this what Mom meant? Will I be the Queen of… the animals?
My mind wanders through the possibilities: servants, messengers, spies, guardians.
Your Highness? The mice pull my attention back to them.
"Yes. Please fetch me lavender, lemon balm, and parsley from the gardens."
As you wish. They scurry back behind the wall, and I can hear the scraping of their miniature claws as they scrabble away from my room.

256

"Huh. This is… unexpected. When Peter and I are finally free, I will begin preparations to become… Queen of the animal kingdom." My heart races. Wonder seeps in where anxiety has been weighing me down.

"This is what you meant, Mom… right? This is what you've been trying to tell me all along. Feed the fire. Embrace the cinders. Remember who you are. If I hadn't begun these experiments, I would never have realized what you intended for me to do. My full potential is beyond just connecting with the animals. It's to rule all of them."

Is it, though? Does that sound like something your mother would have wanted? The thought prickles at the back of my mind.

"Yes. It is. The evidence is everywhere. This is my destiny."

The mice return with my list of ingredients. They are rewarded with a cheek-full of sunflower seeds, and they skitter away.

"It's too late to try this tonight. I'll work on it tomorrow."

Day12

Unable to connect with family. Will enhance powers again. Memory of the painful transformation makes me averse to trying again. Besides, I'm not sure drinking the potion and enhancing my abilities on the same day are such a good idea. Powers today, appearance tomorrow.

Dear Jessamine,
I will be able to sneak away tomorrow to come see you.
Anxious to hear how things are going.
Ever yours, Peter

Peter,
Meet me where you asked me to marry you.
Can't risk you being seen outside the castle.
Love, Jessamine

257

Anticipation keeps my nerves on edge. What if his father catches him trying to leave? What if something happens to him on the way here? What if all our plans fail and we won't be able to spend our lives together?

The thumps of hoofs on the forest floor to my right make me jump. His black horse breaks through the underbrush, and Peter slides from his back before the horse has even stopped moving.

He rushes to engulf me in his arms. My own arms squeeze him as tight as they can.

"You made it, I was so worried."

He brushes a tear from my cheek. "I will always make my way back to you."

Words can't break through the tightness of my throat, so I simply nod in reply.

He takes my hand and leads me away from the palace and toward the hillside where we picnicked on my birthday. He distracts me by telling tales of where we will live when we run away; and how many children we'll have, which makes me blush.

On top of the hill overlooking the city, Peter asks me about my plan.

"It's only been a couple of days… but it's working. I just need a little more time to work out some of the details."

"Thank you for doing this, Jessamine. I don't mean to rush you; I just want to begin our lives together. I don't want to have to wait any longer."

"Me too." Should I tell him about the transformation? About how painful it was? But that will only make him worry. I don't want to give him any reason to change his mind, so I keep the information to myself.

Day 14
Even with stronger abilities, still not able to connect to people.

However, rumor has reached me that an aquatic puma has moved into the swamp. This is my chance to prove my abilities. I will honor my mother's agreement with the kelpies and convince him to leave so they can keep their home.

My abilities are stronger than ever. Influencing the mind of an aquatic puma should be no problem for me now.

Will test potion when I return.

The wolf pack follows me through the woods as I make my way toward the swamp.

You've changed, the alpha says.

"How so?"

He side-eyes me. *I'm not a fool.*

I grin. "I know."

Your powers have grown. I can sense you enter the woods now, even if I'm very far away.

"I've been… practicing."

That look again.

"Alright! I've learned how to enhance my abilities."

What other things have you been able to do?

Does he know about the potion? How could he?

Do not hold back from me, little one.

I glare at him.

If wolves could smirk, he would be smirking back at me.

"I can temporarily change my appearance."

I wish to know more.

"Maybe another time. Today I am working on another project."

The aquatic puma.

"Yes… how did you know?"

I didn't. But you are walking toward the swamp with purpose. And I know that the puma is there.

"Your assumptions are correct. Will you join me?"

We will not involve ourselves with such a being. But we will stay close.

"Are you worried about me? Because I can assure you, you shouldn't be."

We shall see.

The water level in the swamp is much higher this time. And it's much quieter than usual, too. The puma's presence must be making the others who live here reluctant to go about their lives.

"This will not do."

My riding boots protect my feet and ankles from the thick water. My hands on my hips, I scan the surface with my eyes. Where is he?

A massive blue heron takes to the sky, startling a handful of frogs to jump into the water with a chorus of plunks.

"Mr. Puma, this swamp is home to a family of kelpies. They are under my care. I respectfully request that you leave and find a new home for yourself."

My words are muffled from all the moss dripping from the trees, the plants that cover the surface of the water, and the tall sedges and cattails that grow in clumps around the perimeter of the swamp.

After a few long minutes, the water on the other side of the swamp ripples. The lily pads on the surface shake. The sedges and cattails rattle. A wake forms in the water behind a row of scaly spikes that slice the surface and glide smoothly towards me.

I take a hesitant step back but remind myself to hold my ground. I am in charge here today.

My mind tries to connect with the creature. I can see the swamp from below the surface. I can feel a sense of superiority. But I cannot communicate with the aquatic puma.

With a splash, the enormous cat-like creature breaks the surface not five arm lengths in front of me. Water drips from the fur on his face and legs. Looking like shimmery scabs, scales mingle with the fur at the creature's shoulders. A row of spiked fins line it's spine, the scales matching the blackness of its fur. The back half of the puma is all scales that shine iridescent in the dim light.

He lets out a menacing cat-like roar, exposing his long, sharp teeth. His red eyes rest on me in challenge.

I have claimed this swamp as my own. You do not command me.

I will not obey.

"The kelpies have lived here for generations." I keep my voice firm and continue to reach for him with my mind.

They will have to find someplace else to settle. You must leave now.

I gasp. The minds of a dozen water snakes, some venomous, surround me. With my mind I can feel them. I command them to stand down, but they do not comply.

The puma licks his lips with his large tongue. *Leave, or my pets will strike.*

How is he controlling the snakes?

You did not know about this ability of mine? Tsk, tsk. That's a shame.

With a flick of his whiskers, he commands the snakes to attack.

Christine Marshall

Chapter Thirty-four

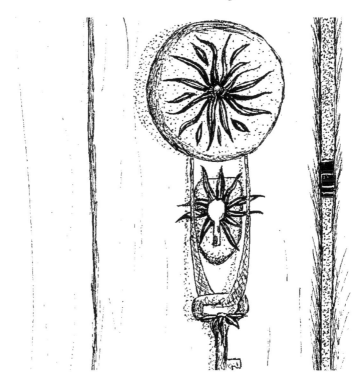

With a shriek I leap backwards, tripping on the muddy floor of the swamp and landing on my back on the moist ground just beyond the water's edge.

Growls emanate from the shrubs around the swamp. My pack.

The aquatic puma purrs. *More meat. Excellent.*

The alpha lunges forward to stand between me and the puma. His mate tugs at my blouse with her teeth, encouraging me to stand.

I scramble to my feet and back away.

She nudges me with her nose and whispers in my mind to hurry.

The pack surrounds me, and I do as she says.

When I'm a safe distance, the alpha joins us.

"I have no idea what just happened. How could I not command the puma? And the snakes? It doesn't make any sense."

The wolves accompany me as I make my way back toward home. They don't have any answers though.

"I assumed I'd be able to connect with his mind. But it's as if he was too in control of his own thoughts. He didn't allow me in. And the snakes listened to him more than me. Were they afraid?"

When we reach the edge of the forest, I haven't figured out the puzzle. But I do know one thing.

"You saved me. Thank you," I say to the alpha pair, bowing my head slightly to show my appreciation.

They nod back.

"How can I ever repay you?"

There is one thing...

An image of the alpha bigger, stronger... scarier... enters my head. He wants me to enhance him.

"I will see what I can do."

The pack pads away. My mind spins. One more thing to figure out.

"Hi Jessamine, I haven't seen you out here in a while," Juliette catches up to me as I cross the meadow.

I smile politely. "I've been... reading."

"Have you noticed a change to the animals around the palace?" She jogs to keep up. "The ravens are much more active lately. And the mice aren't as present as they used to be. Like they're busy, or have found a new home, or something."

"Nope, haven't noticed."

"Are you feeling better about things?"

"Better about... what things?" My pace increases.

She keeps up. "You know, everything with Amelie, and that prince."

"Peter. His name is Peter. And we are in love. And no matter what Henry or his father say..." I take a deep breath. "It doesn't matter,

Juliette. You shouldn't worry about all of that. Or me. I'm fine."

"I just… if you say so." She stops following.

I don't even look back over my shoulder.

Over the next week I test the transformation potion. The additional ingredients help with the discomfort, but some of them seem to cancel out the change, too. I can't try it every day. It's just too much. But I work on it when I can.

The alpha gives me a small amount of his blood for his potion, which I blend with the kitsune fur, the other ingredients, and his own hair. I have no idea if it will work. It's like transforming him into himself… but better? He says he wants to try.

The puma is still a problem, too. As is trying to connect with other people. When I try, it's like bumping against a wall. I cannot enter. Apparently, my abilities do not extend that far. Which goes along with why I couldn't control the puma, either. His mind was too close to the sentient-level of a person. It's a limit that I don't know how to surpass. No amount of reading or research in *The Keeping* produces any hints. I have to put it aside, for now.

The alpha wolf finds me. He can sense that I'm looking for him.

He bows his head when he emerges from the trees. He offers me the respect he would offer another alpha of his kind.

It is ready?

"Yes."

What is in it?

"It contains pennywort extract which will sharpen your mind and improve your memory. Chamomile acts as an antispasmodic."

He gives me a wary look.

"I know it sounds strange but trust me. There's poppy seed oil to temporarily dull pain. The midnight caladium…"

That's toxic. He recoils.

"The plant is, but the steam is not. I've steamed the plant with a lid and collected the condensation to add to the potion. Remarkably, it has all the healing effects of the steam but in liquid form. It will ensure a smooth recovery."

Recovery?

"Besides a drop of your own blood, and a piece of your own hair, the final ingredient is kitsune fur. Your bones and muscles will grow. The transformation can be uncomfortable, but the other ingredients should offer some relief."

The wolf ponders. *Is it permanent?*

"It can be. There are different potencies. Some are temporary, but others are permanent. You can choose which you prefer."

I can smell the potion in your bag. Which did you bring?

"I carry both."

Permanent.

"Perfect."

The wolf leads me closer to his den, far away from the castle. We cannot risk anyone seeing what we are doing. He drinks the more condensed version of the potion. Almost instantly the change begins.

I sit with him and rub his fur. He grunts with pain but does not lash out. His pain tolerance combined with the medicinal properties of the potion allow him to transform without the pain being too intense.

"How are you doing?"

Uncomfortable.

"Is there anything you need?"

No.

"It should be over soon."

No response.

When the transformation is complete, Alpha, as I've decided to call him, relaxes beneath my hand.

It is done.

He stands on his longer, thicker legs. The muscles beneath his fur bulge. His ears are bigger. His teeth longer and sharper. And his eyes. They have turned yellow.

"How do you feel?" My hands slide over his body, studying the changes and making mental notes to add to my book.

Flawless.

My arms wrap around his neck, now taller than my shoulder.

"Thank you for trusting me. And accepting me. You have no idea how important this is. All of this."

Of course, my Queen. He nuzzles my neck with his new, oversized nose.

Henry is irritated at me. I'm late for supper. I knew dinner was approaching, but I stayed longer with the wolf anyway.

"If you refuse to behave with respect, then perhaps you should no longer join the family for meals, Jessamine."

"Father," Juliette gasps beside me. She rests a hand on my arm. "Jessamine is part of the family."

"This is none of your concern, Juliette."

Amelie keeps her eyes on her food. She knows better than to give her opinion when Henry is being all high and mighty. But Juliette keeps trying.

"But she's... like a sister."

"Enough, Juliette. You simply do not understand."

"It's alright, Juliette." I glare at my uncle. "If Henry no longer wishes to treat me as family, that's fine with me."

Henry growls. "You will address me as King or Your Majesty or Sire."

"Right." I pick up my plate. "Well then, *Your Majesty.* I will just take my meals in my room."

"Jessamine," Dahlia gives me a warning look.

"You will do no such thing. That food is for the family. If you refuse to eat with the family, then you will eat what the servants eat."

"Dear," Dahlia lays a hand on Henry's arm. "Perhaps..."

He glares at her. She backs down.

"Great. I don't like your food selections anyway." Food jumps off my plate when I drop it onto the table. The silver edged ceramic dish cracks down the middle.

Henry's face turns so red I'm surprised steam isn't pouring out of his ears.

I walk out of the room with my head held high. He thinks he's won. But he has no idea that he has just given me even more freedom to finish what I have begun.

Day 23

Henry is an idiot.

Since I'm unable to connect my mind with the family, we will have to rely on transformation to sneak away. Must come up with a plan. Must speak with Peter.

My powers have not diminished. My connection with the animals has remained solid. Except for the puma, I can command them to do almost anything, and they obey.

If Dahlia or Henry knew how much my power has grown, they would behave a lot more respectfully towards me. That's alright. They may think I'll never be Queen, but I know better.

If Peter and I can escape… no. *When* Peter and I escape and begin a new life far away from this place, I have the potential of being the Queen of the entire animal kingdom. I'll have to start small, like I have with the creatures here. But in time, I could have it all.

Something whispers that this is dangerous. That I need to give in. Give up. Move on.

But then my mother's voice reminds me, *"You are the Queen."*

My time needs to be productive if I am to have everything ready before Peter's father announces his betrothal to Amelie. Dosages altered. Other ingredients added to stave off some of the unpleasantness of the transformation. Further experimentation and testing. On myself. I must be careful. But with the successes I've had so far, I will be able to pull it off.

I summon the mice to retrieve more hairs from a couple of servants in the palace.

As you wish.

I could get used to this.

Dear Peter,

My abilities with the animals have grown remarkably.
But my inabilities with people have remained the same.
The other part of our plan is coming along.
I will let you know as soon as it's ready to implement.
Love, Jessamine

My Love,
I would leave tonight with you if you gave the word.
Please know that. As soon as you are ready, I will
be at your window.
Ever Yours, Peter

Animals become my servants. They are either respectful or submissive. They know my powers have grown. They know that I could make them do things for me if I wanted to. I won't, of course. I'm not a monster.

Magnolia would say that none of this is right. I shouldn't be commanding the animals. They are my equals. And I agree with her. But this is a desperate situation. She would understand that, wouldn't she?

Alpha requests two more doses of the potion. One for him to change even more, and one for his mate. I prepare the exact same potion as last time, with a little more poppyseed oil, and the transformations go faster and smoother than before.

Days pass. I ignore the family completely. I don't complain about the food I am brought. Anthony doesn't approve of Henry banishing me from the dining room and brings me extra treats whenever he can. I retrieve my food from the kitchens at mealtime, sometimes even eating with the servants.

Henry can't stand my defiance. He's afraid I'll mess things up for Amelie, now that he knows that Peter and I both wish to be together.

I wake up to find that the doors to my suite have been locked. I'm informed by Anthony that the servants are instructed to deliver the food and linens through the dumbwaiter in the wall that I've literally never used before.

My aunt knocks and tries to speak with me through the doors. She apologizes for Henry's behavior. I tell her to leave me alone.

Henry may think he has restrained me, but I just sneak out my window whenever I want. I'm not a prisoner. But I let Henry believe he's in control.

When I tell Peter about my locked doors in a letter, he is livid.

> *I will break down the doors if I must. I will break down the walls of the entire castle to be with you. Henry will not stand in my way. I promise.*

His words bring warmth to my heart. I write a quick response. The raven huffs at me when I call him back so quickly. "You're getting paid, I don't know what you're complaining about."

> *Dearest Peter,*
> *No need to knock any walls down. The ladder out my window will suffice.*
> *Always and forever yours,*
> *Jessamine*

Later, after the sun has set and the stars are bright, the lock of my door makes a loud click just as I climb into bed.

"Jessamine?" Juliette slides through the door and closes it quickly behind her.

A suitably dejected face greets her when she approaches.

"I am so sorry for the way my father is treating you. It's not right and I will continue to do my best to stand up for you. You've already

270

lost so much. You don't need to lose us, too."

My eyes well up. Totally fake.

She hugs me tight. "Hang in there. We'll figure a way out of this."

After she leaves, locking the door again, I grin.

"It's alright, Juliette. I already have."

Christine Marshall

Chapter Thirty-five

"Jessamine? Are you awake?"

It sounds like… my mother.

Am I dreaming?

I stayed up way too late last night thinking about mine and Peter's escape. I've been troubled all night long with dreams of our plans working. And of our plans failing.

And now I'm hearing my mother?

I sit up and rub my eyes.

Someone unlocks the outer door and comes into my bedroom.

"Jessamine?"

My heart sinks. It's only Juliette.

I sigh and throw my feet off my bed.

Juliette sits beside me on the edge of my bed.

"I've brought you breakfast. I know they're not giving you enough to eat. You've lost weight. Your eyes look tired. Please, eat this?"

She produces a plate overflowing with leftover vegetable pie, thick gravy, fluffy potatoes covered in melty cheese, and a tall glass of almond milk.

My stomach grumbles. She's right, I haven't been eating much. I've been too busy.

"Thank you," I say.

She smiles and watches me eat.

"There, that's better." She sets the mostly empty plate aside. "Father has given me permission to take you outside for a while. I know you love being in the meadow and woods. I'm sure you miss the animals."

"Um.. I'm good."

She takes my hand. Well, this just got more awkward. I bite my tongue and keep my sarcastic thoughts to myself. But I don't smile. I'm not going that far.

"Jessamine. I'm worried about you. You haven't been outside for ages."

"It's only been a few days…"

Juliette ignores me. "You've been in here, all alone. I'm sorry for what I said to you in the woods, about… well, about my sister."

It's like she's afraid if she says Amelie's name I'll break. Or maybe ignite. I keep my eyes from rolling.

"You were right, Jessamine. I have no idea what you've gone through. We all could have tried harder to be more understanding. I want to do whatever I can to make it up to you."

I almost… allmmmooooost let out a sharp laugh. What could she possibly do to make any of the past four months of my life up to me?

I pat her hand. "It's fine, Juliette. It's not your fault."

Hopefully my words sound more sincere than they feel.

"Everything will turn out as it is meant to." That part, I believe.

Juliette smiles her sickly-sweet smile. I know it's sincere, she doesn't have a mean bone in her body, but I'd like to see her get mad just once in her life. Then she would be more relatable.

"Well, if you change your mind, let me know."

How am I supposed to do that if I'm locked in my room? I don't point this out to her.

I let her hug me, and she skips out the door. She'll have a good day now that she thinks she's solved all my problems. If she only knew.

Later in the afternoon, a bulbous silver carriage arrives at the castle. The heralds sound their horns, announcing an important guest to the kingdom. Bells ring across the city in response. I lean out the window to get a good view until it turns the corner toward the front of the castle.

It's a carriage from Peter's kingdom.

I quickly climb down the ladder and skulk along the edge of the castle, behind the shrubs, and peer around the corner.

An important looking messenger steps out from the fancy door. Our own butler, Anthony, greets him at the top of the palace steps. They bow at the waist toward one another, and the other guy hands Anthony a fancy, fat envelope. What could it possibly be? An invitation to something? If it was an official betrothal thing it would have been a meeting between Henry and Peter's father. This is weird.

The man from Bennfaran makes a sharp turn around, and marches back into the carriage. Then the horses pull him back the direction from which he came.

After Anthony shuts the front door, I sneak into the palace.

Servants whisper questions and make excited comments. My eyes are fixed on Anthony and that envelope. He places it on a silver tray and turns to deliver it to my uncle.

I follow. I'm sure I'm not *allowed* to be in on whatever this little secret is. Anthony either doesn't notice I'm following him, or he just doesn't care. He makes no indication he is aware of my presence whatsoever.

After delivering the envelope to my uncle, Henry tells Anthony to fetch his wife and daughters so they may look at the contents together.

From my hiding place in a dark corner behind a statue, I can see and hear everything. No one even tries to find me. So much for being "part of the family."

After they've entered the king's study, I sneak closer.

"Shouldn't Jessamine be invited to join us?" Juliette asks in her timid voice.

"Nonsense," Dahlia replies. "She wouldn't want to come anyway."

My eyes couldn't roll any further back into my head.

In his most official sounding voice, the king reads the announcement to the rest of the family.

Donalbain and *Vanora*
King and Queen of Bennfaran
formally request the presence
of
King Henry and *Queen Dahlia*
of *Dragovalon*
Along with their daughters
Amelie and *Juliette*
To a ball
in celebration of
Princess Amelie of Dragovalon's
Betrothal
to
Prince Peter of Bennfaran
On the last day of the twelfth cycle
at sundown.
Any and all families of title
from *Dragovalon*
are invited to attend
this momentous event.

My legs give out. I slide down the wall and sit on the floor. I can barely breathe.

This can't be happening. I'm so close to having our escape sealed. And now this? This is going to change everything. I have exactly one week before Peter will officially belong to someone else. How can this even be real?

"This doesn't seem fair. Peter and Jessamine…" Juliette starts to argue on my behalf.

Dahlia doesn't let her finish. She gushes about how wonderful the news is.

Amelie's sniffles reach my ears.

Why is she so upset about this? She's so ungrateful!

Dahlia's voice gets louder. Before they can burst out of Henry's office, I scurry back to my shadowy hiding place.

"We have so much we must do to prepare!" Dahlia claps her hands, gathers as many servants as she can, and starts making assignments.

Then she turns to Amelie and places her hands on her daughter's shoulders. Her eyes are misty. "I am so happy for you, darling. This is a dream come true. Congratulations." She squeezes Amelie tight, then hurries away to "prepare."

Amelie stands there like she's in a daze. Then she floats away the opposite direction as her mother.

I sneak back outside, up the ladder, and into my room, where I throw myself on my bed and scream into my pillow. I'm all out of tears by now. All that's left is red hot anger.

As I seethe in my secret room, I combine ingredients. I need to get the formulas exactly right. I probably shouldn't work while I'm angry, but what else am I supposed to do?

Peter should be announcing his betrothal to *me*.

But my plan will work. I just need a little bit more time.

I push the animals to work harder and faster. I also command a few of them to begin gathering some other supplies that I will need, that have nothing to do with the potion, and everything to do with my escape.

Then, I start to pack. It's a bit premature, but I don't care. A week can go by really fast. I cannot stay in this place even one second longer than I absolutely must.

> *Peter,*
> *I heard the news. My nerves are on edge.*
> *Will you come see me?*
> *Love, Jessamine*

My heart aches as I watch the ravens carry my letter to Peter.

> *Jessamine,*
> *I will sneak away after dark.*
> *Tonight.*
> *Watch for me.*
> *Ever yours, Peter*

By the time he enters the forest, the nearly full moon is high.

He waits in the shadows of the woods; I hurry across the meadow.

I rush into his arms. Both of our cheeks are wet with tears. He holds me close against him with both arms.

"I am so sorry, my love. This meeting should be thrilling and romantic. But after the ball announcement, everything feels like it's happening too fast." Peter's voice is filled with despair.

"Peter, I've done it. I have our way of escape."

"Tell me, Jessamine. I'll do anything." His words are tight. He's barely holding his emotions together.

"I've created a potion that will alter one's appearance." I lean back and look into his eyes.

Does he trust me? I see no hesitation. No doubt. I continue. "I have not been able to cloud the mind of any person."

He looks crestfallen.

"It's alright, maybe even for the best. This way no one will realize anything is amiss with the kings. We won't be doing anything to anyone except ourselves. We can drink it tonight. Slip away after dark. We don't have to wait."

He furrows his brow. "I want to. More than you can know. But if we cannot cloud their minds, they will surely realize that we've run away. How will we do this without arousing suspicion? We need some sort of distraction."

My mind spins. I was sure we'd be leaving tonight. I've already begun to pack. But Peter's right. Someone would notice. Anthony, or Juliette when she comes to offer me food that she thinks will make me feel better. And Peter's father would surely notice his absence, since he's been watching his son so closely lately.

"What about… the ball?"

His eyes meet mine. "What are you thinking, my love?"

"What if we take the potion at your palace when I arrive for the ball. Everyone will be busy with the party. We can blend in with the crowd. We'll look like totally different people. No one, and I mean *no one*, will be able to recognize either of us."

Peter nods. He squeezes my hands. "That will work. The ball is the perfect distraction."

"You can meet me in the gardens, we'll drink our potions together, have our bags packed. We'll leave and never look back." My heart beats faster. We're going to do this. In one week's time we will finally be free.

"If we do this," I can practically see Peter's brain visualizing the evening. "We can't transform ourselves before the announcement. They would begin looking for us immediately. It would be better to wait. Let everyone see me there, get all excited. Then, I'll… I don't know, pretend to be sick and leave for the night. No one will think twice if I retire before the ball is truly over. You can meet me in the outer halls."

My heart sinks, just a little. I don't know if I can stand to watch him be with Amelie. To watch everyone celebrate his betrothal.

Peter's brows come together. "You've tested it? You're sure it's safe?"

"It works, Peter. And the results are temporary. It's slightly… uncomfortable, but it will give us time to escape. To truly be together at last."

He shakes his head. I'm afraid he's about to say no. But he surprises me. "I don't know how you do it, my love. I can handle a bit of discomfort if it means I will have you by my side for the rest of my days."

"And I can wait until after the announcement, if I must."

Our eyes lock. He kisses me. It's urgent, and passionate. He needs me.

I wrap my arms around his neck and hold him so tight.

It feels like the last time we'll share a kiss.

But we both know that in less than a week, we'll be sharing our entire lives.

Before he leaves, he asks one more time. "You're *sure* this will work? I can't go through with this marriage, Jessamine. I love *you*."

"I'm no midnight-pixie with sparkly magic and a silly song full of magic words. But this I can do. I promise."

Chapter Thirty-six

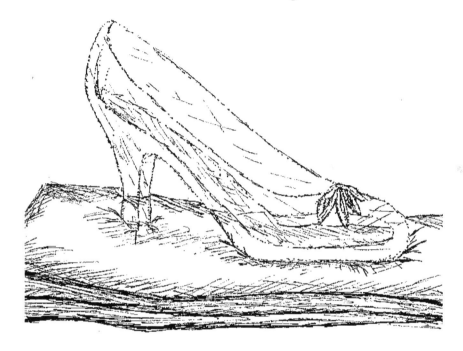

I receive love letters from Peter daily, sometimes more than once. I'm sure the ravens have so many shiny things by now they don't know what to do with them all!

Peter is distraught about the preparations being made in his palace. He must pretend to be agreeable, but he is seething inside. The same as me.

I desperately urge the animals to work harder and faster to make sure everything is ready for the night of the ball.

The morning of the ball, I receive my last letter from Peter.

The next time we see each other,
my love, we will be free.

I'm so nervous. And so excited.

I don't want to go. But I can't wait to get there.

I'm in my closet, finishing up the last little bit of packing I need to do, when I hear a soft knock on the door to my bedroom and the key scrape in the lock.

Juliette.

I can do this one more time. She can't know that anything is amiss.

Juliette's arms are overflowing with a huge, pillowy bundle of cream-colored cloth, tied with an enormous red ribbon.

"What's this?" I ask, genuinely curious. ·

"It's a gift, for you." She enters my bedroom, slides past me, and gently lays the package on the bed.

She turns toward me and smiles so wide.

I take cautious steps toward the gift.

"Open it," she claps her hands. She almost squeals the words.

A sinking feeling fills my gut. I hesitate too long.

"Here. I'll help!" Juliette pulls the ends of the ribbon, untying the bow. The silky ribbon slides off the soft fabric.

When I push the fabric aside, my breath catches.

Inside is one of the most beautiful dresses I've ever seen. The bodice is pale blue, with matching gemstones covering almost every open space, except the sleeves. The flowy cap sleeves are just the pale blue silk. The skirt of the gown has an ombre effect, matching the blue bodice at the top and fading into white at the bottom. Layers upon layers of tulle hold the silk up, like a cloud.

"Do you love it?" Juliette asks. She's so excited.

I honestly don't know what to say. A past-me probably would have died three times over to wear such a beautiful gown.

"And here, look!" Juliette reaches beneath the soft layers to unveil a pair of beautiful shoes. "They look like they're made of glass! It's some kind of sea magic, or something. But they are very sturdy. They won't break." She holds them out for me to take.

I've never seen anything like them before. I turn them over in my hands, blown away by the craftsmanship.

"And these," she presents me with white silk gloves that will stretch up my arms, above my elbows, leaving a modest gap between my sleeve and the glove.

"What do you think?" Juliette's voice is airy.

This is when I should squeal, giggle, grab her hands and swing her around with a huge thank you. But that's the last thing I feel like doing right now.

How can she expect me to be excited about the ball tonight when she knows... she *knows* that I'm in love with Peter?

I stare at her, mouth agape.

Her smile fades. "Jessamine?"

I shake my head. I don't want to be mean, but this is seriously so inconsiderate. "I don't want it. I don't want any of it, Juliette. Why would I?" I gesture at the whole get-up.

"I know my father said you can't come. He doesn't want any... distractions, or whatever."

I stiffen. I didn't know that.

"But I thought... maybe you'd want to come with me?"

"Does Henry know about this?"

"Well, no. But we can invite anyone we want. I want you to come. I mean, what can he do if you just climb into the carriage with me?"

I set the shoes down on top of the gown and rewrap the cloth around it. "I don't think that's a good idea." I shove the bundle back into Juliette's arms.

She stares at me in disbelief. "But I thought..."

"We're not little girls playing dress up anymore, Juliette." I try to keep my voice even. The fire is burning in my heart again. I'm barely keeping it under control. "This isn't some fairy tale, where things always turn out happy in the end. People get hurt." I rest my palm on my chest. "They die." I gesture to the painting of my parents on the wall.

"But..." Juliette starts to plead.

"No, Juliette. It's over. I'm not coming with you to the ball. Please, just go."

She shifts the fabric bundle in her arms and stares at me.

I return to my closet.

From the corner of my eye I watch as she sets the dress back on the bed.

"Just in case you change your mind," she whispers. Then she leaves without another word.

When I hear the lock click, I turn around. She's laid out the whole outfit. There's even a sparkly tiara to go with the ensemble.

I shake my head. "I don't need her charity, or 'gifts' as she calls them. Besides, I already have my own dress for the ball. And it's going to light the room on fire."

Within the hour the family departs for the ball. The carriage rattles and the horses' hooves clop as it slowly rolls away from the palace.

"Finally!"

The pots and dishes I have accumulated are disposed of. The dried herbs and plant bundles lie in separate wrappings beside the vials and packets of other various concoctions in my over-the-shoulder bag.

All the various potion bottles are sealed tight, each one wrapped in a soft cloth to prevent them from jostling in my bag too much. The ones for me and Peter rest on top of the others, so they will be within easy reach.

Also in the bag are two pairs of my pants and blouses. My riding boots are strapped to the outside. I look around. The space is empty. Only a couple of bits and pieces are left behind. I close the secret door. The closet is a disaster after I've sorted and resorted everything that I had thought I would want to take with me. Turns out, I don't need much. Just Peter. I slip my mother's soft blanket and my father's hand-carved donkey into my bag and close the closet door.

Now it's time to get myself ready for a ball.

The animals have done a superior job creating my gown. I never knew mice and birds could be so handy with collecting long swaths of fabrics and sewing implements. Or turning my vision for my gown into a reality with careful snips and stitches. They seemed happy to help, and even hummed tunes in their heads as they worked.

A thought crosses my mind. If I show up looking like me, wearing that dress, Henry is going to have me murdered. But if I take my potion now... I have a lot. If my appearance starts to revert, I can drink some more. Then no one would recognize me at all.

But Peter wouldn't recognize me at all, either.

I scribble a quick note:

> *There's a last-minute change of plans.*
> *I will take my potion before I arrive.*
> *I will not look like myself.*
> *But, trust me, you'll know it's me.*
> *If you have any doubts, my dress is the exact same silk*
> *you wrapped my birthday gift in.*
> *I love you and can't wait to be with you forever.*
> *Love, Jessamine*

"Deliver this to Peter as fast as you can. Just you. We don't need to draw any attention to the fact that he's receiving a message. He may not be in his room. You will need to find him and make sure he's the only one who sees the note."

Yes, Your Majesty.

The raven tells his conspiracy to stay behind, and he will be back before the hour changes.

"Perfect."

My potion bottle is out of my bag and in my hand. The color of the liquid reminds me of blood. I can almost smell the irony scent of blood just from its appearance. But when I pull the cork out of the vial, a sweet, floral scent wafts into my nose.

"That's not so bad."

We were supposed to take our potions together, Peter and I. But this new plan will work out better. Way less risk at getting caught. Henry and the others believe I am locked in my room at home, crying my eyes out at my lost love. Juliette knows I don't want to be at the ball.

The thick potion runs down my throat. A warm, glowing sensation washes over me from head to toe. My muscles relax. I carefully lower myself to the floor, so I don't fall and hit my head or something. My heartrate slows. My eyes get heavy. All my worries about everything slip from my mind. My skin tingles. Freckles appear on my arms. The hair resting on my shoulders lightens several shades. My bones stretch, just a little.

When the transformation is complete my reflection almost surprises me. A different woman returns my gaze. Hazel eyes, slightly darker skin tone. Light brown hair a totally different texture than mine. I'm a little taller, but not enough to be a problem for my dress.

I smile at her. She smiles back at me. I hurry into my ballgown, secure my new hair into a twist on the back of my head, shoulder my pack, and head for the door.

I considered climbing down the ladder, but I want my leaving to be intentional.

The lock is easy to pick. I could have escaped long ago if I really wanted to. The metal wire that the mice delivered to me during preparations clinks when it lands on the floor at my feet.

Pausing in the doorway I look around my room for the last time. Memories of long nights with my mother sitting with me when I was sick, small arguments over unimportant things, and crying on her shoulder flood my mind. Also, of my father kissing me goodnight when I was small, his scratchy beard rubbing on my face and making me giggle. His warm hugs, stupid jokes, and amazing smile that crinkled the corners of his eyes.

My breath catches in my throat. This is it. I'm really leaving. Forever.

"Goodbye," I whisper to the ghosts of the past.

My two little mouse friends that have been my personal servants these past few weeks want to help more. They want me to succeed, to be with my true love. They insist that they are ready to help in any way they can. I send them on a reconnaissance mission.

Henry has taken the large carriage and the whole retinue of palace horses with him to Bennfaran. There are a couple of the guards' horses in the stables, but they would definitely be missed if I take them.

We *would be happy to help, your majesty.*

"What do you mean? I can just ride Alpha, he won't mind."

Oh, no. That is no way for a Queen to arrive at a ball! You must arrive in style. One mouse says.

Please, his wife agrees. *We will be your horses.*

"I don't understand."

Apologies, ma'am, we never intended to pry, but you have been open in our presence. We know what you've been working on in your secret room. We have brought you two horse hairs. You may change us into horses, and we will whisk you away to the ball. There is still a small carriage in the carriage house that the two of us can pull with no trouble. At least, I think. I've never been a horse before!

The two mice twitter with their squeaky laughter.

"Oh, no, I couldn't. I haven't tried changing any animals into something else before. I don't know what will happen."

The mice scurry up my dress and settle in my hands. *We would do anything to serve you. Please, allow us to do this.*

I hesitate. It's probably a bad idea. But they *want* to help. I wouldn't be making them do anything.

"Embrace the cinders."

"Alright, let's do it."

Christine Marshall

Chapter Thirty-seven

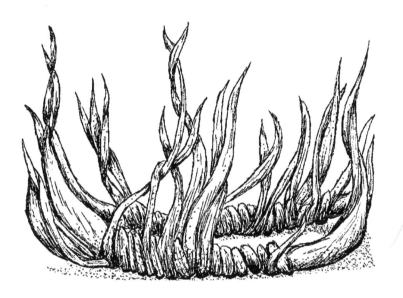

My wolf pack is gathered at the edge of the wood. Alpha looks more menacing standing beside the other, normal sized wolves.

When they see that my appearance has changed, they all lift their noses into the air. Alpha approaches and circles me slowly, his nose brushing against my hands.

Your Majesty. He dips his head. The others imitate his submissive pose.

Then he peers at the horses and small carriage waiting in the courtyard beyond the castle. The shiny silver trim twinkles in the light from the full moon.

And them? He can tell they aren't actually horses, then.

I shrug. "They wanted to."

He nods. *Then it is time.*

He escorts me to the carriage, and I rest my hand on his shoulder that is now taller than my head. He stabilizes me as I climb into the carriage.

We will lead the way. He bounds forward with a howl. The other wolves howl in response.

The ravens call from above. My messenger has returned, and they have chosen to follow me back to Bennfaran. To the ball. To my love.

My bag bounces beside me in the carriage

The mice-horses do not know the way, but Alpha does. He assures me that he can follow the scent from Peter's trips back and forth time after time.

"Thank you," I tell him with my mind.

The moon is high and round. The clouds are thin. Glimpses of stars peek through as we make our way at full speed toward the ball. We pass through a river valley and over several steep hills. The mice-horses have no trouble pulling the light carriage.

Animals begin to follow as we go. They must sense my anxiety. Or they recognize my authority. They have come to support me. Bats squeak in the air, owls hoot and swoop above the carriage. Creatures from every species, large and small, follow my path toward my future.

When we arrive at the wall around Peter's palace, the carriage rolls to a stop.

"This is it," I tell them all with my mind.

They all offer words of encouragement and support.

After I dismount from the carriage, Alpha by my side, the animals surround me, and they bow. I sense fear, respect, and awe.

"You may return to your homes," I tell them. "Your continued presence is not necessary."

With bows and whispers of "*Yes, Your Majesty*" and "*As you wish*," most of my subjects comply. The ravens stay, lining up on the wall in an ominous row of oversized, dark, shifting shadows.

I rub Alpha's side. "Stay close. Be ready," I tell him. "I'll see you soon."

Thunder rolls in the distance. The clouds have begun to thicken. I can no longer see the stars. The light of the full moon is still visible through the growing darkness.

The ball has already begun. Music, talking, and laughter lead me through the palace to the ballroom. Just as I planned, I stash my bag behind a pillar in the hall, deep in the shadows.

Around the corner, the massive doors of the ballroom are carved with intricate designs. They are firmly closed.

I slip on my short black satin gloves. I place my twisted, dark tiara on my head and smear purple berry juice onto my lips to tint them a little. I smooth the front of my dress down. I put one black satin slipper in front of the other and push on the doors.

Just as the doors swing open at my touch, a loud crack of thunder echoes from the sky.

All eyes turn to me, as if the thunder has announced my presence. A flash of lightning blinds the audience for a moment. When they've regained their vision almost everyone in the room gasps.

This is exactly what I wanted.

I step down the marble stairs and onto the polished wooden floor of the ball room.

Women murmur about the inappropriate dress I'm wearing. The animals have prepared it exactly as I had wanted.

The dress is fashioned from a silk the deepest shade of purple imaginable. It shimmers in the flickering candlelight, giving it highlights of violet and lavender. The length isn't the problem, it trails on the floor behind me as I walk. It's the shape. Every other woman in the room wears a traditional ballgown, fitted at the bodice, wide and full from the waist down.

My dress, however, is a design no one has ever seen before. Because I designed it myself. Instead of a two-piece bodice and gown that covers almost every bit of exposed skin, except for a small gap between the tops of their long gloves and their sleeves, my dress allows my skin to glow. The sweetheart neckline plunges just a smidge too low to be appropriate. The cap sleeves are shredded to give a fluttery appearance over my shoulders.

The skirt is fitted to my shape, hugging my hips and flaring out at the knees. It gathers and swings and brushes the floor with each step.

There is a split in the outer lower on the back from my thighs down, which allows the flowy, matching underlayers to billow out, and makes it easy to take confident steps through the crowd. Between the design and cut, this dress leaves practically nothing to the imagination.

Over one shoulder is a matching cape of sorts, just long enough to reach my right elbow, with an uneven hem giving it an edgy look. It's light and airy and floats as I move. My midnight black gloves reach only to my wrists, leaving the entire length of my arms immodestly bare. I've smudged charcoal around my eyes and smeared the purple berry juice on my lips.

And my tiara. Oh, my tiara. It is a halo of dark, twisted branches formed into a crown on my head. With my unfamiliar hair in a twist pinned to my head, and long strands of curls hanging around my face, I must look fierce.

The men, for the most part, can't take their eyes off me. A sly grin pulls at one side of my lips.

The crowd parts for me. I hear whispers.

"That gown!"

"Where did *she* come from?"

"Mysterious woman."

"Indecent."

My confidence is through the roof as I saunter between the men and women in their "proper" ballroom attire. I wink at a young man who gapes. He snaps his jaw shut and the woman at his side glares at him. Then she glares at me.

The royals stand together at the far end of the ballroom. Peter looks dumbfounded. In a good way. My smile grows. His eyes crinkle in the corners and his cheeks flush.

My aunt looks scandalized.

Amelie just stares at the floor, and Juliette looks confused.

Uncle Henry, however, looks positively livid.

When I arrive before them, I curtsy deeply to all the royals, then stand with my hands demurely folded in front of me.

"Je… Miss," Peter clears his throat. "You look…"

His brother nudges him in the ribs.

"Oof," Peter reacts. He glares at his older brother, the crown prince and heir to the throne of Bennfaran. His brother's wife, the crown princess, smirks beside him, covering her mouth with her own modestly gloved hand.

Henry glares at me. He can't figure out who I am, but Peter's reaction certainly gave him suspicion. He studies me, trying to find something he'll recognize, I'm sure. He won't. The transformation is flawless.

"I don't know who she is," Dahlia whispers loudly to Henry. "But we can allow nothing to disrupt Amelie's night." She glares at me as a woman challenged.

The truth is, I don't plan to disrupt the party. Not any more disruption than my entrance has caused. I plan to disrupt their lives *after* the party. But they don't need to know that.

The orchestra has continued playing through all this supposed drama, and most of the couples have returned to dancing.

Peter hasn't taken his eyes from me. When the orchestra begins a new waltz, he steps forward.

"May I have this dance?" His eyes shine.

I nod, and he takes my gloved hand in his and leads me onto the dance floor.

His parents look confused, but unconcerned. Henry looks angry and suspicious. Dahlia looks affronted. Amelie doesn't look at us at all.

Peter swirls me around until I'm just in front of him. Then he places his hand on my lower back and pulls me just a hair too close for propriety. "Even though you appear different, I can tell it's you. And … well. Let's just say, you're driving me wild tonight." His eyes are full of desire.

While we dance, we plaster smiles onto our faces, and discuss our plan for the evening.

Peter whispers, "We will meet in the hall outside the ballroom."

"I'll give you your potion. I've stashed my bag behind a pillar."

"We will leave together and never look back."

People stare at us. We do make quite a handsome pair. I move in a little closer to the prince.

"It's going to be fine, Jessamine. Don't worry. We're in this together." His voice is thick with emotion.

"To the end." My words come out all breathy. He's so handsome. And I love him so much.

A man clears his throat behind me, and I snap out of my daze. Apparently, the music has stopped, but we are so wrapped up in each other, that we haven't noticed.

We stop and look around. I giggle. "Oops."

Peter bows. "Thank you for the pleasure of your company this evening, miss." He winks at me, then returns to his brother's side.

The stranger asks me to dance the next waltz, but I refuse and slip away to observe from the sides.

The dancing goes on and on. It's hot and stuffy, plenty of women's hairstyles are beginning to wilt. Some of the middle-aged attendees have settled into chairs along the perimeter, clearly done dancing for the evening.

Finally, not too long before midnight, the orchestra dies down and Peter's father stands on a raised platform to make the announcement.

"Thank you all for attending our party this evening. As most of you know we are here to celebrate the betrothal of our Prince Peter of Bennfaran…"

The crowd claps.

"… to none other than the stunning Princess Amelie of Dragovalon."

I almost gag. He's laying it on pretty thick. I clench my jaw. Peter loves *me*, not her. I tamp down my fire. There's no need to be jealous.

Peter behaves as a perfect gentleman. He gives Amelie a hand up the two steps and joins his father on the platform. Amelie stands beside him, but not very close. She doesn't look at anyone, just the floor. Peter's eyes search the crowd until they find me. I wink. He smirks.

"Let us all have the pleasure of watching Princess Amelie and Prince Peter share their first dance." The king motions to the orchestra.

Peter is all propriety as he leads Amelie around the dance floor. He speaks softly to her, and she barely makes eye contact when she responds. Everyone has gathered in close to watch them dance. I can barely make him out through the crowd.

I move around behind the people, trying to get a glimpse of him. It's as though if I lose sight of him our whole plan will fail. I must be able to see him.

Pushing my way between a few layers of people, I finally catch a glimpse. I can tell his smile is forced. The dance steps take him away from me, and then back again. He turns my direction. Our eyes meet. It's time.

The music ends. Prince Peter bows, then returns to his father's side. He leans in and whispers something to his mother. She pats him on the arm and gives him a sympathetic look. He nods and makes his way out a side door.

The party continues. It will probably last long into the early hours of the morning.

I push my way back through the crowd and exit the ballroom from a different door, hurry through the halls in the direction that he should be coming from, turn a corner, and jump. We almost crash into each other.

"Jessamine!" He scoops me into his arms, swings me around, then sets me down and kisses me hard. "We've made it. Finally…"

I want to be excited, too, but this is going to be the riskiest part. "Almost, Peter." I squeeze his hands. "We're almost free."

Christine Marshall

Chapter Thirty-eight

I pull him down the hall and behind a tall pillar, where I retrieve my bag. When I sling it over my shoulder, Peter says, "It's a shame you have to cover up any part of that dress."

"Shh, Peter. Not now. Sit on the floor, so you don't fall and hurt yourself. The change is uncomfortable, but not too painful. It should be quick."

He rests a gloved hand on my cheek and gazes into my eyes. His smile is confident. "Don't worry, my love. It worked perfectly for you. It will work for me. Then we will escape and never return."

My eyes sting. "The wolves are waiting. We'll retrieve your bag, and they will carry us away from here."

He kisses me again. Sweeter, gentler. "I love you, Jessamine."

A gasp comes from the other side of the pillar.

My back stiffens. Peter freezes, his eyes look shocked.

I hold a finger to my lips to tell him to remain quiet. I gesture for him to stay here.

As I slip around the pillar, Peter's hand reaches into my bag to retrieve the vial.

At the same time that I find myself face to face with Juliette.

"Excuse me, miss," I curtsy and maneuver around her.

Peter has retrieved the potion. I must draw Juliette's attention away from him so he can take it and transform without her noticing.

I only make it a few steps toward the doors to the ballroom when her hand gently, but firmly grips my arm.

"May I help you with something, Your Highness?" I don't meet her eyes.

"Jessamine?" She studies my eyes, my face. "Is it really you?"

Panic grips me for just a second, but I hide it quickly. "I'm sorry, miss, I think you have me mistaken for someone else."

"I know it's you…"

"Excuse me." I pull my arm free and retreat into the ballroom. She can't confront me if we're surrounded by people. I'll wait just inside the door. When she leaves me alone, I'll return to the hall for Peter.

She follows me through the side doors.

"Jessamine," she hisses in my ear.

I keep a smile on my face and pretend I don't hear.

"I don't know how you did this, or even what this" she gestures to all of me, "even is. But it's not a good idea. Someone will find out."

"You don't know what you're talking about," I say through gritted teeth, pretending to still be enjoying my view of all the partygoers.

"I know you've been up to something. The alpha wolf is bigger than he should be. The ravens have been acting strange, and the mice have all but disappeared. I know you said you hadn't noticed, but I know you're behind all of it…"

How does she know these things? I guess she's been busier trying to keep an eye on me than I thought.

"It doesn't concern you, Juliette, just leave it alone." I finally turn to face her.

A loud groan comes from the hallway. I want to rush to Peter's side, but she blocks my path.

"Do you think this will really work?" she quizzes me.

My eyes lock onto hers. She takes a half step back. My anger must show on my face.

I lean close and whisper for only her ears. "You have no idea what

I can do. Your abilities are nothing compared to mine. I have done so much more than what you think you've seen. I may not be the future queen of some stupid human kingdom, but I will be Queen of the animal kingdom. It's already begun, Juliette, and there's nothing you can do to stop it. Please, don't get in my way. I will have my love. And I will have my crown."

Juliette is about to say something to me, but I don't get the chance to find out what it is.

The side door to the ballroom opens with a bang.

People around us gasp. A woman screams.

It's…

"Peter?" My mouth forms his name, but no sound escapes my lips.

The clock tower adjacent to the castle begins to chime. The midnight hour has come.

Peter's eyes are wide. He clutches his stomach.

I grab his arm with both hands to steady him.

"I think it's working," he gasps.

My heart is racing. I know it's Peter, and the potion is working, but he doesn't look like himself. His eyes are wild. Thick silver fur slowly spreads across his skin. His fingers stretch into claws.

His hair changes from golden blonde to a silvery white and grows several finger lengths past his chin. His shoulders broaden and the muscles double in size.

"Peter… are you alright?" I whisper. My eyes search his face for any signs of trouble.

He pinches his eyes shut. His face is contorted in pain. He grunts.

He gains several hand lengths in height in a matter of seconds. His cry sounds like a… howl.

People around us start to panic.

"Jessamine, what did you do?" Juliette stands beside us, her eyes wide.

Peter groans and slumps to the floor.

"Peter!" I shake his shoulders. He is not conscious.

Just as the last, slow strike of the clock for midnight rings across the palace, the full moon breaks through the clouds. My eyes are drawn to it through the skylight openings in the ceiling of the ballroom. The moonlight illuminates the potion bottle that falls from Peter's hand and clinks to the floor.

"Oh, no." I whisper.

I yank open my bag. Peter's potion, labeled correctly, is still in my bag. My last vial of wolf-enhancing potion is gone. My legs shake as I stare at the red potion that would have transformed him into a mere palace servant. He grabbed the wrong one!

Peter makes a strange noise. His clothes have torn at the seams and hang off him in rags. His new physique is too large for them. Fur covers every part of his body that I can see beneath the scraps of cloth. His legs are misshapen.

"Peter?" I whisper, kneeling beside him on the floor. "Peter, are you awake?" I shake him again.

His face turns towards me. I gasp and recoil. My hands fly to my mouth. His face no longer looks like Peter, just as we planned. But it no longer looks human at all.

He has the face of a wolf.

He opens his eyes. They glow yellow.

The music has stopped. I look up from the floor. Men and women scurry around in a frenzy. Calls for the castle guard ring out. Other cries to protect the royals reach my ears. The noises are deafening. I squeeze my hands over my ears.

"Jessamine?" Juliette's quiet voice cuts through all the noise.

I open my eyes and look at her. "I don't know what happened, Juliette. It wasn't supposed to do this." Tears stream down my face. Where fires of anger burned not very many minutes ago, ice has engulfed me.

Juliette kneels beside me.

Peter growls. His jaw snaps in her direction. His wolf-like lips curl. She jumps away.

I look back and forth between my love transformed, and Juliette.

"Stay there," I whisper to Juliette.

She doesn't move a muscle. I've never seen anyone look so afraid in my life.

The ballroom swirls with hectic activity, but Juliette stays still as a statue.

I help Peter stand. He is so much taller than me. And he looks nothing like the man I love. He sniffs the air. Saliva drips from his muzzle. Snarls come from deep within his too-wide chest. His posture lowers and he locks his eyes onto Juliette.

"Peter!" I shout in his face.

He doesn't take his eyes off her. The hair on the back of his head and neck stands on end, like the hackles of a dog. He lowers his stance and stretches out his claw-like fingers.

Juliette whimpers. "Jessamine?"

"Peter, it's time to go now," I say to Peter, talking to him as I would a young child. I hope he still understands me in there.

He growls in reply.

He lunges forward.

Juliette screams and collapses to the floor.

People around us react. The sounds of all the shouts and cries draws Peter's attention. Green flashes across his eyes. He looks panicked. But then they glow yellow once more. The animal has returned.

I block this animal version of Peter and push him away from the crowd.

"Let's go now, Peter." I push my will onto his. If he's more animal than person now, I may be able to control him as I do the others.

He complies.

"Stay here, Juliette," I beg my cousin.

She just shivers on the floor, making herself as small as she can.

I command Peter with my mind to follow. I grip his hairy arm as we leave the castle and head for the ravens and wolves.

The ravens don't stay long. They must be able to tell something is wrong. They caw and yell and take flight, circling a few times before flying away.

The wolves take wary steps away from me and Peter.

"Peter? Are you still in there?" His eerie yellow eyes lock with mine. "I love you, Peter."

My heart breaks. What have I done? This is not how it is supposed

301

to turn out. "We were so close." I whisper. "We were going to be together. Forever." I gaze into his inhuman face.

He whimpers a little. Does he understand?

Then his nose lifts into the air. A couple strolls through the castle gardens. They have no idea that everyone inside the castle is in an uproar. Of the danger that lurks in the shadows. The woman giggles as the man speaks in low tones in her ear. Peter turns his head toward the sound.

"No, Peter," I command. "Eyes on me. Stay with me. The change is temporary. It's supposed to be temporary." My words squeeze out between sobs.

He looks at me but is distracted by the couple again. He howls, face pointed toward the full moon, half hidden by clouds.

The woman screams. The man shouts for help.

"You have to go now, Peter." I'm sobbing now. "Go, before they find you. Before they…"

I know what will happen if the palace guards find him. They will kill him. He can't stay here.

"Run. Go. And do not return." I command him with my voice and my mind.

He jolts, and then turns and runs away on all four limbs. Like an animal.

"Goodbye, Peter," I sob. Then sink to the ground.

The guards rush to the couple in the garden, who point them in my direction. They hurry to me and ask if I am in danger. I tell them no; they may return to the castle. They look around as if they aren't sure, but then comply.

Juliette makes her way to where I have folded in on myself.

"Jessamine, what did you do? Was that thing… Peter?" Her eyes are wide. Her cheeks are stained with dried tears. Her dress is rumpled and her gloves dirty from the floor.

I have no answer. I can't speak. My heart has shattered inside of me.

"Jessamine, they found the glass vial. You must tell someone what you've done so they can try to save Peter." She reaches a hand down to help me stand.

I look up at her, but do not take her hand. "Juliette, if I tell them what I've done, they'll have me banished… or worse."

I know the truth. They'll probably execute me. "We were going to run away together. We were going to marry, have a family…" my throat closes. I can't breathe. This has all gone so terribly wrong.

I hear shouts from inside the castle. They've begun to search for Peter. And for me.

I allow Juliette to help me stand. She makes her way back to the castle.

I reach for the alpha wolf with my mind. He pads to my side on silent feet.

By the time Juliette turns around to help me up the stairs, I am long gone.

All that's left of either Peter or I is the glass vial, stained red from the potion.

Alpha carries me away from the castle. I don't know where he's taking me. I don't really care. I collapse onto his back and bury my face into his fur. My body shakes with sobs. The wolves howl, sharing in my grief.

"Stop," I tell Alpha.

I hold Peter's potion in my hands. Tears drip down my face. How could I have let this happen? The potion bottle slides from my hand and drops to the ground. It shatters when it hits a rock. The red liquid seeps into the dirt.

If I could only go back, prevent this one mistake, this whole thing would have worked. I have ruined everything.

Or maybe, a voice whispers at the back of my head, *you shouldn't have been meddling with this kind of power to begin with. You should have left well enough alone.*

"Leave me!" I shout.

Alpha doesn't flinch. He knows I am not speaking to him.

"I no longer wish to hear thoughts that bring me shame and guilt! I no longer wish to be told I am wrong! About anything! I am tired of feeling sad. Of feeling bad for wanting to make my life better. For wanting a happily ever after. I don't need some other version of myself reminding me of my failures over and over again. I just want her to go!"

As if I can control my own mind, as I do with the animals, the voice fades away. I wait for it to talk back to me. To guide me down the right path of how to fix this. How to find Peter. How to make this right. But she's gone. Somehow, I've pushed my own conscience right out of my head.

The earth rumbles beneath my feet. I feel my physical form transform back into my original self. I shriek at the pain, and the power.

Like a wildfire burning them away, the feelings of remorse and embarrassment for all the mistakes I've made dissipate. My desire for power spreads to take its place.

In a voice that sounds like mine- but different, I announce to all the animals who are within my sphere of influence. And there are many.

I am power.

I will rule over everyone. Everything.

I am the Queen.

Epilogue

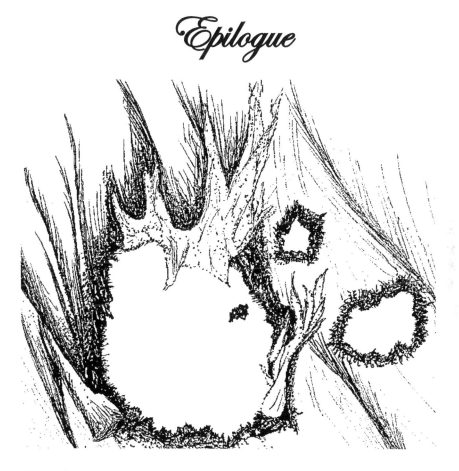

The door to my shop opens with an ear-splitting squeak. I like that the hinges make noise. Then I can tell when someone enters.

A scruffy looking man with shifty eyes enters. He doesn't even pretend to browse the mismatched shelves, but heads straight for me.

Most women would be afraid of a man like this. He's big, unkempt, and angry looking. I lift my chin and wait for him to approach.

"It is done." His voice is low, rough.

"Very well. Any complications?" I give him a sharp look, expecting the worst.

"No, ma'am. All went as planned. The creature is secure. It will arrive in the night."

I retrieve his payment and drop it in his hands. "Speak of this to no one. Do not contact me again."

He hefts the money pouch as if he can tell how much is in it by its weight. He nods once, turns, and leaves.

My experiments are progressing. I have discovered many secrets within the walls of the City of Dorian. My pawnshop is the perfect place to connect with some of the… lower class citizens of this place.

I busy myself reviewing the latest "contracts" I have arranged. Others would call them bribes. It doesn't matter.

The door opens once more. A woman enters, small of frame, a cloak covering her head. This is fairly typical for the kind of customers I receive. Most do not come here because things are going well in their lives. They prefer their identities to remain hidden.

I cannot see the woman's face, but I am not currently conducting any… let's say… business with anyone that matches her general appearance.

An actual customer, then. Perhaps selling something for desperately needed money? Perhaps purchasing an item that is required for some unwholesome purpose?

I approach and welcome her to my shop.

"May I help you find anything in particular?" I ask in a sweet voice.

The woman turns to face me and lowers her hood. Her long, blonde curls cascade down her back. It can't be…

"Hello, Jessamine," Juliette says in a quiet voice.

She holds herself with perfect posture, hands clasped nervously in front of her.

Juliette. What is she doing here? How did she find me? My mind races. I mask my thoughts with a cross between a smile and a grimace.

Juliette looks around the shop but doesn't move from her place. "It looks like you have done well for yourself."

I roll my eyes. And I don't hide my annoyed expression. "What are you doing here, Juliette?"

Her eyes return to meet mine. "I have searched for you far and wide. I did not expect to find you... here."

I grin a mischievous grin. "The best place to hide is in the middle of nowhere, in the middle of everything."

Satisfaction wars with annoyance that she has discovered my whereabouts. Hopefully she knows nothing of what I've been able to accomplish with the animals.

"Jessamine... you do not have to stay here." She reaches her hands out as if to take mine, but then thinks twice and drops them to her sides. "No one else knows what you have done. Everyone has assumed Peter fled to avoid the marriage to Amelie. It's been long enough. It is all over. I have come to ask you..."

She hesitates.

"What Juliette? What could you possibly want from me anymore?" I cross my arms and wait for her response.

"Please... come home with me." She reaches out a hand to me. Her eyes are so sad. I can tell she has suffered to keep my secret. She has treated me as a true friend. A sister.

If my heart had any softness left in it, I might take her up on her offer.

"It's too late. That bridge has burned. It's nothing but ashes now." No regret mingles with my words.

"It does not have to remain that way," Juliette pleads. Her voice is thick with emotion. "There is still a place for you."

"It IS that way, Juliette." She flinches at my harsh response. "You can't change what has happened. You can't bring back my parents. Or Peter. It's over. I've moved on."

Her eyes fill with tears. She must be able to see the indifference on my face. I'm no longer angry. I just... don't care.

"What has become of you? Please do not be this way, Jessamine," she begs.

"Stop." I hold my hands out and close my eyes, as if I can block her words if I can't see her.

"Please do not let your heart become destroyed."

My eyes are hard when they return to her face.

"Jessamine?"
I turn away from her.
"If my heart has become as cinder, so be it."

Read more of Jessamine's story

in the *Charlie and the Giants* series.
(Hint... she's the villain!)

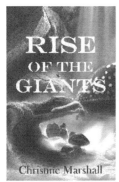  

Available on Amazon

Christine's **Charlie and the Giants** books are filled with magic, mythical creatures, and an *awesome* female protagonist that has to figure out who she wants to become.

If you love books that will help you forget the real world for a little while, are full of surprising characters, and will keep you guessing, then these are the perfect books for you!

What happens to Jessamine next?

Why does Juliette ask Jessamine to come home?

What happened to Peter?

Jessamine
(Cinderella)

Juliette
(Snow White)

Sariah
(Sleeping Beauty)

The first three books in the *Charlie and the Giants* series. Learn why Jessamine became so wicked. Find out why Juliette loves the giants so much. Read Sariah's inspiring but heartbreaking story. These origin stories for three of the critical characters in the *Charlie and the Giants* series are framed as fairytale retellings full of twists and turns that you'll never see coming.

Available on Amazon and

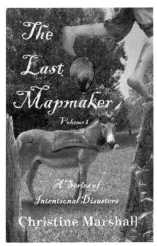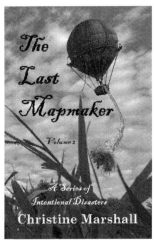

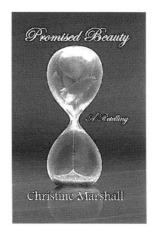

Get ready for another exciting fantasy adventure!

Steampunk? *Check!*
Pirates? *Check!*
Dwarves? *Check!*
Peter Pan vibes? *Check!*

These books are perfect for readers young and old who love friendship, family, and adventure!

Becoming Cinder
Sign up for Christine's e-newsletter!

Check out Christine's website!
www.ChristineMarshallAuthor.com

Christine's Amazon author page:

E&O Creative's Etsy shop
Featuring art by Steve, signed books by Christine,
and other awesome swag!

Coloring books featuring illustrations from Steve including
chapter heading art from Christine's books!

Thanks for Reading!

I hope you enjoyed this book!
Please leave a review on **Amazon** and **Goodreads**. For indie authors like me, reviews are our lifeblood. Help a girl out, it'll only take a few minutes!

Check me out on social media!

Facebook: Christine K. Marshall-author
www.facebook.com/christinemarshallauthor

Instagram: @the_christine_marshall_24
www.instagram.com/the_christine_marshall_24

TikTok: www.tiktok.com/@christinemarshallfantasy

Email: christinemarshall24@gmail.com

Acknowledgements

No book is written alone! *Becoming Cinder* would not have been possible without a lot of amazing people.

Beta readers: Steve, Belle, Sophie, and Pepper. Y'all rock!

Moral support: Sumedha and Shaylen, you guys are my BFFs!

Original cover art & chapter heading art: my amazing husband, **Steve**, thanks for reenacting some of the Peter and Jessamine scenes with me.♥ And thank you for the collaboration on the story and the art. I love you too much.

Amazing ARC Team: I was blown away with how many people on social media signed up to read this book and help market it before release. Seriously, the success of this project would not have been possible without you!
Here goes!
Lacey, Winter, Cassandra, Jennifer, Tracy, Britanny, Sureeta, Samantha, Brie, Connie, Neoma, Brooke, Stephanie, Keziah, Marsha, Rachel, Jenny, Izzy, Crystal, Nikki, Kristen, Tiffany, Samantha, Sally, Virginia, Alma, Tarah, Destiny, Jana, Shaylen, Courtney, a_slavinskas, Kelli, Meira, Michelle, Niki, Jessica, Veronica, Katherine, Anne, Liesel, Ashley, GG, Jenifer, Hillary, Jennifer, batmanlovebug, Sumedha, Kyle Natalie, Keegan, Emily, Marie, Susan, Laura, and Ashley.

About the Author

When Christine isn't spinning tales on her laptop, she probably has a book and a chocolate chip cookie in hand. She loves all kinds of books: fantasy, sci-fi, historical fiction, non-fiction, and even textbooks.

She also loves to play her ukulele, stand in the rain, stay up late, and try new foods… but not all at the same time! Christine has moved over 20 times in the past 20 years, and firmly believes that people are more important than things.